LIAM BROWN

SKIN

Legend Press Ltd, 107-111 Fleet Street, London, EC4A 2AB
info@legend-paperbooks.co.uk | www.legendpress.co.uk

Print ISBN 978-1-78955-0-405
Ebook ISBN 978-1-78955-0-399
Set in Times. Printing managed by Jellyfish Solutions Ltd
Cover design by Kari Brownlie | www.karibrownlie.co.uk
Chapter illustrations by Ed Homer | edhomer@live.co.uk

Liam Brown's debut novel *Real Monsters* was longlisted for the *Guardian*'s Not the Booker prize in 2015 and followed by *Wild Life* in 2016. His latest novel *Broadcast* was optioned by a major Hollywood film studio and sold into multiple languages. *Skin* is his forth novel. He lives in Birmingham with his wife and two children.

Stalk Liam
on Facebook, Twitter or Instagram
@liambrownwriter

For my mother, who carried me first. Who carries me still.

Emergency Alert

CITIZENS. FOLLOWING THE RECENT SPELL OF DISRUPTION, WE CAN CONFIRM A LARGE-SCALE RELIEF EFFORT IS NOW IN PROGRESS. NORMAL ELECTRICITY, WATER AND INTERNET SUPPLIES HAVE RESUMED. DETAILED INFORMATION PERTAINING TO YOUR SAFETY AND HEALTH FOLLOWING THE OUTBREAK OF PH1N2(C) VIRUS (CEBU FLU) IS EXPECTED IMMINENTLY. IN THE MEANTIME, THE MINISTRY FOR HEALTH RECOMMEND THAT YOU:

1: AVOID ALL PHYSICAL CONTACT WITH LIVESTOCK, PETS AND PEOPLE.

2: MINIMISE EXPOSURE TO OTHERS, EVEN IF THEY APPEAR WELL.

3: STAY INDOORS. KEEP DOORS AND WINDOWS SEALED.

4: REMEMBER TO WASH YOUR HANDS REGULARLY.

5: STAY CALM AND AWAIT FURTHER INSTRUCTIONS.

THANK YOU FOR YOUR COOPERATION AND PATIENCE DURING THIS DIFFICULT TIME.

PART ONE

ONE

IT'S HARD TO think of you as anything other than an egg. I'm sorry about that. I know some women like to imagine their donations as babies-in-waiting. Or else picture a near-future nirvana, where ruddy-cheeked, dimple-bottomed sons or daughters sit bouncing contently on their knees. Eyes shimmering. Immune systems fully functioning. But try as I might, I just can't buy it. It's been five years since my lap has been used as anything other than a cradle for my computer. I'm not expecting that to change any time soon, either for me or anyone else on the programme.

And so, I refuse to get sentimental about you, dear Egg. As far as I'm concerned, your fate is to sit frozen on the shelves of some distant laboratory for an indeterminate eternity, lined up amongst a million other hopeful samples. Mislabelled, maybe. Forgotten. Lost. Or perhaps, if you're really lucky, to be meddled with by some anonymous scientist. Your DNA decoded, mapped and modified as they attempt to edit out the harmful mutations and save the species. And then a few weeks later, when they inevitably discover that it hasn't worked – that your life is *unviable* – they'll simply scrape you away like yesterday's omelette. Down the pan with all the others. Off to the incinerator. Flushed out to sea.

Still, as cynical as I am about your prospects as a miracle, I nevertheless acquiesce to do my biannual bit for humanity, just like every other woman of childbearing age. I nod and I smile as I wedge myself into the tiny quarantine tent that constitutes our front porch while a government gynaecologist offers pinched-nose platitudes through their scratchy respirator:

'You're a superstar for agreeing to do this, Mrs Allen…'

'You're really helping to build a brighter tomorrow, Angela…'

'Sure thing, Doc!' I say, gritting my teeth like a trooper as a stranger in a hazmat suit and breathing apparatus goes to work between my legs, prodding at my reproductive organs nervously, as if defusing a weapon of mass destruction. Which I suppose, in a funny way, is precisely what I am now.

We all are.

Of course, I'm never really relaxed about the procedure, even after the local anaesthetic and a mild sedative. Despite the dust extraction unit running full blast and both of us clad in protective gear, it is still exceedingly risky. Every minute of every day, the average human sheds between thirty and forty thousand dead skin cells. A sort of invisible aura that follows us around. It would only take a single stray airborne particle to make its way into my suit or, heaven forbid, into the house…

Well, you know the rest.

Anyway, now that the doctor has left for her next appointment, I'm stuck here for at least four hours while I wait for the drugs to wear off and the red light above the quarantine door to blink green. As ever, I note that Colin doesn't have to endure any of this physical discomfort or inconvenience. No, when it's time for my darling husband to proffer his donation, it's simply a case of tossing a sparsely filled sample cup into the quarantine area before sloping back to his living quarters to carry on with his work. Or whatever else it is he fills his time with these days. Which, if the muffled grunts and groans that occasionally escape through the walls are anything to go by, mostly seems to be rehearsing for precisely these visits.

I roll over onto my side and bring my knees to my chest, attempting to dull the spasms in my bruised uterus. It's difficult to get comfortable in here. Despite constantly nagging Colin to order an upgrade, our quarantine tent is still the standard-issue model we first had fitted four and a half years ago. It's claustrophobic with just me in it, let alone when it's being used as a makeshift medical clinic. Coupled with the full body suit and respirator mask that I'm obliged to keep on until I'm safely back in my living quarters, it's almost unbearable.

And then there's the heat. While it's always pretty warm in our apartment due to the additional insulation between rooms, in the tent it's like a sauna. Despite the ventilation, the walls are misted with condensation, while inside my suit my skin prickles with perspiration and my mask has fogged up, rendering everything a vague smear of white and grey. After a while I give up staring at the blurry light above the door, which remains a stubborn shade of red, and instead close my eyes, thinking perhaps I'll try and sleep.

It's funny. When it first became apparent that the world was ending – or at least coming apart at the seams – I remember that, as bad as everything was, part of me was actually relieved. At least things would slow down a bit now, I thought. Back then everyone was just so tired all the time. It was a way of life. We'd actually get competitive about it, as if there were a correlation between our moral fibre and our level of sleep deprivation. *Four hours a night*, we'd brag. *Five at a push*. We took pride at being the first at our desks in the morning and the last out of the door at night. We'd mainline coffee just to keep going. Leave meetings to splash our faces with cold water. Take power naps in toilet cubicles. Drive home in the dark with the windows rolled down and the music turned up just to prevent ourselves from falling asleep at the wheel. And then we had childcare to contend with. Nutritionally balanced meals to prepare. Gym sessions to slay. A social life to maintain. Family. Friends. Marriages. And when, finally, we crawled into bed at the end of the night, the headboard already rattling with our partner's apnoeic snores, we still couldn't sleep. No. We just lay there, bathed in the permanent murky brown twilight of the city sky. Unable to wind down. Our bodies vibrating as if electrified. Our heads still spinning as we chewed over the day or drafted imaginary emails, disturbed by the sporadic cricket chirrups of our devices, squinting through sticky eyes to decipher urgent messages, the night punctuated with the arthritic clicks of predictive text, until the next thing we knew, the sun was coming up and it was time to start the whole crazy cycle again.

But here's the thing: I'm still tired. I'm permanently exhausted. Because although everything has changed, nothing has changed. Not really. Obviously, there's no commuting any more. And I don't have to worry about shopping. I don't even really have to cook, what with the majority of our food arriving as vacuum-packed, robotically prepared ready meals. Everyone just takes care of themselves.

Even so, there never seems to be enough hours in the day.

Work is still the biggest drain on my time. After the initial outbreak, things got back on track surprisingly quickly. Everything is done remotely now, of course. Meetings. Appraisals. Sales. It turns out there's very little that I did at the office that I can't do at home. In fact, pretty soon I found myself even busier than before.

And then there's the insomnia. It's still as tough to relax as ever. Regardless of the hour, my phone still rattles with the furious impatience of a wasp under a glass. And, while I no longer have to share my bed with anyone, I still have to put up with the laboured rasps of my husband's snores coming through the layers of plasterboard and plastic sheeting that separate our rooms.

Like I say, both everything and nothing has changed.

•••

WHEN I OPEN my eyes, the light is still red. I haven't slept. I lie here, staring blankly at the rivulets of condensation running down the inside of my mask. The anaesthetic is starting to fade now, sharp cramps stabbing through my abdomen, like the worst period you can imagine. Somewhere beyond the tent a low rumble starts up. *Thump-thump-thump*. Still slightly sedated, I initially mistake it for footsteps. I picture Colin coming to see how I'm doing. Fighting his way through the layers of canvas to bring me a cup of tea. A kind word. A kiss.

Then I remember.

No one is coming to see me. Colin is locked away in his room, too busy working to even remember I'm out here. In the room beside him, through a few inches of plaster that might as well be a few thousand miles thick, is Charlie. At fourteen he takes isolation in his stride. It's a way of life for him now. He can't really remember anything else. He'll be plugged in too, of course. Headset on, controller in hand. His eyes flitting from his phone to his tablet to his computer screen as he blasts away at whatever homicidal video game he's playing when he should be doing his homework.

And then, just down the hall in what used to be our living room, is Amber. That's where the sound is coming from. My eldest child, pounding away at the treadmill. This is what she does now, for five, sometimes six hours every day. It's sad really. She's like a hamster on a wheel. All that work and she still never gets anywhere. I understand, of course. It's hard enough being seventeen without having to spend your life under house arrest. At her age I was out every night. Getting myself into all sorts of trouble. It's different for her. There's no outlet. Just exercise. The treadmill. Skipping rope. Yoga. The punchbag. All that energy. Wasted.

And maybe it's the last of the sedative turning me soft, but as I lie here and listen to Amber grinding away on that imaginary road, I wish I could throw my arms around her. Just once. To mop her sweaty brow and crush her body to mine like I did when she was a baby. To hold her and say, 'Hey, it's okay. Things are going to get better. Everything will be all right in the end'.

And now I know it's the sedative talking. Because in my

heart, I don't really think things are going to get better. No. This is it. Not the world we wanted or deserved, but the only one we've got. And in this world, I've got about as much chance of hugging Amber again as I have of hugging you, my poor sweet Egg.

Which is to say, there's no chance at all.

TWO

I REMEMBER THE first person I actually saw die. This was still a good few weeks before the outbreak officially arrived here. Back when the news of a strange virus that had originated in the Philippines was still the stuff of news feeds and social media timelines. Back before phrases like 'hazmat suit' and 'immunodeficiency' were part of our everyday vocabulary.

I was in a shopping centre when it happened, a cloud of carrier bags cutting off the blood supply to my fingers, Charlie and Amber skulking close behind me. This was around April, the tail end of what had felt like an endless Easter holiday. The skies filled with a cold, relentless mizzle. The kids jacked up on chocolate and stir-crazy after being cooped up in the house for a fortnight. We were normally more organised than this. We had childminders during the school holidays. Day camps. Sports clubs. Ordinarily the kids were wrapped up and shipped out for a minimum of ten hours a day, returning home suitably subdued each night. For whatever reason, though, our arrangements had fallen through that year, and seeing how Colin's job was so much more important than mine – or at least, better paid – I'd bitten the bullet and arranged to work from home so I could babysit the children.

Not that they were babies any more. Even as a toddler, Amber had displayed a fiercely independent streak, batting me away whenever I attempted to brush her teeth or get her dressed. Now she was twelve, you couldn't tell her anything. Whether it was her school work or baking or gymnastics, she would rather get something wrong – or in the case of her swimming lessons, nearly drown – than take advice. It was as though she saw asking for help as a weakness. A form of cheating. As if an achievement only had any value if you did it entirely alone.

Perhaps that was why she had recently started placing such importance on her privacy. Her bedroom, in particular, had become a battleground. Overnight, hand-drawn signs had been stuck to the door. Keep Out. No Entry. Forbidden. Suddenly she would scream at anyone who entered her room without express permission. Now to some extent, I could understand this impulse. She'd started her period the year before, and although she tended to dismiss our 'little chats' about her body with a loud huff and a shake of the head, as if what I was telling her was the oldest, most embarrassing news in the world, I nevertheless detected a trepidation in her as she transitioned from child to teenager. It was unsurprising she wanted her own space and, while we drew the line at her demands for a lock on her bedroom door, we did concede to knocking before we came in.

Things weren't quite as tough with Charlie. Not yet anyway. Three years younger than Amber, he had yet to fully master the less agreeable qualities he would hone as a teenager. That's not to say he was an angel. Even then, he was prone to sulking, showing flashes of what would later become his trademark cynicism, as if he'd already seen everything the world had to offer and found it all insufferably boring. More worrying was his propensity towards cruelty. I lost track of the times I caught him plucking the legs from a spider. Or pouring salt on a slug, watching the pitiful creature as it fizzed and hissed into a brown puddle on our balcony.

Still, these horrors were interspersed with moments of sweetness. I remember evenings where he'd lower his guard and curl up on the sofa next to me to watch TV, his head resting on my hip, my fingers teasing at the blond tangles of hair. Or nights when he'd wake up terrified in the dark, eyes wide with the nameless terror of some fast-fading nightmare. Nights when he'd thunder down the hallway into our room and I'd simply hoist him into the air and engulf him in the duvet, pressing his tiny body to mine until he eventually stopped shaking and started snoring instead.

Sadly, those fleetingly sweet moments were in notably short supply over the course of that holiday. In fact, relations between the three of us had pretty much broken down by that point, the kids constantly squabbling while I was stuck in the middle, desperately trying to work, a frazzled and despondent referee. I remember moaning to Colin each night about the situation. As crazy as it sounds now, I was desperate for personal space. Just like Amber, I wanted a lock on my bedroom door. I felt smothered in the house. Hot and fidgety. At night, I'd lie awake and fantasise about moving out to the countryside. To a house with six bedrooms. Ten bedrooms. Somewhere expansive enough that I would never have to see another person again. Where I could hole up by myself, with no distractions. Or else I pictured a long, winding garden where I could build my own studio, far away from the beasts I shared my life with. I imagined a beautiful, monastic existence. Total silence. Utter isolation.

If only I knew.

Towards the end of the holiday there was a break in the incessant rain and I decided the time had come to give in and book an actual day off work. Abandoning my laptop, I dragged the kids out of the house, intending to take them to a local park and force them to run off their cabin fever. By the time we got to the end of the road, however, the sky had curdled black. Rain pummelled the pavement with a renewed sense of purpose, forcing the three of us to sprint back to the car. Which is how I ended up traipsing around a cramped shopping centre with two grumpy children in tow.

SOMETIMES IT'S DIFFICULT to remember just how busy the world used to be. I guess because of the school holidays, the shopping centre was unbearably full. The escalators churning. The walkways heaving. Wet people, dry people, old people, young people. Business people on their lunch break and young mums with pushchairs and old men with dogs and cyclists carrying fold-up bicycles and workmen in high-vis waistcoats and security guards with cheap black blazers and tattoos on their necks and teenage girls with blue dreadlocks and guitars strapped to their backs.

People shopping. People looking. People moving. People stopping.

All races, shapes and sizes.

Pressed together. Mushed together. Mixed together.

Merged and funnelled and sheltering from the rain.

And the sweet awful stink of it all. Expensive perfume mingling with cheap aftershave. Fresh coffee and stale cigarettes. Minty breath and morning breath and garlic breath and dog breath. All of us breathing each other's air. Stepping in each other's spaces.

People, people, people.

A confluence of life. A huddle of humanity. Everyone shuffling along the polished channels of the mall, like some weird, multi-headed, thousand-limbed organism.

Wriggling. Writhing. Rushing.

Together.

As soon as we arrived, I realised I had made a terrible error of judgement. This was a thousand times worse than being home. Nevertheless, I doubled down, insisting we make the most of it as we fought our way through the hordes, traipsing from shop to shop to shop. After a miserable hour, in which the children bickered constantly and I mostly ended up buying clothes for myself, I decided there was nothing for it but to pacify them with sugar.

As we stood in the food court on the top floor, the kids finally silenced by ice cream sundaes, a scream rang out nearby, cutting through the chatter of the nearby diners. One by one, the crowd turned their heads. Seconds later another cry echoed off the polished marble floors. Louder this time. Female, and filled with panic.

Instinctively, I reached for the children, pulling them close to me. Preposterous as it seems now, my first thought was terrorism. Back in those days, our timelines were regularly filled with news of atrocities. There were 24-hour streaming bulletins showing the aftermath of attacks. Tearful interviews with the families of victims. Wreaths of flowers strung around lamp posts and the balustrades of bridges and the railings of school gates. Earnest warnings from politicians that another attack was inevitable. Imminent. That it would be bigger and bloodier than the last. It's funny to think we used to expend so much energy butchering and bombing one another. If only we knew that Mother Nature would turn out to be so much more efficient at finishing us off.

Holding on to Charlie's hood, I took a step backwards. It was no good, though. Already the crowd had swollen behind us. Everyone jostling, pushing, shoving, straining. Craning their necks to see what was going on.

I tried again, excusing myself, trying to force my way through the cage of bodies. As I did, though, there was another cry. This time, a man.

'Move back! For God's sake, give her some space. She can't breathe!'

There was a ripple of movement around us, and suddenly the crowd parted, affording me a clear view of the terrifying tableau playing out close by. On the floor of the dining area, a man in a blue shirt was kneeling over a middle-aged woman. At least I think she was middle-aged. Her face was swollen up so badly it was difficult to tell. Her lips like pink balloons. Her eyelids so fat and puffy they had closed over completely. It looked as if she had toppled backwards off her bench, a tray of food left untouched on the table above her. Now she lay sprawled on her back, clawing at her throat, her face purple, her skirt ridden up around her waist, just one more indignity to add to a catalogue of miseries.

Embarrassing as it is to admit, I can clearly recall a wave of relief sweeping over me. We were not under attack after all. While this poor woman had clearly suffered some kind of medical emergency, a serious allergic reaction from the looks of it, we were going to be just fine. This was not something that would affect me or my children in any meaningful way. Sure, we might discuss it in the car on the way home. Charlie might bring up the boy in his class who was allergic to peanuts and so had to take his lunch break alone. But by the time dinner was served tonight, the drama would be forgotten, replaced by other, more immediate concerns. In other words, everything was going to be okay.

There was another scream, and for the first time I noticed a teenage girl wailing above the ill woman.

'Mum? Mum? Somebody do something. Oh my God, oh my God, oh my God...'

I watched as the woman on the floor began to fit violently, her body shaking, a thick white froth seething between the grotesque pillows of her lips. The man in the blue shirt was attempting CPR now, thrusting down on her chest with both hands, pressing his face to hers as he attempted to administer the kiss of life.

Somewhere by my side I felt a small hand reach for my own, pumping it anxiously. I looked down to see Charlie, his eyes wide with terror.

'I'm scared, Mummy.'

'It's fine,' I lied. 'She's going to be fine.'

Still, we'd seen enough.

Taking them both by the hand, I dragged them away, squeezing through the tight circle of bystanders. As we headed towards the escalators, I turned to steal one final glimpse of *the woman. She was motionless now. Her face drained white. Then the crowd shifted again and I lost sight of her.*

As we made our way towards the ground floor, I saw a flash of green on the opposite escalators. A pair of young paramedics fighting their way up towards the food court, a portable defibrillator slung over one of their shoulders.

'You see?' I smiled. 'They're going to take her to hospital now and make her better.'

Charlie gave a small nod. He didn't look convinced.

As we reached the ground floor, I stopped and glanced behind me. Already, the screams from the top floor had faded away, drowned out by the drone of the crowd. Down here, it was like nothing had happened. People went about their business, utterly oblivious to the woman dying fifty feet above their heads.

'Mummy, what was wrong with that lady?'

I turned to Charlie. To them both. They each looked pale and impossibly small.

As the shoppers weaved and bobbed around us, I knelt down and put my arms around the two of them, squeezing them tight to me, chest to chest, cheek to cheek, as if trying to absorb them.

'It's okay. I know it was upsetting to watch. It was horrible. But it's over now. Really, there's nothing to worry about. I promise.'

Of course, back then I had no idea how wrong I was. There was everything to worry about. Everything. And as for it being over? It hadn't even begun.

THREE

YOU MIGHT FIND it hard to believe, but in the old world Friday night actually used to stand for something. Back when I was in my early twenties, it was all we lived for. We'd drink until we were half blind. Laugh until our bellies ached. Dance until our feet hurt and our heels cracked. And even when we were eventually thrown out of the pubs and the clubs, staggering blinking onto the filthy streets, it didn't stop there. No. We simply kept going, chasing the moment. Desperate not to squander a single second. We'd bundle into a taxi and head back to someone's house. We'd light a fire to keep warm and someone would bring out a stereo or a guitar. There'd be more drink. A joint might go around. Powders and pills. Perhaps we might even meet a nice boy or a girl to cuddle up to and fall in love with. At least until the sun came up and the spell was finally broken…

Even when I was a little older, once I'd settled down with Colin, Friday night was still the finish line we hurled ourselves at. Though my partying days were long behind me, Friday was still a chance for us to relax and reconnect. To open a bottle of wine and argue over what to watch on Netflix. To curl up on the sofa and eat a takeaway, before collapsing into bed, too exhausted to do anything but hold each other in the darkness.

These days, though, Friday is indistinguishable from any other night of the week. And so tonight, just like every other night, I'm sitting in front of my computer with the remains of my ready meal for one. Tonight, it's just you and me, Egg.

And you don't even exist.

The evening started promisingly enough I suppose. For the last few months or so, Colin has been on a crusade to bring us 'closer' as a family and, as laughable as I might find this exercise, I have nevertheless made an effort to support him. To present a united front. Part of his strategy involves us eating together again in the evenings. Of course, to physically get together around a table would be illegal – not to mention suicidal – and so in practice we have agreed to switch our webcams on during mealtimes, our screens divided into four equal squares. A sort of culinary conference call.

Naturally, the kids are less than enthused with this arrangement. I guess they're so used to doing what they want, when they want, that any attempt to cajole them into an artificial social situation was always doomed to fail. During meals, they each sit looking off screen, distracted. Watching something else, maybe. Or playing a game. Staring at their phones. Most days, Charlie refused to take his headphones off at all. Still, Colin persists, seemingly blind to their resentment. He sits there smiling, relentlessly cracking jokes and asking open questions until his attempts to force a conversation eventually unravel, leaving only the sounds of us chewing our decontaminated food. It would almost be sweet if it wasn't so futile.

After the first few weeks, Charlie stopped logging on altogether, his quarter of the screen remaining a deep, impenetrable black. While I have sent him a couple of half-hearted messages explaining the importance of participating, emphasising how much they mean to his father, my pleas have so far been met with a wall of silence. What else can I do? It's not like I can force him to come to dinner. I guess this is the reality of remote parenting. I have no idea what he gets up to beyond what he tells me. I don't know if his room's tidy or if he's done his homework, let alone what he gets up to online. Not that I'd want to know. I have friends who have taken extreme measures to keep tabs on their children, even going so far as to pay hackers to secretly install spyware on their kids' computers. I have no interest in going down that route. As far as I'm concerned, ignorance is bliss. Besides, even if I did discover he was up to mischief, what could I do about it? Ground him? There is no realistic threat I can make. Nothing I can cut off that hasn't already been denied to him by the circumstances of our lives.

Anyway, you can imagine my surprise when I logged on for dinner this evening to find Charlie's square lit up. Seeing him for the first time in weeks, I was once again struck by how rapidly he seems to be changing these days. A fresh spray of wiry hairs along his top lip. His eyebrows thicker and darker than ever before, almost meeting in the middle now. Hard as it is to admit, he is fatter, too. Though food is still technically rationed, it is not exactly in short supply, and without an Amber-style exercise regime in place, the heavily processed ready meals make it easy to pile on the pounds. Charlie, though, is bordering on obese. Meaty rings of flesh bunch up around his chin, as if his head is sinking into his neck, while a too tight T-shirt strains to contain the swollen mounds of his bosom. The pale little boy I used to scoop up and press to my own chest, whose heart I could feel fluttering like a baby bird beneath the delicate nest of his ribs, has long gone. Still, at least he seemed to be in a good mood for once.

'Oh hey, Mum. Nice day?'

I nodded, instantly suspicious. 'Um… sure?'

Glancing over at Amber, I found myself weirdly relieved to find her looking as unhappy as ever, her shoulders hunched around her ears, her expression barely masking her deep contempt for the world. At least she was acting normal.

Colin on the other hand was predictably delighted, beaming into the camera as he spoke. 'Charlie! So glad that you could join us. Hey, now that you're here, would you mind passing the salt?'

I stifled a groan. This is one of Colin's favourite jokes. It wasn't funny the first time he made it. Hearing it again for the hundredth time was enough to make me want to smash my face into my computer screen. Judging by Amber's expression, she felt the same way.

To my disbelief, however, Charlie splayed his lips into a gummy grin. 'Good one, Dad.'

Encouraged by this response, Colin moved on to the next gag in his comedy routine, reaching for a napkin and pretending to polish his webcam. 'Gosh, I must have a word with that window cleaner of ours. These things are filthy!'

This time Charlie actually laughed out loud. The kind of yelp a dog might make if you were to accidentally tread on its paw. A shiver ran down my spine. Something was very wrong here. Charlie was evidently relishing some cruel private joke, of which I suspected we were all the punchline.

'So, how was your day, Dad?' Charlie continued, his smile stretching, becoming a smirk.

Oblivious to the sarcasm in his tone, Colin prattled on, telling Charlie about his latest triumphs at work, about the struggles he's facing, about a new project he's working on.

When we first started dating, Colin was a computer engineer for a car company. Obviously, there isn't much call for that line of work since the collapse of the automotive industry. While we do still technically have our car – one of those boxy, first generation self-driving models – it lies rusting in the parking bay beneath our apartment building with all the other abandoned vehicles. A grim monument to a simpler time, when the only safety equipment you needed to worry about was a seat belt.

Fortunately for us, however, Colin's skills proved to be eminently transferable in the new economic landscape that rose from the rubble of the old world. For a year or so, he found work with a drone manufacturer, before he settled in his current role at a company that specialised in virtual reality.

Even before the virus, VR had been booming. Now it's everywhere. I have friends – grown men and women – who

27

spend entire days online in virtual chat rooms, talking and flirting with strangers who seem close enough to touch. The project Colin is currently working on seeks to take this a step further. His company have been working on a sort of virtual vacation spot people can visit. Digital beaches and pixelated palm trees or something. But apparently that's not the exciting bit. According to Colin, they've developed some kind of new technology to create the illusion of touch. You simply put on a pair of special gloves that are fitted with sensors and then pop on your VR headset. Then, when the computer detects you touching something on the screen, a series of air-filled sacks mimic the sensation of actually holding something in your hands, while a series of targeted vibrations, pulses and pinches trick the brain into being able to feel its texture. The effect, Colin assures me, is mind-blowing. You can run your fingers through an imaginary child's hair. Or walk hand in hand with a loved one along a virtual beach. And that's not all. The gloves are only the first stage. Colin has said they're working on a new prototype, full body suits that can simulate the feeling of being hugged or massaged.

'Just imagine the possibilities,' I've heard him gush more times than I care to remember. 'A mother could feel her child curled up on her lap for the first time in half a decade. You could put your arms around Charlie and Amber again and they'd actually feel it. We could hold hands again.'

Whether or not this is anything other than wishful thinking, I have no idea. Still, the work is well paid, especially compared to my meagre contributions to the family budget. This is important. The things we need to survive in this environment are eye-wateringly expensive. Just the bare minimum modifications we've had to make to our home – hiring professionals to insulate each room and fitting them with their own independent air filtration system – cost almost double what we originally paid for the whole apartment. Add to that our day-to-day expenses, such as medical bills, food, water, Internet and electricity, all of which have spiralled outrageously in recent years, and we find ourselves struggling just to stay afloat.

Well, relatively speaking.

I'm aware of course that we're still obscenely more comfortable than most.

I have seen a few documentaries online about poorer communities who have created improvised quarantine stations using sheets of tarpaulin to divide their homes. Adapting old desk fans to create makeshift air purifiers. Drilling wells. Powering their lights with diesel generators. I suspect these people, however, are the exception rather than the rule. That for every family who has successfully filmed their own DIY house conversions, there are ten thousand more who didn't make it.

No, as much as things have changed, the paradigm still remains. The more money you have, the better and longer your life.

To be poor is to be miserable.

To be poor is to be dead.

And so, as much as I might privately mock my husband's dull work anecdotes, I am nevertheless grateful for the money he brings in and, by extension, for our continued survival.

Charlie, on the other hand, looked less impressed. By the time Colin finally broke off from his monologue about the finer points of hydraulic pressure pads, I was pleased to see that his enthusiasm had visibly waned. His smirk frozen in a pained rictus. His eyes glazed over.

'And how about you?' Colin asked at last. 'How was your day, buddy?'

This seemed to be just the moment Charlie had been waiting for. His eyes swam back into focus. He licked his lips. 'Oh, my day was just swell. But why don't you ask Amber what she's been up to? I bet she's got loads to share with us all. Isn't that right, Sis?'

Amber looked up sharply.

'That's a good point,' Colin blundered on. 'How *was* your

day, sweetie? I feel like I haven't caught up with you in ages. Are you well?'

Amber's scowl darkened, her teeth clenched so tight I was amazed she could get any words out at all. 'I'm fine,' she spat.

'Well that's *great* new*s*, honey. And you're staying on top of your college work?'

For the thousandth time that night, I marvelled at my husband's capacity to completely miss the subtext of a situation. How liberating it must be to be that oblivious. That insulated from the emotions of others.

Amber shook her head once, violently, as if jerking her head from a bee. 'I'm fine,' she repeated.

There was an awkward pause, before Charlie spoke again, his voice a teasing sing-song. 'Hey, Sis. Why don't you tell Dad about Jamal? I'm sure he'd love to hear all about him.'

For a single beat, Charlie's words seemed to hang in the air, like smoke after a gunshot.

And then Amber exploded.

'You little shit! You've been into my machine, haven't you? You and your ratty little hacker friends. I swear to God, I'll kill you. I'll fucking KILL you—'

'Hey!' I said. 'That's enough. I know you're angry, but there's no need to talk to your brother like that. And Charlie, how many times have I told you about respecting your sister's privacy?'

Charlie held up his hands in a half-hearted defence, but he was laughing too much to pay me much attention. 'Amber and Jamal, sitting in a tree, K-I-S-S-I-N-G...'

'I mean it, it's not nice. How would you feel if—'

Before I could finish, Charlie's screen went blank. He'd killed the feed.

We all fell silent for a moment, and then Colin cleared his throat. 'So who's Jamal?'

This time Amber's scream was so loud I could hear her through the wall.

30

Her screen went black, too, followed a few minutes later by the familiar thud of her treadmill.

Colin frowned. He looked confused. 'What the heck just happened? Do you know anything about this Jamal character?'

I let out a long sigh. 'You know, I've actually got some work I need to catch up on...'

I switched off my camera and finished my food in silence.

That was hours ago. Now I'm sitting at my desk, the plastic container that contained my dinner still lying beside me, a greasy scab congealing over the leftovers. A couple of minutes ago Colin texted:

Hey. Sorry about earlier. Kids, eh?

I didn't answer.

A minute passed before my phone vibrated again:

Wish you were here with me now x

I stared at the message, my finger hovering over the screen as I tried to think of what to write.

Seconds later another message arrived:

I miss you.

Then another:

What are you wearing?

Then another:

I'm so hard.

I hurled my phone across the room.

Killed the light.

Went to bed.

FOUR

FOR WEEKS, IT *was all anybody spoke about. The virus had spread from the Philippines to Indonesia. Then from Malaysia to Thailand. Then to China. India. Russia. New cases were appearing by the day, with no sign of stopping. The death toll doubling by the hour. Then the minute. Pretty soon we lost count. It was simply millions.*

At first it was unclear exactly what was happening. For some reason, the government seemed hesitant to use the word 'pandemic'. While the symptoms were similar from region to region – the nettle-sting rash, the shortness of breath, the sudden swelling of the eyes then tongue then throat, followed by an agonising, choking death – it was difficult to establish the exact cause of the outbreak. Overnight, we all became amateur virologists. Armchair epidemiologists. Perhaps it wasn't a disease at all? It might be something in the atmosphere. Or in the food chain. Air pollution from vehicle emissions. A build-up of toxins from illegal pesticides. A secret leak from a nuclear reactor. A biological attack by a terrorist state. Plastic microbeads. Nobody knew. And in the vacuum of uncertainty, rumours blossomed.

The news channels had a field day, of course. Frowning reporters offered grave dispatches from capital cities. Istanbul. Athens. Kiev. Minsk. Every now and then they'd flash up a map of the world, the infected countries – more than half the planet at that point – bathed in an ominous red glow, with animated arrows suggesting the direction it was travelling.

Right towards us.

In between interviews, footage showed locals wearing dust masks as they rode the subway. Sardine-packed hospital waiting rooms, overworked receptionists weeping at their desks. Supermarket shelves swept clean of supplies. Bottled water. Tinned food. Powdered milk. Batteries. In America, there were pictures of empty gun shops. Men in khaki-coloured clothing and wrap-around sunglasses with mountains of heavy-duty artillery piled up in the back of their utility trucks, as if they were planning to shoot the disease to death.

Then there were the pictures the regular broadcasters couldn't show. The stuff that would sometimes pop up on your social media timelines and that you couldn't help looking at, no matter how quickly you tried to scroll over it. The close-ups of the victims. Their faces ballooned beyond recognition. The scratch marks around their throats from where they'd fought for a final breath. And the mass cremations. The bodies stacked up under white sheets, taken out to burn in fields and deserts around the world, thick towers of noxious brown smoke coiling up towards the sky, visible for miles around.

Still, there was no real sense of panic. Not yet. Rather, there was a strange sense of unreality about the whole thing. After all, we'd spent decades at the cinema watching this stuff. We'd flicked through it at the local bookshops a thousand times before. We knew the narrative arc by heart. The apocalypse was hackneyed. Old hat. Besides, as bad as things were, they still weren't happening to us. It might have been creeping closer by the day: Croatia, Austria, Slovenia – even the odd case in Italy and France! – but it still wasn't here. No, this was something that was happening to foreign people in exotic countries. It was a mudslide in Bangladesh.

A famine in South Sudan. A terror attack in Lebanon. Just another pan-global atrocity playing out in montage on our mobile devices. Something to scroll and share while we rode the train to work.

So blasé were we that, even when the first sporadic cases did eventually reach our shores, we still didn't connect the dots. The janitor they found in our office building when we came into work one Monday morning? It was probably just a heart attack. The woman who dropped dead in the canteen of the shopping centre weeks earlier? She'd simply choked to death on her chicken sandwich.

Even when social media exploded with footage of local deaths and the red tops' headlines grew increasingly hysterical, it was still easy to pretend that it was all going to blow over. That everything was going to be just fine. After all, hadn't there been scares like this before? Bird flu. Swine flu. SARS. And look at how those had turned out. An anxiety attack over nothing. No, pretty soon the government would announce a vaccination programme and whatever this was would be relegated to a false-alarm, just like all the others. All hype and no teeth. Until then, it was simply a case of keeping calm and carrying on, just like the tea towel said.

And so that's exactly what we did.

We went to work. Sent the kids to school. Visited the shops.

We switched off our news feeds and stayed away from social media. Changed the channel to cartoons and talent shows and episodic dramas, binge watching our way to serenity.

We talked about the weather. Holiday plans. Career goals.

It wasn't until people we knew started disappearing – colleagues, a child in Charlie's class, Colin's aunt – that we started to appreciate just how serious the situation was shaping up to be. That things might not be all right after all. That maybe we should start doing what our paranoid neighbours had been doing for weeks. Securing the apartment. Hoarding food. Petrol. Water. Weapons. Or else just loading up the car with supplies and driving away. Getting out of the city altogether. Heading out to the countryside or the coast or somewhere remote. Lying low until the whole thing blew over.

By the time we got our act together, though, there were no supplies left to buy. No food or petrol or water or weapons to gather. The shops were empty. The roads were closed. The electricity was off and the taps had run dry. By then, around half the city had been infected and there were soldiers on the streets.

In other words, it was already much, much too late.

FIVE

WHICH CAME FIRST, the woman or the egg?

I'm serious. Well, semi-serious. You see, I've been thinking about you again this morning, Egg. You and your two million or so other unfertilised sisters. Did you know that women are born with all the ova they are ever going to have? If that's true, I guess that means that I didn't make you at all. Rather, you were stitched together at the same time as me, in my poor old mum's womb. Just as the egg that became me was made by her mother, my grandma, who was made by her mother, and her mother before that. And on and on it goes, a biological production line stretching back millennia. A microscopic torch passed from ovary to ovary over millions of years. Back before my ancestors were even 'people' at all. Back when they weren't much more than proto-organisms, a few cells swimming around in the primordial swamp.

And before that?

It's hard to say. My grasp on evolutionary theory is shaky at best, but I like to imagine I'm looking backwards through the telescope until I reach the very start of the chain. The very first egg, floating there in that silent darkness at the beginning of the world. Encoded within her tiny shell all the secrets needed to build a planet full of people. My earliest relative. And yours, too. Though I fear that you, sitting there in your top-secret government medical facility, may actually represent her diametric opposite. The very end of the chain. A genetic cul-de-sac.

The place where it all finally stops.

Anyway, all this talk of ancestry brings me round to my own darling daughter, who this morning has already been the source of a hundred headaches.

It's Saturday the something. February, maybe. Or perhaps April? I stopped paying such close attention to the calendar a few years ago now. With the windows and balcony sealed up, I hardly know what season it is, let alone the day. Dates, I decided long ago, are for people with plans. Holidays. Events. Celebrations. I hardly even bother keeping track of my own birthday any more. Cake and candles for one is just too depressing for words.

Still, while I may have given up counting the days, my computer hasn't. My online assistant 'helpfully' taking note of every email I send or receive, prompting me whenever a rare obligation does come up. Which is the reason I woke this morning to the high-pitched trill of a new notification:

NEIGHBOURHOOD WATCH DUTY: 09.00–11.00

I first stumbled across our local neighbourhood watch scheme on an online forum last year and instantly I was hooked. In return for a few hours of basic health and safety training, you were given a licence from the government to break curfew and roam the city streets by yourself for an hour or so every fortnight with a camera strapped to your chest, the idea being that you could let the authorities know should anything untoward be taking place locally. Sure, you had to stick to a designated patrol route and then type up a detailed report for your group leader (in my case a lady called Fatima, who lives in the apartment block opposite ours.) But what a trade-off! For four years, I hadn't been further than the ration drop-off point in the basement of the building. Suddenly I was free to walk out of the front door of the apartment as if it was the most natural thing in the world.

I remember the night before I was due to go out on my first patrol. I lay restless on my bed, unable to sleep. Of course, by then I had a fairly good idea of what to expect out there. In the immediate months after we'd sealed ourselves away, the Internet was awash with rumours. Gossip. Hearsay. The world was a dystopian wasteland inhabited by the dead and the dying. Fires raged day and night. Buildings lay flattened. Corpses lay stacked in the street by the dozen. People posted clips from *Mad Max* and *Dawn of the Dead* and passed them off as documentary footage. No one knew what was real and what was Photoshop. After a few months or so, however, official drone footage began to leak in from what was left of the media. Then we all saw what was out there. To my surprise, it wasn't as extreme as I'd expected. For the most part, the world looked the same. Only without the people. Sure, there were some iconic shots. The Arc de Triomphe empty. Times Square deserted. Tokyo Station abandoned. In truth, though, it all seemed a little anticlimactic. There was nothing we hadn't seen before in the cinema. None of it looked... *real*.

As the years went by, more and more footage was beamed back to our bedrooms. And admittedly, some of it was pretty dramatic. Who can forget the shots of the Eiffel Tower, its lower legs now entirely engulfed by thick foliage? Or the London Eye lying on its side, its carriages rusting, its spokes bent in on themselves? Perhaps it's images like these that have convinced Colin that the neighbourhood watch scheme is a terrible idea. Honestly, the way he talks about it, you'd think I was going off to war rather than for a mid-morning stroll around the neighbourhood.

'What if you get into trouble?' he'd fretted when he first found out I'd signed up. 'What if someone attacks you?'

'Who's going to attack me? There's no one out there.'

'What about soldiers? You've seen what they do to people.'

I patiently explained about my training again. About the protocols we had in place. About the special set of digital credentials I'd been given, authorising me to pass freely on the off-chance I should run into any military personnel. Though of course there's not much danger of that ever happening. In fact, in the six months I've been on patrol, I haven't once needed to show my ID to anyone. While I've seen online footage of heavily armed soldiers in various trouble spots around the country, our neighbourhood is almost embarrassingly safe. There's never anyone out there but me, and the only traffic on the roads are the huge, automated lorries that criss-cross the country, delivering groceries and medical provisions to residents, or dropping fertility doctors to their appointments.

While it's comforting to live in such a quiet neighbourhood, the downside is that I never have anything to write up. Having read a dozen or so of the bone-dry reports from some of the other members on my team, they seem to have the same problem as me. It's almost tempting to start inventing things, just to make it worth reading.

Not that any of this seems to make much of a difference to Colin, who all these months later still frets about my participation in the scheme. One of his biggest gripes is that we undertake our patrols alone, rather than in a group. Apparently it hasn't occurred to him that walking alongside a stranger with only the thin fabric of my hazmat suit for protection would potentially pose a far graver risk.

Incidentally, this is exactly the same point I made to Amber when she texted this morning with the unprecedented request to accompany me on patrol. It's a shame, really. While I appreciate her unusual willingness to spend some time with me – or to do anything outside of her obsessive exercise regime – I nevertheless declined her offer, reminding her of the multitude of dangers it would entail. *All it would take*, I typed, *is a small rip in your suit. If you caught it on a rusty nail or a shard of shattered window, there'd be nothing anyone could do for you. Besides, does that old suit even still fit you?* I inserted a winking emoji then finished the message with three crosses:

Kiss kiss kiss.

She didn't reply.

After breakfast, which as usual consisted of a small, vacuum-packed pot of porridge, I picked up the cup containing the government-issued pills we are required to swallow each day in order to stay healthy. I rattled the six small tablets against the plastic. There's Vitamin D, obviously. That's for the lack of sunlight. Then there's B12, which we take due to the scarcity of meat. There's also a supplement for iron, and another containing niacin and calcium, though I forget which is which. The final two are medications. A beige one for anxiety and a small green capsule containing a low dose of anti-depressants.

Again, for obvious reasons.

I tipped my head back, washing them down with a gulp of orange juice. Then I put on my suit, pausing to strap the small digital camera into the harness around my neck, before finally slipping on my mask. Then I headed for the front door.

Even now, six months after I signed up, I still get a tingle of anxiety at the thought of leaving the apartment, and as I stooped to enter the cramped tent of the quarantine zone, I felt my heart beginning to race. We upgraded our front door a couple of years ago to a thicker steel model secured by an electronic access code. Although I know the number by heart, my hand was shaking so much that I got a digit wrong, resulting in a sharp buzz and a red light. I took a deep breath and tried again. This time the lock flashed green. As I depressed the handle, the door gave a slight hiss as the airtight seal broke. And then I was stepping out into the hallway.

Alone.

WHEN WE FIRST moved into the apartment building, almost a decade ago now, the communal areas were maintained to an incredibly high standard. Freshly watered plants lined the halls. The corridors were vacuumed daily. The stairs swept and mopped. Today, however, the state of disrepair is overwhelming. The building is only a third full these days, and with the majority of families permanently sealed away, no one has yet volunteered to take responsibility for the clean-up. Even if they did, it's difficult to know where they'd start. Most of the lights overhead are broken. Those few that still work tend to blink on and off at random, casting the halls in a stuttering fluorescent gloom. The potted plants are long gone, the only trace of them a few shards of broken terracotta, adding to a crackling topsoil of dirt and glass, as well as the odd belonging lost in the initial evacuation. A mobile phone. A set of car keys. An inhaler. A child's toy.

As I made my way towards the exit, I did my best to tread lightly, tiptoeing through the filth so as not to disturb the deadly dust that coats everything. I kept moving, past the lift, which is broken, permanently jammed between floors, and instead headed for the stairs. In order to get there I had to pass Mr and Mrs Chen's old apartment. As with every time I go out there, I told myself not to look. Yet, as always, I found I couldn't help myself, craning my neck to peek in at the charred remains of their home.

The Chens were a young family who moved into the building around a year after us. Jin, Lucy and their son, Wei. While I didn't know Jin well, I always made an effort to stop and talk to Lucy whenever we bumped into each other in the hall. We weren't friends exactly, but Charlie was only a few months older than Wei, and so we had some common ground. She was nice. Smart, with a dry sense of humour. I remember one of the last times we spoke she told me they were trying for another baby and that she was nervous because Wei was already such a handful.

'You'll be fine,' I told her. 'Second time round is a piece of cake. Trust me.'

I didn't see her again after that. Like us, the Chens had decided to stay and try and wait things out. They weren't worried either. What was the worst that could happen?

After they died, a group of neighbours broke in at night and doused their apartment in petrol before setting it on fire, presumably in the misguided belief they could burn away the virus. If it wasn't for the sprinkler system, the entire building would have gone up.

Peering in at the blackened, smoke-damaged shell, I could almost see Lucy standing in the doorway. Could almost hear the high-pitched gurgle of Wei's laugh as he and Charlie swapped toys or babbled to one another. I swallowed hard. Blinked away the ghosts. Kept walking.

When I reached the ground floor, I saw the main entrance was blocked off. This wasn't unusual. Despite crime being virtually non-existent these days, some of the older residents here are still convinced we are about to be ransacked by a post-apocalyptic biker gang, or something equally ridiculous. Although I have posted a number of polite messages on the online communal message board requesting that people keep the exits clear, I still regularly come down to find a ramshackle assortment of furniture stacked in front of the main doors, as if this easily disassembled barricade might somehow deter the fearsome zombie hordes who are allegedly lurking around each and every corner.

It took me a couple of minutes to clear a path to the door, and as I stepped out onto the front steps, I found I'd broken into a sweat. Still, the moment I looked up, I forgot all about the unnecessary exertions. Even though it had only been a few weeks since I'd last been outside, the world had transformed completely. Colourful explosions of flowers sprang from the cracks in the concrete. Crocuses. Daffodils.

Lily of the valley. Bumblebees bobbed and flies flittered and butterflies beat their quivering wings. Somewhere above me, a pair of amorous squirrels scampered across the drooping line that somehow still clung between telegraph poles. Everywhere there was life.

Hitting record on the camera, I crept forward into the crisp morning. To my surprise, I felt an unexpected pang of sadness as I realised the visceral thrill of my very first patrols was already a distant memory. Now that the novelty of just being out here had faded, I'd begun to feel frustrated with the limitations of the set-up. From behind my mask, everything seemed muted. The colours less vibrant. The details blurred. The sounds muffled. It was like watching a wildlife documentary on TV. Or staring at video footage of Niagara Falls. It was pretty. But it wasn't the same as actually being there.

It's funny. In the old world, I had suffered horribly with hay fever. My eyes and nose streamed at the first sniff of spring. The whole season filled me with dread, as I looked forward to months of crumpled tissues and scrabbling around in my bag for blister packs of antihistamines. This morning, though, I would have given anything to peel off my mask and breathe in the sweet, spring air. Just for a second. Just to feel the sunshine on my face one more time. Just to be truly outside again.

But of course, I didn't.

No. I kept my mask firmly in place, peeking out through the protective screen. The only thing I could smell was warm plastic and the faintly astringent sting of disinfectant spray that I use to keep my respirator clean.

In the courtyard outside our apartment building, there had once been a large ornamental fountain, the pump of which had long since broken. Peering into it this morning, I saw there was now an entire shoal of silverfish living there, scattered like a handful of loose change through the murk. I wondered how they had got there. It didn't make any sense. The pond was totally cut off from everything else. And yet there they were, clinging on in their own self-contained bubble. Defying the odds to survive.

I pressed on, moving out of the courtyard towards the wide road where my patrol begins. Five years ago, this stretch of concrete was one of the major routes in and out of the city. Traffic would thunder along here day and night, an endless procession of noise and fumes. This morning, though, the only thing I could hear was the chatter of birdsong. Even muffled by my mask, it was louder than I ever remember it being in the old world.

Years ago, I watched a documentary about the dramatic resurgence of wildlife inside the Chernobyl exclusion zone. Without humans to hunt them down and destroy their habitat, the animals there had apparently thrived, despite the supposedly deadly levels of radiation. Where once workers had spilled from factory gates, now bison and boar snuffled through the tangled undergrowth that had consumed the buildings. Where decades earlier schoolchildren had lined up for class, wolves and wild horses roamed across the crumbling playgrounds.

It seems a similar phenomenon has also occurred here. Indeed, as I cut across the forecourt of a derelict petrol station, I glanced up to see a colossal colony of black-feathered birds scowling down at me from the faded awning. It was an eerie sensation, to be watched like that. There must have been four hundred of them up there, slowly tilting their heads to track me until I'd safely passed. I'm not quite sure what they were. Crows, maybe. Or ravens? Rooks? I never learned the difference. One of the other members of my team is a keen twitcher, his reports littered with breathless descriptions of the latest formally elusive breed he'd spotted that day. Wood warblers. Goshawks. Willow tits. Nightjars. They've all bounced back apparently, their populations thriving now that we are the endangered species.

It's not just birds that have enjoyed a resurgence in

our absence. Now that they pretty much have the land to themselves, the mammals have crept back from the fringes, too, claiming the streets for their own. Even in the daytime, I've lost track of the number of foxes I've seen, far fatter and redder than any of the pitiful grey things I remember prowling around our bins at dusk and at dawn. Huge colonies of rabbits sit grazing at the jungle-like lay-bys and traffic islands, utterly unbothered by my presence. There are badgers, too. And hares. I've even read reports of polecats and pine martens padding through the overgrown parks, though I'm yet to see them myself. Down by the canals there are stoats and voles and shrews.

The city crawls. It slinks. It glides and slithers and gallops.

And then there's the livestock. Meat is a rare commodity these days, mostly confined to just poultry and pork. Animals that can be bred indoors, processed more or less autonomously. The other animals were simply left to die when the farmers abandoned their fields. The cows and the sheep and the goats. And while presumably many of them did indeed starve, many more escaped, crashing through their pens and leaping over fences and out into the world. I've read stories of vast itinerant herds of cattle lumbering down the motorways in search of food. Of entire suburbs invaded by sheep. Shopping centres overrun with goats.

These aren't the only rumours I've heard.

There are whispers of other, non-native animals, too. Wild and exotic species.

Dangerous beasts.

After the outbreak, the various zoos and safari parks around the country were supposedly ordered to euthanise their stock. According to some reports, though, many of the keepers simply opened the cages, releasing the captive animals into the wild. Elephants and rhinos. Monkeys and zebras. Lions and tigers and bears.

Oh my.

Of course, I'm not sure how much truth there is in these

stories. Even with the media up and running again, you still tend to hear all sorts of crazy things on the Internet these days. Even so, I find myself freezing at the slightest flicker of movement, certain that any second a hungry leopard will launch itself from the shadows and tear me to pieces.

Fortunately, the most threatening animals I came across that morning was a pride of scrawny kittens, a dozen or so of them strutting through the gardens of an old office block as I turned right off the main road to avoid them. These days, pets of any kind are strictly forbidden. They are deemed a risk of spreading potentially fatal allergens. While we were instructed by the government to dispose of them humanely, like the farmers and zookeepers, many pet owners across the country simply turfed their animals out onto the streets. Millions must surely have perished, too domesticated to feed and fend for themselves. Some pets, however, did make it. These days packs of feral cats and dogs are a common sight in the city, though I make sure to give the latter a wide berth, for fear of being bitten.

ON MY FIRST few expeditions into the city, I kept religiously to my designated patrol route, terrified that deviating even an inch or two would somehow flag me up to the authorities, and that my newly minted freedom would be snatched away from me. As the weeks and months wore on, however, I began to grow a little bolder, especially once I realised that I could simply pause the camera strapped to my chest if I decided to explore somewhere further afield. While, I still didn't dare to wander too far from the main road, it was fun to visit some of the places I remembered from the old world.

I remember a few months ago standing outside a supermarket, the same store I used to visit religiously each Saturday morning. While the front windows of the building were all smashed, probably during the initial wave of lootings, the structure still looked in reasonably good shape. Of course, I didn't dare venture inside. Still, if I squinted past the dirt and the plants and the rusting trolleys that lay scattered across the car park, it wasn't hard to remember the store as it was before. The weekly trudge up and down the heaving aisles. The impromptu meal planning and mental arithmetic as I juggled various promotions and special offers. The staccato bleeps and the stilted conversations at the checkout. So dull, so drab, so everyday.

Until suddenly, it wasn't.

This morning, however, I was in no mood for nostalgia, instead deciding to stick to my official route. I kept walking, deeper and deeper into the city, abandoned apartments giving way to derelict shops, before I finally reached what used to be the financial district. This marked the halfway point of my patrol. I paused, peering up at a tall, modern office block set back slightly from the road. By some quirk of programming, my route took me directly past the place where I used to work. Even though I've seen it a dozen times now, I still never quite got used to the sight of it. Where once teams of acrobatic window-washers abseiled down its sides, buffing the glass and chrome frontage until it gleamed, today it is a scuffed, grimy mess, more like a gravestone than the headquarters of an international social media conglomerate. Near the front entrance, someone had scrawled a message in red paint, the huge letters still just about legible all these years later:

The end is nigh!

And then beneath it:

Repent, ye sinners, else hell awaits thee!

I turned my gaze upwards, counting until I found the fourteenth floor. My old office. I could still picture it all so well. Water-cooler gossip with colleagues. Meetings with my boss. Lunch with friends. It's hard to get my head around what it must actually look like up there now. The carpets rotten. The walls peeling. The computers strung with cobwebs. Everything happened so quickly, there was no time to pack anything away. I left work one Wednesday lunchtime and never went back. Presuming the floor hasn't caved in, or that it hasn't been ransacked by animals, my desk must still be there. A layer of dust thick enough to write my name in. A half-drunk mug of coffee still beside my monitor, the surface blistered with spores of mould. One of my old blazers still hanging over the back of my chair, the fabric decomposing, eaten away by moths. Paperwork. Pens. Diaries. All of it faded and forgotten.

I shook away the memories, ready to carry on my route, when suddenly I froze. There was something there, a little way down the street. A trickle of movement. A shifting in the shadows. I struggled to keep my breath steady, fighting against the surge of adrenaline to stay calm. Rational. Telling myself I was being ridiculous. That a ferocious big cat definitely wasn't about to appear. A tiger or a lion. A jaguar or a leopard. That it was probably nothing more than a straggling kitten. Or perhaps nothing at all. My tired eyes playing tricks on me.

Only it didn't look like a kitten.

And it didn't look like nothing.

I pushed my glove up to my mask, wiping away the layer of grime that had settled on the visor, then squinted again into the distance.

And then I heard it. Not from the direction I'd been looking, but from right behind me.

Close.

And getting closer.

The unmistakable slap of rubber on concrete. The swish of fabric.

I turned.

Just in time to see someone sprinting.

They were heading right towards me.

PART TWO

SIX

I TURNED AND ran. My body a jangle of disjointed limbs. My protective suit crackling with static. It had been years since I'd moved so fast. It would almost have been exhilarating if I hadn't been so scared. The jolt of hard tarmac on my toes. The sudden burn in my chest. The rubber band twang of my hamstrings stretching.

But then, seconds later, it all went horribly wrong.

I hadn't appreciated quite how much the suit constricted my movement, and within a couple of seconds I felt the fabric pulling taut around my knees, knocking me off my stride. For a split second I flailed helplessly, clawing at the air as I tried to regain my balance, before my momentum sent me sprawling to the ground.

For a moment I lay there, too stunned to move. Then the pain arrived. Though my suit was miraculously untorn, my knees and elbows were grazed, the sharp sting bringing with it a fleeting memory of childhood falls in the playground. Balls of cotton wool dipped in witch hazel. Cold compresses. Sticky beige plasters.

Then I remembered where I was.

Why I was running.

Seconds later, a shadow fell over me, and I looked up just in time to catch a glimpse of a suited figure bearing down.

I braced myself and waited for the end. Then the figure called out.

'Mum? Mum? *Angela*.'

It took me a few seconds to understand what was going on. That rather than being attacked, someone was calling my name.

I unfurled myself cautiously, then sat up, trying to make sense of the face that was staring back from behind a mask identical to my own. A warm flood of relief crashed over me. 'Amber? Is that you?'

As I climbed to my feet, Amber suddenly threw her arms open, embracing me in a tight squeeze.

Instinctively, I thrashed to get away from her, shoving her so hard she almost toppled over. 'Jesus! What the hell do you think you're doing?'

'I'm sorry. I was just so pleased to see you that I wanted to... I'm sorry.'

Having recovered slightly from the shock of physical contact now that I'd put some space between us, I forced a smile. 'It's fine. I understand how you feel. But you can't just go around *hugging* people. It's too dangerous. You know that. Even in our suits, it isn't worth the risk. All it would take is one microscopic rip and... Wait a minute. What am I saying? What the hell are you even doing out here?'

Amber shrugged, staring at her feet.

'Hey, I'm talking to you, young lady. Do you have any idea how dangerous it is to be out here without permission? And how in the world did you squeeze into that old suit? Are you sure it's still airtight?'

'It fits fine.'

'What if somebody had seen you then? Did you think about that? You could have been picked up by the police or anything. What then? You think life in your bedroom's bad? Try a prison cell.'

'Whatever,' she said, still refusing to meet my eye. 'You're the one always moaning about how there's no one out here.'

'That's not the point. You deliberately disobeyed me. What do you think your father's going to say when he finds out?'

Amber shook her head defiantly, but when she finally looked up, I saw her eyes were glossed with tears. When she spoke again, her voice sounded thin and pinched. 'I just couldn't take being in there any longer.'

'So what? You thought you'd run away?'

'What? No! It was nothing like that. I was just going for a walk around the block. Just for a couple of minutes. But then this dog started sniffing around me. And at first it was kind of cute... but then it started barking and I started to run... and then I saw you... and I thought... I thought...'

Amber trailed off, dissolving into a dry retch of tears. As she did, she took a step towards me. I flinched. For an awful moment I thought she was going to try and hug me again. Instead, she just stood there, her arms hanging pathetically by her sides.

'Hey. Come on.' I took another discreet step backwards. 'Being cooped up in that house is hard on all of us. I know that. But it's not safe for you to be out here. That's why I don't let you come with me. It's not because I'm mean, or I want to keep you locked up. It's because I care about you and I don't want anything bad to happen. I mean, there are worse things than dogs. Trust me. What if your mask malfunctioned? I have to say, that suit does look a little tight, sweetie.'

I smiled at her, conscious to keep my tone level. Reasonable. Rational.

Naturally, Amber exploded.

'If it's so unsafe, then what the hell are you doing out here? Why take the risk? It's not like there's any point in your stupid little group anyway. Who the hell do you think you're protecting us from? You said it yourself, there's no one out here. Or perhaps you're secretly hoping that something terrible does happen to you. Maybe you *want* your mask to break, so that you'll die out here and then you won't have to go back to your stupid room in the stupid apartment. To your stupid family—'

'Now you're just being hysterical. I come out here because I believe it's important to look after our local community. And you're right. It is a risk. But it's a risk that I've weighed up and decided is worth taking. That's what adults do. And when you're an adult you can make your own decisions. But until then, it's my job to keep you safe.'

'When I'm an adult? I'm seventeen, Mum, but you still treat me like I'm a little kid. You keep saying that I need to take responsibility for my actions, but how can I if I never get to make my own decisions? I never get a choice in anything, and I never will. I'm going to be stuck in that fucking room until I die.'

'That's enough, Amber. Do you have any idea how lucky you are? The sacrifices we made so we can carry on living?'

'You call this living? Because I don't. And as far as sacrifices, I don't remember ever being asked if we wanted to be saved. Because if anyone had taken the time to consult me, if they'd given me the choice between dying of some virus or living out the rest of my days like a battery hen, I'd have walked into the nearest crowd and taken a nice, deep breath.'

'Why you spoilt little—'

But before I could finish, I froze.

Behind Amber, I'd spotted something. Something moving.

Amber's eyes widened as she turned to follow my gaze, her rage replaced with fear.

She let out a whimper. 'The dog…?'

I didn't move. Didn't answer.

I just kept watching.

Not blinking. Not breathing.

My eyes scanning the deserted street.

Seconds passed. A minute. Then another.

'Mum? Should we—'

'Shhhh!'

We kept watching.

Silent.

Still as statues.

And then, just when I was ready to blame whatever I'd seen on my imagination, something stepped out from an alleyway.

An animal.

Not a dog, or a leopard, but a deer. A baby. A fawn.

Somewhere nearby I heard a gasp escape from Amber's mask as the animal trotted out into the middle of the road, teetering uncertainly on matchstick legs. It was close enough that I could make out the dappling of pale spots along its back, as if it had been lightly powdered with icing sugar. It couldn't be more than a few days old.

Suddenly it stopped dead, its comically large ears swivelling like satellite dishes, before it turned its head so that it was looking directly at us. I held my breath. The fawn gave a couple of slow, sleepy blinks. Once. Twice. Its eyes as black and glassy as marble. It twitched its nose, sniffing the air. And then, just as suddenly as it had appeared, it was gone again, drifting across the road and disappearing into the undergrowth.

'Oh my God!' Amber cried. 'Did you see that? That was the most amazing thing *ever!*'

Even behind her mask, I was able to make out the look of wonder on her face, her eyes sparkling with excitement, before they suddenly widened with fear. 'Will it be okay?' she asked, turning back to look in the direction the fawn had disappeared. 'I didn't see its mother anywhere.'

'I'm sure it'll be just fine.'

Amber shook her head, still fretting. 'But what if it's an orphan? What if it can't find anything to eat?'

'Really, sweetie. It'll be okay. I promise. There's probably a whole family of them nearby. Now, why don't we get you back to your room before anyone notices you're gone, eh?'

Amber carried on looking at the deserted alley for a moment, as if hoping for another peek of animal. 'Okay,' she nodded when it didn't appear. 'Let's go home.'

ALL THE WAY back to the apartment, Amber talked breathlessly. Not just about the fawn, whose wellbeing she continued to fret about, but over every tiny creature we encountered. Every bird and butterfly and bee. Having spent more than a quarter of her life indoors, the natural world both fascinated and confused her. At one point, she actually got down on her hands and knees to watch as a procession of ants marched across the fractured paving slabs.

'How do they know where they're going? How do they find their way back home?'

I shrugged. Shook my head. I had no answers for her. I was taken aback by this version of Amber, so different from the brooding teen I had become accustomed to staring at on my computer screen. Though she had the body of a woman, she was still disarmingly naïve, her development slowed by the years spent alone. She was twelve when we sealed ourselves away. In some ways she's never moved on. She's still that same frightened little girl frozen in time. A relic from an extinct world.

Once the novelty of her new environment had eventually worn off, Amber began telling me about college. Of course, she doesn't physically attend. All of her studies take place online in a virtual classroom, along with thousands of other students from around the country. Unlike Charlie, Amber is actually a pretty committed student, achieving consistently high grades and commendations from her teachers. At least she did until recently. Over the last year, she's floundered, becoming increasingly despondent whenever either Colin or I have attempted to ask her how things are going or, God forbid, what she might like to do when she finishes studying. I suppose this is hardly a surprise. No matter how many times Colin repeats the line about 'being armed with the skills you need to thrive when all this blows over', we all know that in reality her 'job' will hardly differ in any meaningful way from either school or college. It will take place in her room. In front of her computer. Alone.

I was therefore taken aback when Amber initiated a

conversation about her favourite classes (history and English lit.) and her favourite tutor (Mr Hopkiss), mentioning the names of a dozen or more friends I'd never heard her talk about before. Hearing her chat away like a normal teenager was reassuring. I hadn't been sure she even *had* a social life, and yet here she was telling me all about the intimate struggles of her cohort. To my amazement, Amber sounded not only popular, but wise. She seemed to be the person her friends turned to in moments of crisis. Trusting her with their most intimate secrets. Counting on her for guidance. As we approached our apartment, I found myself overwhelmed with pride. In five years, I can't remember ever feeling so close to her.

Perhaps that's why I decided to try and prolong the moment.

'Hey, do you want to do something a little crazy?'

Amber turned to me, perplexed. 'What do you mean?'

'Come on,' I grinned, abruptly changing direction, so that I was walking away from the apartment. 'I'll show you.'

'Wait. Mum. Stop. Won't we get in trouble?'

I laughed. 'It's fine. Trust me. I've done this loads of times.'

With my camera safely shut off, I led Amber down a side street, past the crumbling remains of what used to be our local swimming pool, until we reached an innocuous-looking patch of bushes at the side of the road.

'Do you recognise it?' I asked.

Amber shook her head, perplexed. 'It's just a bunch of… Wait. What *is* that? Is this… Oh my God. Is this the parrot park?'

Just visible through the thicket was a green metal fence, though the paint had mostly flaked away. Beyond that, if you looked hard enough, it was possible to make out the rotting remains of a wooden climbing frame. Elsewhere, the top of a warped metal slide protruded from a tangle of brambles, along with a warped set of swings.

'I can't believe you found this place,' Amber said, before she began pointing excitedly. 'Look! There he is.'

Over in the far corner, almost totally obscured now by

foliage, was the eponymous 'parrot': a purple and green fibreglass bird fixed to a large spring rocker.

'It's been so long. I can't believe you remember.'

'Of *course* I remember. This place was the best.'

Amber had always been an early riser and I have vivid memories of standing in the park with her at some obscene time on a Sunday morning while I pushed her on the swing or the parrot for what felt like hours. Even when she was older, too big really for the babyish rides, she still begged to come here, contorting her body in order to squeeze down the slide or into the basket of the swing. Strangely, Charlie had never taken to the park in the same way as his sister, preferring instead to play computer games inside than to join us on our chilly early morning expeditions.

Amber stood silently for a few minutes, staring off wistfully at the ruined play park, until eventually we turned back towards the apartment. This time we walked in silence, Amber seeming lost in her memories. Desperate to rekindle the connection I'd felt with her earlier, I decided to bring up the subject of school again.

'So what about this Jamal boy I've heard about? Is he in your class, too?'

The moment I spoke, I realised my mistake. Instantly, Amber's shoulders hunched protectively around her ears.

'I don't want to talk about it.' Her voice was so low it was difficult to hear her through her mask.

'I'm sorry. I wasn't trying to pry. It's just that I know how tricky things can be with boys. Especially at your age. Anyway, I just want you to know that if you need any advice, I'm right here for you.'

Amber's scowl only darkened, though. Even behind her mask, I could make out her lips puckering. Her nostrils flaring. And then she started shouting. 'Jesus! I am *sick* of this family! Everyone is obsessed with everyone else's business. There's no privacy. Not online. Not out here. Nowhere. I've had enough. I've had enough of it all.'

'Amber, wait…'

It was too late, though. Already, she was storming ahead of me towards the apartment. By the time I made it upstairs and through the front door, I saw she'd installed herself in the far corner of the quarantine tent, so that she was facing the wall. I tried a few more times to initiate conversation with her, but it was no good. That fleetingly happy, talkative Amber was once again a thing of the past.

After that, we sat in silence, counting the minutes and hours until the red light eventually turned green, at which point Amber stormed from the tent without so much as a glance over her shoulder.

A few seconds later I heard her bedroom door slam shut behind her, before the treadmill started up again.

Thud.

Thud.

Thud.

●●●

AND SO HERE I am again. Just you and me, Egg. It's late now. Way past my bedtime. Yet I'm sitting at my desk wide awake, watching the footage from this morning's patrol. I've been running it backwards and forwards for hours, but still I can't decide exactly what it is that I'm looking at.

Neither Charlie nor Amber turned on their webcams for dinner tonight, and for once Colin seemed in no mood to talk. We ate our dinner quickly and in near silence, logging off the second the last forkful slid down our throats. After that, I paced around my room restlessly. Not that there's much room to pace. You can't move more than six or seven strides in any direction without hitting a wall. It's just about large enough to house my bed, my desk, a wardrobe-sized ensuite bathroom and a small kitchenette. It's hard to believe that Charlie's room is about half this size. This was always meant to be a temporary arrangement, and so giving the kids smaller rooms made sense at the time. Now it just feels like an extra kick in the teeth. One more thing for them to hate us for.

Eventually I stopped pacing and sat down at my computer, forcing myself to tackle my neighbourhood watch report while it was still fresh in my mind. After a few minutes, however, I became distracted, unsure of how to cover the part where my teenage daughter illegally gatecrashed my patrol.

While I dithered about what to do, I decided to review the footage from my chest camera. Once I'd hooked it up to my computer, I hit the fast-forward button, watching the butterflies flutter in double time. The bees buzzing like bullets. As it reached the part where I got to my old office building, though, I instinctively slowed the footage down to normal speed. Even seeing the building on the screen felt weird. I reached out to hit fast-forward again, but as I did, something made me stop.

A trickle of movement.

A shifting in the shadows.

All at once, I remembered the fear I'd felt, just before Amber had interrupted me. The sense that I was being watched. I paused the video, straining to make out what it was that was lurking at the edge of the frame. I rewound the footage slightly. Zoomed in. Then again. Closer and closer, so that the image smeared. Bled.

I hit play. Pause. Rewind.

Again and again.

Play. Pause. Rewind.

And then suddenly I saw it.

Or at least, I saw *something*.

The image blown out and distorted, a blurry mass of brightly coloured pixels.

It could be anything, really.

And yet, if I squinted my eyes and tilted my head slightly, I could almost make it out. Though I knew what I was seeing was utterly impossible. A trick of the light, surely. An optical illusion.

Even so, I'm still here, staring at the screen hours later. And no matter how many times I look at it, I can't help but think it looks exactly like a person, crouched in the shadows.

A person dressed in regular clothes.

An orange T-shirt and a pair of jeans.

No suit.

No mask.

Nothing.

What's more – and now I know I sound crazy – but if I *really* squint, it almost looks as if they're staring right back at me.

SEVEN

IT WAS COLIN who decided we should try and make a break for it. His boss, Steve, had a small holiday cottage we could use. A bolthole by the sea that he kept stocked with supplies in case of spontaneous weekend getaways. We'd actually stayed there a few years earlier, when the kids were younger. It was beautiful, if a little isolated. I remember complaining at the time about there being nothing to do. The nearest shop was a good twenty-minute drive away. Now, though, the house sounded perfect.

Especially as Steve and his family wouldn't need it any more.

We waited for night to fall before we left. This was a week or so after the fire at the Chens' apartment, a few days after the electricity had gone out. It was a strange time. I remember going to great pains to act as if everything was normal in front of the children. To pretend that it was all some great big adventure. Wasn't this fun, heating up tinned soup on the camping stove indoors? Wasn't this neat, using torches and candles instead of lights? At least now that the TV and Internet were down, Charlie had stopped asking awkward questions for which we had no easy answers:

What's a global pandemic, Mummy?

What's a state of emergency?

What's martial law?

Even so, it was impossible to shield them from the constant wail of sirens outside the window. Or the screaming and the sobbing through the walls whenever a neighbour heard bad news about friends or relatives. Or got sick themselves. Occasionally there were other sounds, too. Loud cracks that sounded suspiciously like gunshots. Breaking glass and burglar alarms. Distant explosions. Cries in the night.

And then there was the fact that Colin had taken to sleeping with a cricket bat propped at the end of the bed.

We packed what little we had into suitcases and then waited until the children were in bed before we loaded up the car, leaving it until after midnight before we lifted them from their beds. Charlie stayed asleep, still coiled in his blanket as I strapped him in. At twelve, Amber was too big for me to carry, and she stirred a little on Colin's shoulder as he heaved her out into the cold hallway.

'Where are we going, Mum?'

'We're going on a holiday.'

Even in the dim light I could make out the sceptical look on her face.

'We're not coming back are we?'

'Don't be silly, sweetie. Of course we're coming back.'

Amber didn't answer.

IT WAS TOO *dark to see much outside. Even so, we kept our faces pressed to the car windows, our breath clouding the glass as the road unravelled ahead of us. Though we didn't say it aloud for fear of scaring the kids, we both knew what we were looking for. Looters. Carjackers. The diseased and the desperate.*

Then there were the soldiers to worry about.

While officially there was still a curfew in place, there didn't actually seem to be any military presence on the streets to enforce it. Still, before the Internet had gone down I'd read rumours about people being stopped and turned back. Or worse. Of soldiers hijacking their vehicles and stealing their supplies for themselves. It made sense. They were just people, after all. As scared and confused and as desperate as everyone else.

While we scoured the darkness for danger, I heard a rustling from the back seat. I turned to find Charlie sitting up, though he was only half awake, his eyes scrunched tight.

'Will the bad guys kill us if they catch us?'

Colin and I exchanged a glance, before I reached forward to tuck the blanket back over his shoulders.

'Don't be silly, darling. Why don't you try and go back to sleep?'

I leaned in and placed a kiss on his forehead.

At the same time, I heard an unmistakable crunch as Colin activated the central locking.

In the end, we managed to make it out of the city without being stopped, passing through the suburbs and eventually out into the countryside. While not as efficient as the newer generation of self-driving models, the car was surprisingly nimble, gliding around the potholed country roads as if on rails. It was quiet, too, the engine virtually silent, the only sound the log-fire crackle of the wheels on the loose gravel below. Colin and I hardly exchanged a word. It was difficult to know what to say. For weeks, we'd wittered endlessly to one another, putting a brave face on for the sake of the kids. For ourselves. Somehow, we managed to make the disease sound quaint. People were 'feeling poorly' or 'under the weather'. They never died painfully. Mysteriously. Without hope.

Now, though, all the words had dried up.

Now there was nothing to do but drive and pray.

IT WAS STARTING to get light by the time we reached the coast, a slither of slate just visible on the horizon. We passed *through a small village I remembered from the last time we'd been there. A few houses and a church. A petrol station and a post office. A pub: The Swinging Piglet. I had fond memories of the place. We'd ended up eating there a few times, Colin and I sipping our drinks on the decking while the children scrambled over a small wooden play area around the back. Charlie shrieking on the swings. Amber hanging upside down from the monkey bars, a stuntwoman in training.*

As we approached the sign, however, I saw that the pub was boarded up, clumsy rectangles of chipboard screwed over the windows and doors. It wasn't the only change since we'd last been there. The petrol station was derelict. The windows whitewashed. A chain around the doors. As we drew closer, I could see someone had vandalised the place. The glass sign smashed. The hose torn from the pump. The electric charging points bent and toppled.

The rest of the village was in a similar state of disrepair. The houses either boarded up or broken into. Doors hung off their hinges. Windows were shattered. What few cars remained looked like they'd been abandoned, strewn along the side of the road. Some had been set on fire. One was on its roof.

We kept driving.

At last we reached the turning for the cottage. By now, both children were awake, sitting saucer-eyed in the back seat. Charlie was hungry. Amber needed the toilet.

Colin had finally started talking again, filling the air with fatally optimistic prognostications as we rattled down the long, chipped slate drive. 'We can all relax when we get there. Charlie, you can help me build a fire. That'll heat the place up nicely. Then maybe we'll have hot dogs for tea. What do you say, guys? Indoor barbecue? And after that we can…'

As the cottage came into view, Colin fell abruptly silent. He gasped.

We all did.

The car slowed down as it approached the front gate,

before juddering to a stop. Seconds later a robotic female voice rang out from the GPS system.

'You have arrived at your destination.'

We all leaned forward. We all stared.

The car spoke again.

'You have arrived at your destination.'

On the dashboard, a question blinked in blue letters:

Enter Park Mode Y/N?

We ignored it.

The cottage was gone.

Well, almost gone. There was a small section on one side where the wall was still standing. The rest, though, was unrecognisable. A blackened husk. A few timber frames reduced to charcoal. Roof beams bowed and collapsed in on themselves. A pile of ash and twisted metal.

At last, Charlie broke the silence, unbuckling his seat belt and squeezing between the front seats. Close enough that I could smell the faint trace of bubble gum-scented shampoo on his hair, sweet and artificial. 'Is this the place we're supposed to be staying? Do you think we should go and find a hotel instead?'

Neither of us answered. What was there to say? We just kept staring at the burnt-out ruin, while the car droned on, over and over again.

'You have arrived at your destination.'

'You have arrived at your destination.'

'You have arrived at your destination.'

EIGHT

NOW, I'M AWARE I should probably be acting as some sort of role model for you, Egg. Teaching you right from wrong. Providing you with a moral barometer which you can tap on in later life and all the rest of it. But the fact is, it's not always that simple. Sometimes the truth is just more trouble than it's worth. That's why sometimes it's easier just to pause the video camera and pretend you stuck to the route you were supposed to be on. And that's why, in the end, I decided to leave Amber's surprise cameo out of my report to Fatima altogether, blaming the lack of accompanying footage on forgetting to charge the camera. I know, I know. The whole neighbourhood watch scheme is built on foundations of trust and transparency. But this was only a tiny deception really. A lie of omission. And, when you consider that I probably saved your big sister from being thrown into prison, I think you'll agree that it was the best course of action for everyone involved. Besides, by excluding Amber from my report, it conveniently meant I could also leave out whatever – or whoever – it was I thought I'd seen lurking in the shadows.

And just imagine trying to explain *that* particular Rorschach-splodge of pixels.

No, it's far simpler this way. Not to mention potentially less embarrassing. For having watched the video back somewhat obsessively this last week, I am now ninety-nine per cent sure I was mistaken. That the figure is nothing more than a figment of my overheated imagination. That there is absolutely nothing of interest to report to the powers-that-be.

Although I must admit, I haven't simply erased the file from my desktop. No. I've decided I'd better hang on to it. Just for now. Just in case.

Anyway, you'll be pleased to hear that Fatima – aside from castigating me for my failure to bring a spare battery pack – was as pleased as ever with my write-up. She praised my 'vivid descriptions' and 'attention to detail'. I was surprised she didn't go right ahead and give me a gold star. Since then, my focus has been on more mundane things. Mostly work, which for some reason has been even more of a slog than usual.

It occurs to me that I haven't told you about my job yet. Not that there's much to tell. Back in the old world, I worked in the marketing department for a multinational social media company. It was well paid, if not especially inspiring work. Not that I realised that at the time. Though I cringe about it now, back then I thought I was basically doing God's own work.

Despite being valued at several dozen billion dollars, the company was still relatively young. No more than four or five years old when I joined. The people who worked there were young, too. In my early thirties, I was one of the oldest members of staff. Perhaps because of this, I made an extra show of my enthusiasm for the role. My white-hot passion for multimedia marketing. My fanatical fervour for company-client relations. I stayed later than anyone else. Talked louder. Worked harder. Or at least, more overtly. I'd buzz about the building like a Benzedrine-addled bumblebee, spewing worn-out idioms to anyone in earshot. Shooting from the hip. Thinking outside the box. I was such a fucking idiot. We all were. And the inflated sense of self-importance. My God. Because you see, we weren't just there to make a salary. Or to pimp advertising space. Or to make our shareholders richer. Oh no. We were out there making a real difference to the world. We were *shaping relationships*. We were *curating memories*. We were *facilitating meaningful connections in a noisy world*. Jesus. It was like a cult. And I hadn't just drunk the Kool-Aid. I'd filled a paddling pool and was doing backstroke in the stuff. To think we actually thought what we were doing mattered. In the way that food matters. Or shelter. Or water. Or clean air.

What a terrible joke we were.

Of course, once the outbreak happened, it quickly transpired we weren't as essential as we'd assumed. The company folded. Too many dead. Or not enough people alive to make it worthwhile. Whatever. Once things had settled down and businesses began recruiting again, I eventually found myself a similar role, only at a smaller company. A start-up called MeetMee, which thankfully doesn't take itself quite so seriously.

The idea is simple enough, if still fairly trivial. As you can imagine, loneliness is a pretty big issue these days, especially for those people who were unfortunate enough to be single when the virus hit. Meeting new people isn't as simple as swiping right and heading to the nearest bar any more. That's where MeetMee comes in. We provide a safe space for people to mingle and talk with like-minded strangers online, first as part of a group, before providing customers with the option of moving to a private chat if they find someone they like the sound of. Which they usually do. You see the clever thing about MeetMee is that, unlike traditional dating apps, which either force you to wade through mountains of questionnaires in an attempt to gauge your interests, or to simply place a blind bet on a heavily Photoshopped headshot, it automatically scans through your online search history, linking you with others with a shared set of interests. What films you like. What papers you read. Your most perverted fantasies. It's all there, encoded in your search history, your digital genome.

The results are startlingly effective, with our 'match rate' running at above eighty-five per cent. This makes working for the PR department a doddle, our 'Success Stories' page populated with pictures of the latest happy couples, which helps to lure in eager new customers almost every day. Virtual weddings are not uncommon, which might sound insane, considering they'll never actually get to live together, let alone physically consummate the marriage. But then again, some people actually seem to prefer it that way. There's certainly less scope for disappointment. And you save a fortune on catering.

While my role at MeetMee isn't radically different to what I was doing before, I definitely have a more realistic perspective about my work. It really is just a means to an end, rather than a way of defining myself. Something I have to do to collect the money we need to maintain our relatively high standard of living. Having said that, I suppose if I try hard enough, on some days I can just about convince myself that the service we provide does have some small value. While we might not be changing the world, we are bringing a small spark of joy to people's lives.

On other days, though, I'm less generous. Days when I like to look at all the beaming couples we've brought together and shake my head. The fools, I think. Kidding themselves that they've found true love with someone they're never going to share a table with, let alone a bed. They're no more really 'together' than the suckers queuing up to spend a fortune to frolic on Colin's virtual beach. Although, when you think about it, there's not much difference between their situation and mine. Not really. I mean, what practical difference would it really make if Colin was in Nicaragua, rather than next door? Hell, he could be sitting on the surface of the moon and it wouldn't change a thing. For all I see him, he might as well not even exist.

Just like you, my sweet Egg.

●●●

THE DAYS FLUTTER by with a shrug, a flurry of indistinct moments.

Work. Eat. Sleep. Repeat.

I text Amber and she ignores me.

I text Charlie and he ignores me.

Colin texts me and I ignore him.

In other words, life continues *ad nauseam*.

The only slight kink in my routine comes when it is time to pick up our weekly groceries from the designated drop-off point in the car park under our apartment building. Until I joined the neighbourhood watch scheme, this was the closest I'd ever get to going outside, and I looked forward to the change of scenery. Not that there was much to see down there. Low ceilings. Concrete pillars. An oil-spattered floor. Before you reach the drop-off point – a basic polythene tent situated near the exit – you have to walk through the old parking bays. Alongside our wrecked old car, there are around twenty or so other vehicles parked there, all of them in various states of disrepair. Tyres flat. Windows strung with spiderwebs. Sometimes I would sidle up to them and push my mask against the glass, like peeking into a time capsule from another century. There were colouring books and computer games scattered over back seats. Hiking boots and high heels lying in footwells. Coats and cushions stuffed onto parcel shelves. Mouldering cardboard coffee cups wedged into drinks holders. In one of the cars, a dog-eared copy of *Cosmopolitan* magazine lay on the passenger seat, the front cover adorned with a beaming swimwear model, her body recklessly exposed to whatever virulent toxins happened to be floating through the atmosphere that day. Screaming from the margins were the usual hysterical headlines. I've stared at that damn magazine so many times over the years, I can still recite them by heart:

Dress Like an A-Lister (on a Z-list Budget)
14 Sure-Fire Signs He's Planning to Dump Yo' Ass
Flat-Belly Secrets You Need to Know Right Now
Messy Hair, Don't Care – 5 Reasons Fuzzy Is the New Fabulous.

Weirdly, even thinking about that copy of *Cosmo* lying there on the passenger seat leaves me feeling sad. I miss magazines. Sure, you can find a million identical articles on the Internet, but it's not the same. The smell of the new paper.

The free samples stuck to the pages. The ritual of sitting down with a cup of coffee and peeling open a new copy. As a teenage girl, magazines were my first window to the adult world. To fashion, body issues, relationships. Sex. And as easy as it is to sneer at their triviality, they remain a reminder of how much simpler our lives used to be back then. When a girl's biggest concern was how to put the 'O' back in her love life, rather than wondering where to order the best value replacement filter cartridges for her personal respirator. Magazines are yet another reminder of the world that we had and lost.

When I set out for the supply tent a few days ago, however, I only got as far as our front door before I saw a pile of ready meals and toiletries stacked neatly in the corner of the quarantine tent, ready for each of us to collect. Colin had already beaten me to it. At the sight of the supplies, I felt a jab of fury in my gut, cursing my husband for thoughtlessly wasting my time. Why hadn't he bothered to let me know?

As I trudged back to my bedroom, I realised it was actually acute disappointment I was feeling, rather than anger. Not about missing out on my trip to the basement. No. As ridiculous as it sounds, I'd been debating slipping out of the car park and into the outside world again. I wouldn't have gone far. Just around the block. Just in case whoever it was I'd glimpsed crouching in the shadows last week still happened to be lurking nearby.

I laughed at how silly I was being. For days, I'd resisted the urge to rewatch the footage again. And yet here I was, sulking because I'd missed out on the chance to go hunting for bogeymen. It was pathetic. With a snort, I strode over to my computer and, without hesitation, dropped the video file into the little trash can on my desktop, then clicked to empty it. Satisfied, I picked up my phone and tapped out a short text message to Colin:

Hey. Thanks for picking up food. Really sweet of you.

I selected an emoji of a smiling face blushing with contentment and hit send.

There. That was the end of that.

All the same, I couldn't help but look forward to my next patrol. In fact, it was *all* I could think about, a constant sizzle in the pit of my stomach, warm and uncomfortable, so that by the time a fortnight rolled around again I felt so sick I was worried I wouldn't be able to go out at all. The night before the patrol, I hardly slept. I just lay there in a jittery, semi-conscious state, my whole body seeming to thrum with nervous energy. I was up and dressed in my suit and mask before dawn, staring at my phone and willing the clock to speed up until it reached my allotted patrol slot.

When I eventually got outside, I found it was even warmer than last time, the early morning sun instantly sticking my hazmat suit to my back. The plants didn't seem to be enjoying the heat any more than I was, the crocuses and daffodils having wilted into crispy brown heaps, the grass limp and yellow. I squinted down and checked my camera. Satisfied it was recording, I headed straight towards the financial district. By then, I'd given up trying to lie to myself.

I knew exactly where I was going.

Even though my old office is less than a thirty-minute stroll from the apartment, in the old days, I'd never have dreamt of walking there. There was no time, you see. Never any time. Rather, I would take the train from the station around the corner from the apartment. At least, I did the first year I worked there. In the end I got sick of the terrible service. The inevitably over-stuffed carriages. The crush of bodies. My face mashed into a stranger's armpit or crotch. The walls slick with condensation. The noise and the smell and the general sense of carnage. Looking back, it seems perverse that we were ever allowed to travel like that. Close enough to touch. To taste. Even now, I shudder at the things we must have caught from one another. I can feel my throat closing just thinking about it.

Anyway, I eventually leased my own car. A small, sterile, climate-controlled bubble. Tinted windows so no one could peek in at me. The radio turned up to drown out the growl of traffic on the road. A Magic Tree air freshener dangling from the ceiling, saturating the cabin with the scent of artificial pine. At the time, it felt like I'd died and gone to heaven. All that space to myself. All that privacy. Now, though, I'm not so sure. As gross as the train was, some weird part of me would love to experience that chaos one last time, to hell with the risks. To smell the other passengers in the carriage. To feel their textures and weight pressing and pushing, the heat from their bodies radiating out towards me.

Although right then, heat was the last thing I wanted. By the time I reached the financial district, my clothes were saturated with sweat and my mask had begun to fog up. I paused for a second to catch my breath and get my bearings. Squinting past the trickle of condensation, I realised I was standing in almost exactly the same spot where Amber and I had first seen the fawn. Of course, there was no sign of it today. Still, I briefly found myself wondering what had become of it. Had it simply rejoined the herd? Or was Amber right to be worried. Was it still out there, lost and frightened? Was it even still alive? I'd never know.

I peered back down the road. Past my office. Off towards the distant alleyway where I mistakenly thought I'd seen a person crouching in the shadows. I checked the camera one last time. And then I started walking.

As I drew nearer, I saw that it wasn't actually an alleyway at all, but rather a shallow recess between two buildings. If I remembered correctly, this was the back entrance to a mildly pretentious café that used to serve lunch to the local office workers in that area. Quinoa and crayfish frittata. Gluten-free granola bites. I used to see the chef taking deliveries round the back here sometimes. Or vaping on his break, belching great clouds of synthetic butterscotch onto the street.

Today, the whole place was overgrown with weeds, the steel shutter of the back door only just visible through an impenetrable tangle of nettles. I felt deflated. There was no space for anyone to hide there. I'd been mistaken after all.

With a heavy sigh, I decided to call it a day. Before I left, however, I decided to quickly investigate the other side of the café. Unlike most of the shops around there, the building seemed to have survived relatively unscathed, its front window still intact, having apparently been missed by the gangs of desperate looters who'd rampaged through the city following the collapse. I could make out the tables through the filthy glass, cutlery and condiments still laid out, ready for customers who will never come. Beside the till, a specials board was propped up on a small easel, though only the word *vegan* was still legible, the rest reduced to a vague smudge of chalk.

I kept walking, past the café, on towards the next row of offices. Call centres. Banks. Insurance companies. Everything shuttered. Crumbling. Abandoned. Instinctively, I glanced up, scanning the upper floors for signs of life. I'd read stories online about poorer families who had moved into commercial buildings during the outbreak, taking advantage of the chaos and confusion to bag a bigger place. Staring up at the blackened windows, many of them fringed with shattered glass, I struggled to believe it was true. The government keeps a necessarily tight watch on our living arrangements in order to provide basic supplies, water, medical assistance, Internet, education and everything else. To attempt to live outside of that system was unthinkable.

I moved on, the office blocks eventually giving way to a small parade of shops. Here, though, each one had been ransacked, the front of each so comprehensively obliterated that it was difficult to guess what they had originally sold. I stuck to the middle of the road, the gaping shopfronts like sunken eyes, watching me as I passed.

As I reached the end of the high street, I hesitated. I was heading away from the city now, out into the suburbs. The houses there were bigger, five- and six-bedroom monstrosities that had once commanded eye-watering prices, but now lay abandoned, having been deemed too big and draughty to create effective quarantine zones. I was wary of straying so far from my designated patrol route. Glancing down at the camera, I realised I would have to wipe the footage again. Fatima wouldn't be pleased.

I'd just hit the pause button, when a sudden noise made me look up.

A loud crack.

There was something out there. Something close by.

The dappled fur of a leopard stalked through my imagination, its eyes wild. Teeth bared. Ready to pounce.

There was no sign of any animal, though. There was no sign of anything at all. I told myself I was being ridiculous. All the same, I decided to leave. It was time I was getting home.

Before I could move, however, the crack sounded again. Louder this time.

Unmistakably real.

At once I felt my chest tighten. Each breath a dagger slipped between my ribs. The sun, which by now was directly overhead, suddenly felt unbearably hot. I needed to lie down somewhere immediately. Somewhere cool and dark. Alone.

Standing a few feet away from me, I spotted the rusted green tombstone of a broadband junction box. I quickly ducked behind it while I tried to regain my composure. Crouching behind the metal cabinet, I listened closely as the sound rang out again and again. Sharp and insistent. Almost like a gun being repeatedly fired. Resisting the urge to curl into a ball, I forced myself to peek over the top of the box.

Though I knew the sound was coming from nearby, it was hard to pinpoint from where exactly. It seemed to bounce off the buildings and the surface off the road, burrowing its way into my head.

Crack! Crack! Crack!

Suddenly I caught a flash of colour. Something red moving behind the murky windows of the nearest shop.

I held my breath as the sound came again, the red thing seeming to jerk violently with each crack.

And then the sound stopped.

And the red thing shifted into the light.

And then I could see that it was actually orange, rather than red.

It was an orange T-shirt, worn by a man.

A man without a suit or a mask.

A man holding an axe.

A man looking right at me.

NINE

AS LONG AS we stuck together, we'd be fine. That's what we told ourselves as we set out from the ruined cottage. We'd find somewhere to stay for a couple of nights while we made a plan. Hell, we'd sleep in the car if we had to. Whatever it took for us to be safe. To survive.

By then we'd stopped trying to pretend to the kids that this was a holiday. Now we had the radio turned on, scanning through the few stations that remained on air, hoping for advice or answers about what to do next.

'Outbreaks of violence…'

'Extensive loss of life…'

'Millions of refugees…'

We kept to the quiet back roads as we traced the coast. The GPS had stopped working hours ago, and so we'd been forced to switch the car over to manual mode, Colin hunched behind the wheel, his face set in deep concentration as he wrestled with the unfamiliar controls. The clock on the dash read 08.30, the world bathed in gaudy morning light. Just a few weeks earlier, this would have been the most frantic time of the day. The four of us in the throes of the school run. Trying to remember lunchboxes and laptops. Battling traffic. Sprinting for the school gates. Now, though, the roads were utterly deserted.

It wasn't just the roads that were empty. There were no planes in the sky. No boats on the ocean. No ferries. No trawlers. The only movement, other than us, was the occasional flock of sheep or herd of cows pacing uneasily in their fields. It was as if all the other people in the world had simply evaporated.

Every now and then, I would twist around in my seat to check on the children. They looked tired. Their faces creased. Their hair stuck up at awkward angles. To my surprise, neither seemed especially anxious. Rather, they wore the same resolute expression I'd seen on the faces of children in charity appeals following a natural disaster. Famines. Earthquakes. Tsunamis. There were no tear-stained faces. No cries of anguish. No wallowing in self-pity. No. Those Third World children always stared out stoically from the screen. A dullness in their eyes, as if they'd lived a thousand years. As if they'd already seen everything the world had to throw at them.

In some ways, my kids were the same. They no longer moaned about how hungry they were or asked endlessly when we'd arrive. It seemed they'd already adjusted. For them, this was the new normal. Fleeing looted cities and burnt-down cottages. Not knowing where we would spend the next night. Sitting quietly while Mummy and Daddy went to pieces in the front seat. This was just what they did now.

We drove and we drove and we drove.

And we tried to stay alive.

•••

AFTER A COUPLE *of hours on the road, the battery warning light flashed up on the dashboard. The car needed to be charged soon. Colin shot me a look but didn't say anything. What was there to say?*

Gradually, the landscape became increasingly rugged, the road narrowing to reveal a sheer drop down to the sea. There was nothing out here. No villages. No farms. Certainly nowhere we could plug in the car. I was about to suggest we turn around and look for another way, when Amber piped up in the back.

'What about that place?'

We followed her finger until we saw it. A small white house perched on the edge of a distant clifftop. On these winding roads it would take at least twenty minutes to reach. If there was nowhere to charge the car when we got there, we'd be stuck.

Colin glanced over at me. 'What do you think?'

On the dashboard, the small red battery sign seemed to blink more insistently.

'I'm not sure we have a choice?'

Without another word, he pressed the accelerator to the floor.

The four of us held our breath as we hurtled around the blanched-knuckle bends, until at last we pulled up at the top of a long, slate chip drive. The engine let out a high-pitched whine, then shuddered to a stop, the battery dead.

'Well, it looks like this is where we're staying,' Colin said, shooting us a grim smile.

We looked down the drive towards the house. It was smaller than it had looked from the other side of the cliff. A pebble-dash bungalow, set alone in a long, rambling garden. We'd passed dozens of similar places the last time we'd been here. Lonely outposts that originally belonged to fishermen but had since been modernised and converted into holiday cottages to rent to city-sick tourists dreaming of weekends beside open log fires. This one, however, looked empty. There was no smoke burbling from the chimney. No lights in the windows. No vehicle parked on the drive. Still, there was only one way to make sure.

'So who's going to check it out then?' Colin asked.

This was classic Colin. He might sleep with a cricket bat beside the bed, but you can guarantee it will be me who ends up going to investigate the creaking floorboards at four in the morning.

I let out a sigh. 'I'll go.'

'Are you sure?'

'It's fine. I'm a woman. If there is somebody in there, it'll be less confrontational. I'll just explain that we're lost and looking for somewhere to charge the car.'

Colin nods. 'Okay, that makes sense. But be careful, won't you?'

As I unfastened my seat belt, I heard Charlie rustling in the back.

'Do you want me to come, Mummy? I can use my jiu-jitsu if anyone tries to hurt you.'

'Thank you, baby. That's really sweet. But no one's going to hurt me. I promise.'

As I made my way down the drive, however, I wasn't so sure. The closer I got to the house, the less abandoned it looked. In the garden, I spotted a wooden climbing frame. A trampoline. A small blue scooter toppled on the lawn. I looked over my shoulder towards my own family. Forced a smile. Gave them a thumbs-up. Then I turned back to the house, making a conscious effort to look calm. Friendly. Unthreatening. I swung my arms slightly, pretended to whistle, all the time trying my best to block out the thought that there might be a man crouched behind the window with a cocked shotgun. Ready to defend his home from invaders at any cost.

When I reached the front door, I couldn't see a doorbell or knocker, so I rapped my knuckles against the peeling paint. I waited, then knocked again, harder this time, my ears straining to detect movement inside the house. Nothing. I let another minute pass, then pressed my face to the front window. Through the grubby glass, I could make out a small kitchen. A fridge. Oven. Dishwasher. On the kitchen table there was a bowl of rotten fruit. Black bananas. Green oranges. Brown apples.

I felt a flood of relief. The place was empty.

Finding both the door and the window locked, I slipped around the side of the house, trying the other windows until I reached the back door. It didn't budge. For a moment I considered walking away. But then I remembered the flat battery. The burnt-down house we'd left behind.

With a quick glance behind me, I took a step back and swung out my leg. On the third attempt, there was a sharp crack as the lock gave way. I pushed against the wood and the door creaked open.

Instantly, I was hit by a sickening odour. Like spoiled meat, only worse.

It's the bins, I told myself. Whoever was here last obviously left in a hurry. Perhaps the freezer has defrosted and leaked? How else to explain that suffocating stench? Or the low drone of flies that cut through the air?

'Hello?' I called. 'Is there anybody there?'

There was no answer.

At this point, every cell in my body was screaming for me to walk away. But I didn't. Instead, I covered my mouth and nose with my hand and stepped into the house.

It was dark inside. I fumbled around for a light switch but couldn't find one. Undeterred, I felt my way along the wall until I reached a doorway. The smell was stronger here. Almost overwhelming. I reached for the handle, but then changed my mind, deciding to carry on to the kitchen instead.

When I got there, I saw it wasn't just the bowl of fruit that was rotten. The kitchen sink was piled high with festering pans and dishes, the plates glazed with blooms of green mould. Stuck to the front of the fridge was a child's drawing. An indiscernible scrawl of primary colours. I opened the door, braced for the stink of spoiled produce. Inside, however, I was surprised to find the food was fresh.

Then it hit me.

The fridge was cold. The light was on. There was still electricity here.

We were saved.

I slammed the door and rushed from the kitchen, excited to share the good news with Colin. As I hurried down the hallway, though, I once again found myself drawn to the closed door. The place where the bad smell was the strongest. I stopped and stared at it.

Again I was hit by the impulse to flee. To run and not look back.

Instead, I turned the handle.

The smell was so bad it stole my breath, the same rotten stench that permeated the rest of the house, only a thousand times worse. I doubled over. Heaved. Spat. Although my eyes were streaming, I was aware of flies buzzing around me, the air thick and alive. Eventually I straightened up. Even with the blinds drawn, it was light enough to make out the crumpled mound on the bed. Swallowing down a throatful of bile, I took a step closer.

Stop, I told myself. Get out of here. Go. It's not too late.

I couldn't help it, though. I was a rubbernecker at a car crash. A kid poking at roadkill with a stick.

I took another step forward. Then another.

And then suddenly there they were.

Two emaciated figures, lying side by side on a double bed. A woman and a child. A little boy, no more than two or three years old. Both of their faces swollen and disfigured.

Their lips blue.

I gagged again, this time unable to stop myself from throwing up. Doubled over, I fought the urge to burst into tears. I was a little girl again. I wanted my mum or dad. Someone to come along and make things better. To make all the bad things go away. Back in the old world, there were procedures to follow. People to call. Police. Paramedics. Coroners. Now, though, there was no one.

I'm not sure how long I stayed there like that, clutching my stomach, until a sound behind me broke the spell.

'Angela? Is everything okay? And what the hell is that godawful stench? You can smell it from the front door…'

Colin.

I dived for the door, heading him off just as he reached the hallway.

'Nothing,' I said as I pulled the door firmly shut behind me. 'It's nothing. I mean…'

Before I could say anything else, there was a cry from outside.

'*Mum! Dad! Come quickly!*'

Sprinting, we tumbled out into the light to find Charlie standing in the driveway, his face flushed with fear.

'*It's Amber,*' *he panted, trying to catch his breath.* '*She's sick.*'

'*What do you mean? She was fine just a moment ago. What's the matter with her?*'

'*It's her chest. She... She can't breathe.*'

TEN

THE MAN STARED. His back straight. Muscles straining. Had he seen me? I didn't move. Didn't breathe. For a moment I was certain he'd come and investigate. But then he shook his head and looked away, evidently believing he was mistaken.

Still crouched behind the cable box, I watched as the man continued dragging a long wooden beam out of the shop and onto the street. Once there, he laid it across the kerb and raised his axe, severing the beam in two. He stooped to reposition the wood then repeated the action again and again, until eventually eight pieces were lined up on the pavement.

Satisfied, he stood back and stretched. He was filthy, greasy streaks smeared across his hands and arms, and his matted hair still flopped across his face. He looked like the men and women I used to see crouched in the doorways of shops as I made my way home from work, coiled up in sleeping bags with dogs at their feet. Homeless. Only that didn't make sense. There weren't homeless people any more. Not since the virus. With nothing to protect them from contamination, people on the streets had been some of the very first to get sick. And yet here this man was, healthy as anything, chopping wood in the middle of the road, apparently without a care in the world. Even with my mask and suit, being outside for short amounts of time was risky. I had to be fully quarantined after every trip out. To be out here in nothing but a faded pair of jeans and a thin T-shirt was utterly insane.

I watched in fascination as the man hoisted the entire bundle of wood into his muscular arms, before tottering down the road to where a red bicycle and trailer was parked. The trailer was already piled with various other pieces of scrap wood and metal. It seemed the man had been busy.

Once he'd finished loading the wood, he added his axe to the pile, before securing the entire bundle with a length of blue cord, giving it a firm tug once he was done. Satisfied, he took the bike by the handlebars and swung his leg over the saddle, the little trailer rattling and bumping behind him as he pedalled away.

When I was certain he'd gone, I crept out of my hiding place and stepped into the middle of the road, staring after him. For a moment I wondered if I'd imagined the whole scene. If it might all just have been a bizarre hallucination brought on by the heat. When I cupped my hand to my visor, however, I could still just about make the man out in the distance, although by now his bike was little more than a black dot in the distance, getting smaller and smaller by the second.

I stood there for a moment, too stunned to move, before I suddenly remembered my camera. Looking down, I saw that it was still paused. Cursing myself for not thinking to film him earlier, I pulled the camera from its harness and held the small LCD screen up to my mask, zooming in to try to get a better view of the man. It was no good, though. Even set to maximum, he was no more than a faint blur.

Although every rational part of my brain was screaming that I should turn around, to go back to the apartment and immediately contact Fatima, the thought of leaving filled me with a strange sort of dread. After all, what were the chances of spotting this strange man for a third time? Besides, even if I did go back and tell Fatima, would she believe me? Without video footage, there was nothing to stop people thinking I had made the whole thing up for attention.

I checked the camera display. The battery was at twenty-five per cent. That should do it. All I needed was to get close enough to him to capture some irrefutable images and then I could head back home and write up my report.

I cupped my hand to my mask again. By now, the little black dot had faded to nothing. It was now or never. And so, as quickly as I could, before I had a chance to change my mind, I placed the camera back in the harness and started walking in the direction the bicycle had disappeared.

●●●

AS I WADED deeper into the suburbs, the houses I passed grew larger. Once, the gardens of these sprawling family homes would have been beautiful. Their lawns manicured. Flower beds blooming. Weeds selected and destroyed. Now they were sprawling, overgrown jungles that threatened to swallow the decaying buildings altogether. At one point I heard a frantic scurrying from deep within the bushes as a startled cat scrambled out of my path. At least, I hoped it was a cat. I picked up my pace, not wanting to think about what else might be lurking in the undergrowth.

More than once, I considered stopping and turning back. The afternoon heat was almost unbearable by then, and I found myself fantasising about the bottle of filtered water waiting for me in my fridge at home. About the clean comforting chill of my air conditioning unit. Yet for some reason I kept going, marching grimly onwards into the deserted world. Even all these years later, there were signs everywhere of normal life abruptly interrupted. A child's skateboard lying by the side of the road, its wheels orange with rust. A deflated football tangled in the hedges. A flaking red postbox, waiting for letters that will never arrive. Walking by one especially dilapidated house, I spotted a milk bottle still standing on the doorstep, though its contents had long since curdled into a toxic-looking lump. I didn't want to imagine what I'd find if I actually went inside.

The road itself wasn't always easy to follow. Several times it disappeared altogether, consumed by grass or fallen trees or toppled power lines. Where it forked, I was forced to pick a path more or less at random. Every time this happened, I was convinced that I'd gone the wrong direction, that I'd lost the man for good. But then I'd hear a crack in the distance. The unmistakable sound of an axe on wood.

Eventually the suburbs began to stretch and thin, the houses growing even bigger, the distance between them widening. The grey turning to green. In the six months I'd been on patrol, I'd never strayed this far from my designated route before. I found my thoughts wandering back to fanciful rumours I'd heard online about hermits living out in the countryside. Self-sufficient 'preppers' who fetishised the apocalypse, stockpiling weapons and masks years before the outbreak. Dangerous eccentrics who lived alone in bunkers, way outside of the government system. Who roamed the empty streets at night, hunting animals for meat, or else setting traps to catch trespassers. Perhaps the man was one of them?

Just then, I heard the crack of the axe again. Much closer than it had been before.

Too close.

I dropped to a crouch, trying to locate precisely where the sound was coming from. Behind me, set back from the road, was a pair of stone pillars, partially engulfed by a tangle of ivy. Beyond that was an overgrown graveyard, in the centre of which stood a large stone church. Propped outside was the bike I'd seen the man riding earlier, the trailer now stacked unbelievably high with various scraps of wood and metal.

I edged closer, when suddenly I spotted him. He was standing on the church steps, tugging at the thick chain that was looped around the building's enormous wooden door. I groped for the camera. By the time I'd pressed record, however, the door hung open and the man had disappeared. With a curse, I hurried over to the stone pillars, peering through the bushes. I still couldn't see him, though, and so, as quietly as I could, I began to make my way towards the church.

Clawing through knots of nettles, I became aware of the old gravestones pushing up through the foliage. Though the names and dates were mostly faded, I could still pick out the odd word or phrase:

Heavenly Father
Lord in heaven
God's will

I shook my head. To my surprise, religion had enjoyed something of a renaissance in the immediate aftermath of the outbreak. That muddled few months when nobody had any concrete advice or information. I guess back then it seemed that putting your faith in a higher power was as safe a bet as believing any frazzled politician or scientist. I remember hearing about mass public conversions throughout the city. Baptisms in public fountains. Holy men with megaphones. Desperate people flocking to churches and mosques and synagogues and temples, all of them begging for answers. For salvation.

Even today, vast digital congregations still gather online. People who still believe that all of this suffering is part of some divine masterplan at work, rather than the cold indifference of natural selection. Who believe that we can pray our way out of this thing. That if we can just apologise sincerely enough for everything we've done in the past, or promise to deny ourselves the last few things that might conceivably feel good in the present, then everything will magically be reset. That all the bad times will finally be over. That we'll get another shot at life, if not in this world, then in the next.

Not that I blamed them, really. If anything, I was jealous. At least they had something to look forward to. A reason to keep on going, day after miserable day.

As I finally reached the church steps, I began to have second thoughts. There was nowhere to hide out there in the open. Yet the last thing I wanted to do was blunder inside the church only to find the man waiting for me. Checking the camera again, I saw the battery was at less than five per cent. If I didn't get the footage now, there wouldn't be another chance. And so, swallowing down my fear, I stepped over the chain that lay limply on the steps and inched my way inside.

It took a couple of seconds for my eyes to adjust. Even with my suit on, the drop in temperature was immediately noticeable. Standing in the doorway, I scanned the chamber for any sign of the man, poised to turn and run at the first sign of trouble.

Though I'm not religious, there was no denying the elemental splendour of the building, a cavernous tribute to wood and brass and stone. Rows of intricately carved benches stood facing a central pulpit, behind which the pipes of a colossal organ sloped up towards the domed ceiling. Along the walls, sunlight streamed in through huge stained-glass panels, each depicting the various Stations of the Cross, Christ's agony captured in a range of gaudy colours.

Scanning the rows, I saw the man wasn't there and so, with a deep breath, I crept further into the church, acutely aware of the squeak of my boots on the smooth marble tiles. To the side of the pulpit, there was another door, which presumably would have once led to the priest's quarters. Other than the door I'd come through, it was the only other entrance or exit.

He had to be in there.

As I hurried down the central aisle towards the door, the sound of my footsteps ricocheted off the walls. I slowed down, forcing myself to walk on the balls of my feet. Up ahead, a giant crucifix loomed over me. At some point, the cross had slipped forwards, leaving Jesus suspended by the ankles a few feet above my head. I shivered. The quicker I got my footage and got out of there, the better.

When I reached the door, I paused. It still wasn't too late to forget the whole thing. If I left now I could be home in less than an hour. Yet even as I thought this, I found myself reaching for the handle. There was no going back. Not now. Not without proof that I wasn't crazy.

I turned the knob as slowly and as quietly as I could.

Nothing.

I tried again, rattling the handle.

The door wouldn't budge, though.

It was locked.

Before I could do anything else, I heard a clatter close by.

I turned, already knowing what I'd see.

And then there he was.

Floating towards me like a toxic cloud. Like death itself.

His dirty T-shirt. His filthy hair.

The axe in his hands.

Twenty feet away. Then ten. Then five.

Too close.

I turned away, but there was nowhere to run to.

I was trapped.

I looked back.

Just in time to see him raise the axe.

PART THREE

PART THREE

ELEVEN

AS IT SWUNG through the air, the axe let out a whistle. The blade so sharp it seemed to cleave time in two. I closed my eyes and waited for the end.

I waited and waited.

But the end didn't come.

Eventually, I opened my eyes.

The axe blade hung a few inches from my skull. Looking down the handle, I saw the man scowling at me through a mass of dirty blond hair.

I wanted to run but I couldn't move. My entire body had gone into shock, my legs shaking so violently I thought they might disappear from under me. With the axe still quivering above my head, the man shifted his weight slightly, shaking his fringe from his face. To my surprise, he was young. Not much more than a boy, really. Twenty-one? Twenty-two? He looked like he couldn't grow a full beard yet, with just a wispy shadow of moustache above his upper lip. Despite the axe, he looked almost as scared as me, his big brown eyes wet and unblinking. For some reason, I found myself thinking about the fawn again.

'You're a girl?' He seemed to be speaking more to himself than me.

'Please… Please don't hurt me… I have kids…'

'Hurt *you*? You're the one who's been stalking me all

morning. What, you think I didn't notice you back on the high street? At first, I was sure you were Special Branch. But then I realised they'd never let anyone as heavy-footed as you in the forces. So, who are you? And why are you following me?'

Hot tears streaked down my cheeks, pooling at the bottom of my mask. 'I'm no one. I mean, I'm Angela. I work for my local neighbourhood watch. I have legal permission to be here. From the government,' I added lamely.

The man stared hard. The axe twitched in his hands. For a moment I thought he was going to strike me down anyway. One quick blow.

Crack.

But then his face contorted, and I realised he was laughing. 'I don't believe it. I'm being hunted by a fucking *do-gooder*?'

He laughed again, before finally lowering the axe. 'Well then, *Angela-from-neighbourhood-watch*. I'm Jason. Jason Freeman. Or Jazz, as my friends call me. Well, they would if they weren't all dead. Ha! But either way, it's very nice to meet you.'

He jammed a hand towards me. His palms calloused, his fingernails crusted with dirt.

I didn't move. I was scared he was tricking me. That any moment he was going to lash out and attack. Instead, he just stood there, looking vaguely amused by the whole situation, until eventually he lowered his hand.

'Hey, it's fine. I'm not offended. I get it. No one wants to shake any more, right?'

Again, I was struck by the thought I might be hallucinating the entire scene. The man didn't have so much as a dust mask for protection. There must have been millennia's worth of human matter swirling around inside the church, yet here he was cracking bad jokes. It didn't make any sense.

Despite my terror, I found myself fumbling for a question. 'But how are you…? Why aren't you…?'

'Why aren't I wearing one of your funky astronaut outfits?'

He grinned, and for a second I saw a flash of Charlie in him. A slight sneer in his tone. 'How come I'm not dead?'

I nodded.

Jazz only shrugged though, quickly changing the subject. 'You know, I've got a personal rule that I don't leave a new place without making sure I've searched it properly first. You never know when you're going to find something that might come in handy down the line.'

I stared at him blankly.

The next I knew, he had hoisted the axe over his shoulder again, this time sending it crashing into the door behind me.

I screamed, ducking for cover. 'Jesus!'

'No, I'm Jazz. Jesus is hanging out on the wall over there.'

With that, he prised the axe from the door, before raising his boot and slamming it into the broken lock. The door flew open at the second attempt, revealing a set of steps leading down into the darkness.

'So, are you coming or what?'

He didn't wait for an answer before he disappeared down the stairs.

I hesitated. The camera was still recording, though only just, the battery symbol flashing on three per cent. It didn't matter. I had everything I needed. Proof that the man existed. That I wasn't totally insane. I could go back home and write my report now. Fatima would have to believe me. They all would. Yet I still felt something pulling me towards the stairs. Questions I was desperate to ask. Like how long had he been living like this? And how had he managed not to get sick? Was it possible he was actually immune? Most of all, I wanted to know if there were others like him. Other people, living the way we used to, without suits and masks. Together.

Besides, I told myself, the more information I managed to gather, the more useful it would be to the authorities. Reporting a non-suited citizen was one thing. But if I could provide them with a detailed breakdown of where he was living and what he'd been up to, well, who knew? They'd probably give me a medal.

And so, with a check of my camera, I followed the man.

Down, down, down.

Into the darkness.

●●●

AT THE BOTTOM of the stairs, there was a short corridor, which opened up to reveal a small, austere room. Mustard walls. A plain desk. A simple wooden crucifix nailed to the wall. Aside from the dust and cobwebs and some damp, the room looked surprisingly intact. Set in the far wall was an open doorway leading to a small bedroom. As I approached it, I saw Jazz was standing at a wardrobe with his back to me. I watched as he checked over items of clothing, turning out the pockets before discarding them on the floor. The axe, meanwhile, was leant against the wall.

'Well the bad news is they're all out of loaves and fish. There isn't even any wine or wafers. On the other hand, there are some killer threads. Check this out.' He turned around, holding up an ankle-length black cassock. 'What do you think? Priest-chic or pope-nope?'

Before I could answer, he bent forward and peeled his T-shirt over his head. I felt my cheeks burn behind my mask, as next he dropped his trousers, revealing a tiny pair of black trunks.

'You know, you'd be surprised how hard it is to get your hands on new clothes around these parts,' he said as he shimmied his way into the cassock. 'I mean, I've hit a few fashion stores, but most of the stuff tends to have rotted away by now. Damn organic fabrics…'

Having regained my composure slightly, I found myself painfully aware of the camera's fading battery. If I was going to get some information, I needed to do so quickly.

'Look, I'm sorry for following you. I wasn't trying to

scare you. It's just… Well, it's been so long since I've seen anyone outside without a mask or suit that I thought… Actually, I didn't know what to think.'

I watched as he slid a thin white band into his collar, before giving an exaggerated twirl, his robes whipping up around his shins. 'You know I think I like the ecumenical look. Really helps show off my curves, wouldn't you say?'

I forced a smile. 'You know, I can probably get you a suit and mask. If that's what you're looking for? My husband is about your size. I could put an order in for a replacement and no one would notice a thing. If you've got friends, I could get them masks, too? It wouldn't be any trouble.'

Ignoring my questions, he turned back to the wardrobe and once again began rifling through the clothes. 'You ever wonder what it must have been like for the priests? I mean, they gave up everything for God. They spent their lives kneeling on hard wooden floors while everyone else grew up and got jobs and bought big houses and nice cars and had kids and all the rest of it. Still, it was worth it, wasn't it? All of that sacrifice. Those lonely nights. Those *repressed desires*. Especially seeing as how they were going to be first in line when the Big Man finally showed up. And then, out of nowhere, *Blam!* Just a fucking indiscriminate massacre. Old. Young. Sinners. Saints. It didn't make a difference. All those little old ladies who diligently went to church every Sunday and piled up their pension money on the collection plate. God didn't give a shit. He mowed them down alongside the paedophiles and the arms dealers. Like, how did they square that circle? Holy shit, look at these shoes! This was one dapper padre.' He paused to hold up a pair of black-and-white Oxford brogues. 'Ah damn it, size six.'

I glanced down at the camera. By now the battery was down to one per cent. My heart sank. 'I think it's a difficult thing to get your head round whether you're religious or not,' I said, desperately trying to get the conversation back on track. 'Just the idea that things could get so bad so quickly. I mean, I lost so many people I loved. My parents. My brother. I'm guessing you must have lost people, too?'

He turned then, and again there was something of Charlie about him. But not the Charlie of today. The cruel, despondent teenager. No, he reminded me of Charlie as a boy. His eyes wide and shimmering with vulnerability. In a flash, though, it was gone, his chest puffed out. His chin jutted at an angle.

'I've got to go.' He began stuffing items of clothing into his bag. 'There was a military patrol round here a couple of days ago. If they notice the church door is open they'll be in here in seconds.'

'You're leaving?'

He let out a sigh. 'Listen, I'm not stupid. I know what you're doing. Like I'm going to just vomit up my life story to a stranger so you can report me to the authorities.'

'Oh come on. That's ridiculous.'

'Is it? I mean, what are you even doing here? Haven't you got a bake sale or something you should be organising?'

I watched as he gathered the last of his things, before turning to pick up the axe. Squinting down at the camera, I saw the red light was off. The battery had died. It didn't matter. I'd blown it.

When I looked up again, Jazz was moving towards me. I took a step to the side, assuming he was trying to pass. Instead, he stopped and placed an arm on my shoulder. I recoiled at his touch, but he pressed on, keeping his hand on me. 'Hey, I'm sorry,' he said. 'I'm not used to being around people, you know?'

This close, I could see myself reflected in his eyes. My bulky outline reminded me of a deep-sea diver.

'I have trust issues,' he continued. 'It's just this whole situation. I have to be careful, you know?'

I nodded, desperately wriggling to escape his filthy hand. 'Of course. It's just…'

Before I could finish, Jazz pounced, throwing his arms around me, pulling me into a tight embrace. Even through the suit, I could feel his hard body pressed against mine. His arms looped around my back, trapping me.

I closed my eyes. Held my breath. Waited for it to stop.

'Thanks,' he said as he finally released me. 'Thanks for being so understanding. You know, on second thoughts it would be good to see you again sometime. I'm staying in a place not far from here. An old school. If you're ever doing your neighbourhood watch thing again round here, you should drop in and say hello sometime.'

'That sounds nice,' I heard myself say. 'I'll do that.'

And then he was gone, the black cassock swishing around his ankles as he left the room. I heard the echo of his footsteps as he bounded up the stairs.

I looked around, blinking fast, my pulse racing as if waking from a nightmare. I felt dirty. *Violated*. Who did he think he was, risking my life like that? I could still feel my skin prickling from where he'd held me. I needed to get into a quarantine zone fast.

Once I was certain he wasn't waiting for me, I took the stairs two at a time, my boots screeching as I crossed the church floor. Once I was back outside, I leant against the stone wall, catching my breath. My head was spinning and I felt nauseous. For a moment I thought I might actually throw up. Already, terrifying thoughts were hatching in my mind. My throat felt sore and ticklish. My nose blocked. Had Jazz infected me? I should have done more to fight him off. I should have screamed. Kicked. Thrashed. Instead I just stood there and let him kill me.

A minute or two passed before I felt strong enough to stand up again. There was no sign of Jazz in the graveyard, or on the road beyond. It didn't matter. With the footage I had, the authorities would have no trouble tracing him.

By this time tomorrow, he'd be safely locked away in some government institution. That was something at least.

I looked down at the camera.

My stomach lurched.

And it was only then that everything clicked into place. The hand on my shoulder. The weird apology. The hug.

Because in the space where the camera had been, there was now only an empty harness.

TWELVE

AMBER WAS BLUE. *Her eyes were bulging in her head. Her hair drenched with sweat.*

Amber was dying.

With a scream, I wrenched open the car door and dragged her onto the ground.

Somewhere behind me, Charlie was sobbing. Colin, meanwhile, was trying to stay calm. Rational. Offering advice. Giving instructions.

I ignored them both.

The only thing that mattered was Amber.

She couldn't breathe. That was the problem. She couldn't get enough air into her lungs to keep living.

I loosened her collar and checked her airways, trying to see if there was something caught in her throat. It was hopeless, though. She was disappearing before me. Her breath coming in shallow rasps now. Her pulse a fading snare roll.

My poor sweet broken little hummingbird.

In an instant I was transported back to another time, twelve years earlier.

A time of breathing exercises and self-hypnosis and nitrous oxide.

A time of stirrups and callipers and all manner of nightmarish instruments of torture.

Of excitement and fear and screaming and panic.

Of blood and tears and shit and sweat and vomit and a pain so pure it was like a bolt of white light cleaving me in two.

And after that.

Once the midwife had finished with the measuring and the weighing and the counting.

Once she had ticked her boxes and filled her charts; the banal bureaucracy of birth.

Once she had gone, and it was just the three of us.

Two plus one.

Me, Colin and Amber.

My Amber.

Tiny. Hot. Pink.

Brand new.

A shock of black hair still stuck to her face.

Like a blind mouse, she'd nuzzled at me. Skin to skin. Her heart on mine.

Her first few minutes on Earth.

Even then, I remember willing myself to save those moments. Those precious seconds. To burn them onto the hard drive in my chest and set them to Read Only.

Stay with me, I'd whispered then. Stay with me and never leave.

'Stay with me,' I screamed as I rolled her onto her side and began thumping her back. 'Stay with me, Amber. Please. Don't do this. Breathe. Please, just breathe. Breathe—'

'Stop!'

I turned to Colin, who had grabbed me by the wrist.

'What are you doing?' I struggled to get away from him. Slapped. Scratched. Shoved. 'Get the fuck off me. I have to help her.'

'Just stop for a second. I've seen this before. It's a panic attack.'

I looked again at my gasping daughter. At the tears. The bubbles of snot. The terror in her eyes. Then I moved aside as Colin lifted her gently upright and helped her slow her breathing down.

'In-through-your-nose-two-three-four…Out-through-your mouth-two-three-four…'

Until at last the colour returned to her cheeks.

'Is Amber okay now?' Charlie asked, his eyes wide with worry.

'She's fine.' I reached for her hand. 'Aren't you, sweetie? You're all better now.'

Amber gave a small shrug. She looked tiny. Frightened.

'You know we love you, right? Me and Daddy. We love you more than anything in the world.'

She turned to me then. Her voice cold. Her eyes hard. 'If you love me so much, then why don't you tell us the truth? You think we're stupid because we're children. But we're not. We have eyes and ears. We know what's going on. Acting like everything's fun and exciting, when really, you've dragged us out here to die. That's what's going to happen. We're going to get sick and die like everyone else.'

'Stop it, Amber.' Colin's voice was firm enough to silence her. 'Nobody's going to get sick. Okay? Now I need you to be a big girl and stop talking like that. You're scaring your brother.'

Amber nodded, not saying another word. She wiped her face. Took a deep breath.

Still, I didn't think she really believed him.

I don't think any of us did.

●●●

IN THE END we decided to stay in the cottage. Not that we had a choice. Once Amber had fully recovered, I took the kids for a walk along the clifftops, ostensibly to gather firewood, while Colin stayed behind and dug a shallow grave in the back garden to bury the bodies.

I returned after an hour or so to find Colin's face streaked with dirt, a hollow look in his eyes. I touched his shoulder *but he shook me off, reaching for Charlie instead, hoisting him up and squeezing him so tightly that he let out a little squeal. Colin didn't let go, though. No. He buried his face in Charlie's hair and breathed him in. He smothered him with kisses. His cheeks, his chin, his neck. Everywhere. Even once he'd eventually released him, he still wouldn't meet my gaze.*

'Colin—'

'I don't want to talk about it.'

'I know. And I'm sorry. I know that must have been awful for you. But did you at least… you know?'

He looked at me, confused. 'Did I what?'

'You know? Cover your face. Or wear gloves. Or…'

I didn't finish my thought. Instead, both of us turned our attention to Charlie, a muddy handprint still visible on the back of his T-shirt.

'I'm sure it'll be fine,' Colin said quietly.

'I just mean… something killed those people, Colin. And if it was something infectious then—'

'I said it's fine,' he snapped. 'Everything's fine. Now I don't want either of us to mention any of this ever again. Okay?'

I started to say something else, but the look in Colin's eye was enough to make me bite my tongue. 'You're right. I'm sure it will be fine.'

All the same, the first thing I did once we got inside was to strip off Charlie's clothes and hose him down in the shower.

After that, the four of us got to work cleaning the cottage. We tore all the sheets and blankets from the beds and brought them out into the garden. Next, we dragged out the clothes from the wardrobes. The rugs and the curtains. The books from the shelves. We piled it all together with the wood we'd collected on our walk and then Colin doused the lot with a can of petrol he'd found in the shed. Charlie thought it was the greatest thing ever. He whooped and screamed as they ran in circles around the bonfire while Amber watched on apprehensively, noxious black smoke billowing towards the sky.

Back inside the cottage, we scrubbed the floors and walls

with bleach. We bagged up any open food and threw it away. Everything else, the plates, cups and cutlery, we scoured with soap and boiling water. Of course, back then we didn't know what it was we were cleaning. What we were trying to kill. As far as we were concerned, every single thing in the house was a potential threat. It never occurred to us that it might be us that was the biggest threat of all.

By the time we'd finished, it was almost dark again and the kids were complaining of tummy aches.

'Can't we just call a takeaway?' Charlie whined. 'A pizza? Fish and chips? Chinese?'

'What we've got is way better than a takeaway,' Colin said, leading him by the hand towards the car. 'We're going to have an indoor picnic. Here, why don't you help me get the things in while Mummy and Amber put the kettle on.'

Soon after arriving, Colin had discovered the solar panels on the roof at the back, which explained why the cottage had power when most places we'd passed were still without. There was also a small diesel generator in one of the outhouses, which the owners presumably kept as a backup for the winter months. It was a relief to see the red battery sign on the car's dashboard finally restored to a full, green bar. That was, until we realised we didn't have anywhere else to drive to. This was it. At least for now, this was our new home.

•••

THAT FIRST NIGHT we turned what meagre supplies we'd brought with us into a feast. We cooked packet noodles on the stove. We scrambled eggs. We made pasta. We drank lemonade. Sitting and eating together around the table of a stranger's house, the air crackled with a manic tension. Colin told jokes. Charlie talked in silly voices and sang made-up songs. Even Amber seemed to lighten up a little. It was like some weird holiday after all.

Having declared the bedroom we'd discovered the bodies

in 'out of bounds', we tucked both children up for the night in their sleeping bags. We'd decided to put them at the back of the cottage, in what had evidently been the little boy's room. Colin and I would make do with the floor and the couch.

Once the kids were in bed, we opened a bottle of wine and brought it out to the garden, taking a seat on the patio. Though I'd quit smoking more than a decade before, the urge for a cigarette was almost unbearable. Instead I drank too quickly, finishing my glass and filling it again, until my head began to spin.

'Hey. Are you okay?' Colin asked.

'We shouldn't have done that.'

'Done what?'

'The food. Charlie didn't even eat half of his. It just got thrown away. We've only got limited supplies. It's not like we can just pop to the supermarket when we run out. We need to ration. It was reckless. It was stupid. And then there's everything else. My brother. My parents. I can't get hold of anyone. I just can't help thinking…'

Colin pulled me to him. 'Well stop thinking then. You'll drive yourself crazy. Until we hear otherwise, all we can do is hope for the best. And as for the food? Yes, it was stupid. But it's been a long day. A horrible day. We needed to do something to make it better. Otherwise what's the point? Tomorrow we can work out what we've got and make a plan. But tonight, I think we should just… We just need to take a breath.'

I nodded. Swallowed another mouthful of wine. It was a clear night. Away from the city, there seemed to be a million more stars than usual. The sky more white than black.

'Do you think it's the end of the world?' I asked.

Colin didn't answer for a while. 'Honestly? I don't know. For some people, I guess. But then again hasn't it always been the way? The world ending for some while it's just getting started for others?'

I felt his hands on me then. Massaging my shoulders. Working out the tension and the knots. 'All I know is that *as long as we stick together, everything will be okay. We're stronger than you think. You mark my words. The apocalypse is no match for us.'*

His hands slid slowly down my back, then up to my breasts, his lips finding the nook of my neck.

And then we were on each other, the wine forgotten, my top coming over my head, the buttons snapped from his shirt.

The chairs toppled backwards as we fell onto the lawn, grunting and moaning and crying out until the stars and the house and everything else disappeared. Pushing and thrusting and pressing ourselves into one another.

Hungry. Desperate.

As if our lives depended on it.

THIRTEEN

THERE'S SOMETHING TO be said for unfertilised children. There's no drama. No answering back. No tears. No tantrums. Nothing. Just the idea of a child. A blank void to fill with the idealised fantasy of what your offspring might be like. A sweet, cherubic, imaginary bundle of joy. And in my experience, it's far easier to be in love with a fantasy than with the bloated, surly reality of the thing you face on your computer screen at the end of each day.

Especially when the thing you're facing is Charlie.

I realise how that sounds. I'm not saying I don't love Charlie. It's just that I don't like him very much. Not that I'd ever admit this aloud. People would think I'm a monster. But that's unfair. After all, children are just adults who haven't grown up yet. Sure, most babies are cute and smell good. But some of those babies are also miniature bailiffs or bank managers in waiting. Or worse. Murderers. Molesters. To imply we have a biological obligation to like a future sex offender or serial killer just because we accidentally fucked them into existence is just plain crazy.

That's not to imply I think Charlie is capable of murder. At least I don't think he is. All the same, as I stared back at his smirking face this evening, his prematurely thin hair greased to his scalp, his skin the colour and texture of rice pudding, I could hardly mask my repulsion.

As usual, the screen was split into four. One of the quadrants – Amber's – was blank. Colin sat in the other, an inscrutable expression on his face. I wondered if he was secretly wrestling with the same doubts as me. Wondering if our son is not in fact some sort of terrible aberration. A curse that we have inflicted on the world.

The school had been in touch. This in itself was not unusual. Hardly a month goes by without us receiving a report about Charlie's poor attendance or attitude. This time, though, it was not simply a case of addressing bad grades. This time it was the head teacher herself who had contacted us. We listened patiently as she explained that the school website had been hacked. That someone had bypassed their security system, disrupting the learning of forty thousand students. And, while there was no hard evidence yet, they had reason to believe that the person responsible for this mess was none other than our darling son.

At first, Colin made a valiant attempt at defending Charlie. On hearing the school had no proof, he muttered darkly about 'defamation of character' and 'reputational damage'. Fighting talk indeed. Once the head revealed the nature of the hack, though, Colin quickly changed his tone.

Apparently, instead of being greeted by the school home page, visitors to the website were redirected to a new page that had been created. A page that contained a single piece of text. A poem, which the head teacher had ambiguously described as 'erotic in nature'. A poem that was signed, and allegedly authored, by none other than our own daughter, Amber.

While Colin immediately went into damage control, describing the various traumas Charlie had experienced over the last five years, my thoughts immediately went to Amber. I had no doubt whatsoever that Charlie was responsible. He had already admitted breaking into his sister's computer. This, though, was something else. It went far beyond petty squabbles between siblings. This was all-out assault.

Though I have never dabbled in poetry, erotic or otherwise,

I did keep a diary as a teenager. I recall scribbling feverish proclamations of lust in the dead of night, only to wake in the morning and tear the pages out, shredding then burning the evidence, so terrified was I that someone would stumble across it. I can't imagine what I would have done if any of that material had ever been made public.

The head teacher explained that, whilst the website had been fixed within an hour of the attack, screenshots of the poem had already been taken and circulated by hundreds, if not thousands of students. Indeed, it was already so prevalent that later, once Colin had finished grovelling to the teacher not to take any further legal action, I quickly searched for Amber's name online. Within thirty seconds I had located a copy of the untitled poem:

> *I see your mouth,*
> *red and warm as sunrise.*
> *First at my ear, then at my throat,*
> *as the fox takes the bird.*
> *Then lower.*
> *To the twin constellations of my chest.*
> *Licking, sucking, biting.*
> *Teasing*
> *Down, down, down.*
> *Dancing*
> *Your restless tongue*
> *carving me in two,*
> *loosening my secrets,*
> *like a sliver of butter warmed gently in a pan.*
> *I melt with it.*

It was signed underneath with her full name, with a link to her various social media accounts, just in case there was any doubt as to her identity.

Amber May Allen.

Reading my daughter's words, I felt myself redden. It was too intimate. Too *real*. As horrific as it was that Charlie would seek to humiliate her in this way, I was also concerned that the poem was something other than just a hormonal fantasy. Was this about the boy she'd mentioned? Jamal. Was it possible she'd crept out again? Or that she'd actually succeeded in meeting him? That they'd been… intimate?

I shook my head, dismissing the thought. Amber might have been lonely and frustrated, but she wasn't an idiot. Creeping around the streets in a mask and suit was one thing, but to actually *touch* someone? No. She's not *that* stupid.

At least, I don't think she is. I tried to talk to her after we'd finally finished with the school. She didn't respond to my messages and refused my calls. The only way I know she's here at all is the rhythmic slap of her feet on the treadmill that echoes around the apartment. It's been running for seven or eight hours now. Much longer than usual. Earlier, Colin had been down to the drop-off point to collect the latest supplies. When I popped to the quarantine tent to collect my share, I noticed Amber's rations were still stacked in the far corner. I pictured her, sad and hungry in her room. She's already thin. Unlike Charlie, there's not a pound of excess weight on her, the years of obsessive exercise having chiselled her body into something hard and taut. I'd worried before that she wasn't eating properly. Now I'm scared she might waste away altogether. It's awful. And the worst thing is, I can't go to her. I can't hold her hand and dry her tears. I can't tell her that it's all right. That it will all seem better in a day or two. That these things always do, especially once the next adolescent scandal comes along. No. She just has to tough it out by herself. I can picture her in her room now. Not eating. Not sleeping. Drenched in sweat as she hurls herself relentlessly forwards towards an imaginary vanishing point. The place where it all disappears for good.

To my amazement, Charlie did actually answer our request for a conference call. It only took one glance at him, however, to realise he wasn't about to show contrition. No, Charlie was proud of his handiwork. He *wanted* us to know it was him.

'Poor old Amber,' he deadpanned, his eyes wide, eyebrows raised. A parody of surprise. 'Who on earth would do something like that?'

'It is a horrible situation—' Colin started, before I cut in.

'Cut the crap, Charlie. We've spoken to Mrs Patel. She seems to think the only person involved is you.'

Instantly, Charlie's face hardened. His lip curled. 'And would Mrs Patel care to share the *evidence* she has to support those serious allegations?'

I shook my head, too angry to speak.

'Now, now,' Colin said. 'Let's all take a deep breath, shall we? There's no need for anyone to...'

Before he could finish, Charlie's screen went blank. Moments later, a barrage of ferocious bass-heavy music blared through the walls, mingling with the thud of Amber's treadmill.

'You know he is right,' Colin said. 'About there not being any evidence, I mean.'

I let out a sigh. 'You know, I've got a lot of work on at the moment. We'll talk about this later.' With that I killed the feed but didn't move. I just sat there, staring at the outline of my reflection in the blank monitor as I listened to the racket blasting through the walls, angry and indecipherable. Like a storm. A car crash. A city being flattened.

●●●

FATIMA WASN'T PLEASED that I'd lost the camera. I'm not sure she believed my story about the broken harness. Nor did she take me up on my half-hearted offer to go back and look for it. And although she claimed to have accepted my apology, I can't shake the feeling she's holding on to a grudge. For one thing, I received a message about my last report, criticising its lack of detail. She even went as far as to publicly share a link on social media to an online training course to help improve my writing style. The bitch. But that's not all. In addition to her public criticisms, she's also updated our patrol rota. This means that instead of a fortnight to wait, I'm now not scheduled to go back out for almost a month. It's infuriating, but as she's chairwoman of the group, there's literally nothing I can do. Other than forming my own, break-away faction, that is. An independent neighbourhood watch scheme, comprising of a single member. I can't see that going down very well.

And then there's the fact I've been feeling sick ever since I visited the church last week. Time and time again I find myself scrolling through lists of symptoms. Filling out online questionnaires. Checking my temperature. Scouring my skin for signs of a rash. It's irrational, I know. It's already been five solid days since Jazz put his arms around me. If I'd been exposed, I'd already be dead. But that doesn't stop me from worrying.

In an effort to distract myself, I've tried to keep busy at work. Not that I've had much choice. For some reason, it's been relentless recently, with more new members signing up than ever before. Perhaps people can sense the hot weather through their walls. Some primal throwback to a time when the start of summer was a signal to chase a mate, rather than simply reach for the aircon.

Despite the added pressure of work, however, I've struggled to get Jazz out of my head. Late at night, I find myself trawling social media sites, inputting various iterations of his name: Jason Freeman, J. Freeman, Jazz Freeman. Nothing ever comes up, though. The man is a digital ghost. While that alone isn't surprising, especially considering he's trying to keep a low profile and avoid the detection of the authorities, the lack of any archive pages from before the fall is definitely odd. There are no awkward teenage photographs. No dating profile. No work résumé. It could only mean one thing. The name he'd given me was a fake.

Of course, the sensible thing to do would have been to simply send a message to the relevant authorities right then. Having studied various maps and satellite images of the city, I'd narrowed down the school he'd mentioned to two possible sites. I could pass along the details, and within minutes they'd swoop in with their drones and their teams of heavily armed soldiers and capture him. I'd be a hero. And if he did turn out to be immune, the government would be able to use him as a vaccine. His capture would save millions of lives. I'd have single-handedly saved the world. And if he wasn't immune, well then too bad. He'd be just one less crazy person threatening the safety and stability of our society.

But I didn't call the authorities. No. I kept Jazz all to myself. I guess, if I'm honest, I felt possessive of him. Yes, I knew it was dangerous not to report him. It was probably completely illegal. Yet at the same time, it felt good to have a secret. Something that no one else in the world knew about. Something small I could keep scrunched up tight and hidden inside me. To cling to during the hours of endless drudgery in my room. As pathetic as it sounds, Jazz was exciting.

When Colin and I first got together, we courted in total secrecy. This was just after I'd left university, before I'd started my career in marketing, and I was working long hours for little pay in some godawful call centre. As it happened, Colin was doing an apprenticeship with an IT company on the floor below. We first met in a local coffee shop, and although the attraction hadn't been immediate, I'd found his goofy jokes and Dad-like dress sense oddly endearing. I bumped into him again at a bar a few weeks later and, with alcohol lowering my inhibitions, I'd ended up going back to his place.

At the time, I was still technically dating someone else, and so we initially decided to keep our relationship hidden. I still remember the excitement of those early months together. Sneaking around the building. Sending late night text messages. Clandestine meetings after work. It was all such a thrill. So much so, that I remember feeling a slight twinge of disappointment when, a few months later, we began to get more serious about each other and decided to come clean. As nice as it was to be able to go for dinner without constantly looking over our shoulders, there was no denying that some of that early magic disappeared the moment we stepped out of the shadows. In retrospect, I can't help feeling that the early flood of feelings I had for Colin were less to do with him and more the illicit pleasure of keeping him hidden.

And of course, once you're married, you very quickly find there are *no* secrets. There's no space for intrigue or mystery once you've squeezed the blackheads on your partner's back or nursed them through a particularly nasty bout of norovirus. In fact, there's very little space whatsoever. Even when Colin and I weren't physically together, we'd message constantly. He lived in the little square in the corner of my computer screen at work. In my pocket on my phone when I was commuting. Hardly a minute past when we *weren't* communicating.

I remember one time, when Amber was still little, we went to a family party to celebrate my grandparents' diamond wedding anniversary. Sixty years of marriage! I always find it incredible that people can make it through six years without killing each other, let alone six decades. And yet at the same time, I couldn't help thinking about the amount of time my grandparents *actually* spent with each other. For forty years of their marriage, Grandad had worked shifts in a local factory. He would leave the house at eight in the morning and get home at six at night. In those ten hours, they wouldn't hear from each other at all. Nothing. Not a bleep, not a blip, not a buzz. Then at the weekends he'd go fishing, or to the football, and again, they wouldn't speak during that entire time. Measured like that, in terms of hours spent communicating with each other, it occurred to me that Colin and I had probably already spent far, *far* longer together than Nana and Grandad ever had. And I didn't see anyone rushing to buy us a fucking cake.

So perhaps it's the mystery that made Jazz so attractive. Not in a romantic way, obviously. I don't feel the remotest bit *sexually* attracted to him. I mean, he must be almost young enough to be my son. Nevertheless, I recognised the same furtive rush as I did when Colin and I were secretly dating. That feeling of knowing something nobody else does. Of having something that belongs to me and me alone. And the fact that I couldn't just pick up the phone and call him or send him a message whenever I felt like it only added to the appeal. He was like an itch I couldn't scratch, and as the days rolled by, I increasingly found he was all I could think about.

That's what made Fatima's latest petty diktat so frustrating. There was no guarantee that Jazz would still be alive in a month's time. And even if by some miracle he didn't get sick and die, who's to say he'd still be staying in the same place? He said himself that he liked to move around. Like the fawn, he could simply melt back into the city, never to be seen again.

Which is why, in opposition to all logic, I found myself lying in bed one Saturday morning hatching a plan to get my camera back.

I'd slept badly, my dreams filled with nightmarish visions of axe-wielding priests. I woke just before dawn, my mind still fuzzy with sleep inertia. As I lay there trying to clear my head, I found myself thinking about Jazz. It occurred to me that in all the months I'd been out on patrol, I'd never once been asked by anyone to see my clearance. Hell, I'd never even *seen* anyone out there apart from Jazz. No police. No soldiers. What was to stop me, I wondered, heading out on my own for a few hours? For even if, on the off-chance, I was stopped by a patrol unit, surely I could just tell them I was part of a neighbourhood watch scheme? After all, I wouldn't be lying. And even if the worst happened and they contacted Fatima, I could simply claim I'd got mixed up about what day I was supposed to be out there. It was an easy enough mistake to make, especially with the recent changes to my rota.

Outside, I could hear the first faint call of birdsong through the layers of protective glass. No one in the house would be up for hours yet. Even if they did wake up while I was gone, it wasn't like they'd miss me. As long as I was back in time for dinner this evening, they'd have no way of knowing I'd been gone. As for work, I could simply message them to say I was sick. It wasn't as if they were going to demand a doctor's note.

It was ridiculous, I knew that. But sometimes ridiculous is what you need. Sometimes ridiculous is the only thing that is capable of shattering the crushing boredom of life.

And so that is how, early one Tuesday morning, I came to zip myself into my protective suit and mask. And then, as the first thin strains of sunlight streamed into my room to chase the night away, I quietly let myself out of my room and crept down the hall.

And out of the front door.

FOURTEEN

SIX DAYS. NINE *if we skipped breakfast. That was how long we had before we began to starve. We laid everything out again, spending hours juggling our meagre rations into new combinations. Pot Noodles and pizza. Pasties and instant mash potato. It was no good, though. No matter how we split it, we had less than two weeks' worth of food.*

With no obvious solution, we put everything away. Maybe it would be enough? Surely a vaccine would be discovered and rolled out any day now. Then we could return home. Things would go back to normal. Although how we'd know it was safe to return to the city was another problem. Our phones were as good as bricks, and despite the cottage's Wi-Fi router blinking incessantly, the Internet remained stubbornly down along with the TV. Even most radio stations had stopped broadcasting by now, the only message we could still pick up a looped public service announcement, an island in an ocean of static:

Stay calm and await further instructions.

Stay calm and await further instructions.

For the kids, this lack of electronic stimulation was perhaps the most traumatic element of all. For days they were near comatose with boredom, refusing to get out of bed or go outside. They were like two miniature addicts in withdrawal. Not that Colin and I were much better. Every minute or so, we would take out our neutered phones and tap *hopefully at the screens, re-reading the same articles on our frozen timeline, scrolling through the same old pictures on social media until we hit the top of the page, where a small digital cog turned endlessly:*

Loading… Loading… Loading…

Occasionally our frustration would boil over and we'd go out into the surrounding countryside, looking for higher ground as we clutched our phones towards the sky, praying for a signal.

My kingdom for a bar of network coverage!

Of course, we never found any.

Thankfully, after the first few days we began to adjust. Talking face-to-face no longer felt such a strain. The kids began to hold eye contact again instead of constantly glancing down at their laps. Midway through the first week, Colin uncovered a battered copy of Monopoly that had somehow escaped the bonfire. For the next few days we all crowded round the board, staging sprawling financial battles that lasted until late into the night. It was fun, spending time together. Like something out of the past. An idealised, 1950s vision of family life. It was so enjoyable that it was almost possible to forget the real reason we were there. But then the kids' bellies would begin rumbling, and I'd remember that, even with an entire avenue of hotels and a couple of million cash in the bank, I couldn't buy them the one thing they needed:

Food.

On the seventh evening, once the kids were safely tucked up in bed, Colin and I went to the kitchen and laid out the rations again. It didn't take long. Even at a stretch, there were less than a dozen meals left. I cursed myself, thinking of the tins and packets we'd left at home. Why hadn't we brought more? Or made more of an effort to pick up supplies along the way?

'Maybe I could go out there?' Colin pointed vaguely in the direction of the woods behind the house. 'I could, I don't know, hunt something?'

I stared at him. Even back then, my husband was not in the best of shape. A slight paunch already visible through his shirt. His skin pale from too many days spent hunched over a computer screen. And sure, he was good with his hands. He could wield an electric screwdriver or a soldering iron with the best of them. But hunting? I tried to picture him crouched in the scrub, a bandana pulled over his receding hairline, his finger twitching on the trigger of an imaginary crossbow.

'Good idea, Rambo. Maybe you could take your sniper rifle and rustle us up a few seagulls?'

Colin frowned. 'At least I'm being proactive. I mean, the only other thing I can think of is...'

He trailed off. There was no need for him to finish. We both knew that the only other option was to take the car and see what we could find nearby. There'd be no shops open of course. But perhaps there'd be an aid centre or a food bank. Or at the very least, a vending machine we could break into. There had to be something.

'So who's going to go?' I asked, though if I was honest, I already knew the answer.

Colin shrugged. 'Why don't we both go? We can't be more than twenty minutes away from the nearest village. We can be there and back in an hour.'

'And leave the kids?'

'They're asleep. They won't even know we're gone.'

'Until a crazed desperado breaks down the door.'

'Come on, Angela. We're in the middle of nowhere. Besides, we've been here for a week already and we haven't exactly seen many crazed desperados, have we? We haven't seen anyone full stop.'

'Nice try. But not in a million years would I leave them here by themselves for one minute, let alone an hour. So why don't we just cut to the chase, and I'll go by myself. That is what you're suggesting, right?'

'Don't be like that.'

'It's fine. Seriously. It's probably better this way. At least if something does happen, you'll be here to look after the kids.'

Colin frowned, feigning concern. 'I don't know. Maybe we should wait another day or two?'

'For what? Until we're actually starving. We could be here for weeks. Or months. Unless we get some food, we're not going to make it. We'll die. Do you understand that?'

He gave a feeble nod. 'Well at the very least take something with you.'

By 'something' he meant a weapon.

'Don't be so melodramatic.'

Colin wouldn't have it, though. He opened the cutlery drawer and extracted a large carving knife. 'Just in case,' he said, handing it to me.

I snorted. 'Really? What is this, a horror movie?' Still, I took the blade from him and stowed it in my handbag. 'Happy now?'

'Not really.'

'It'll be fine. I'll be back before you know it. Promise.'

By the time I reached the car, however, my bravado had already begun to fade. I sat behind the steering wheel for a good few minutes before I eventually started the engine. The GPS was still down, so I switched it to manual mode, fumbling for the handbrake. Then suddenly I paused, killing the engine and unfastening my seat belt.

Colin looked up, startled as I re-entered the house. 'Everything okay?'

'Everything's fine. I've just forgotten something.'

I'd forgotten to say goodbye to the kids.

I made my way through to the small bedroom at the back of the house. In the dark, I could just make out their silhouettes under the blankets of the single bed. I thought briefly of the little boy whose room this had been before. We'd made a point of burning all the letters and utility bills we'd found without reading them. I didn't want to know who they were. It made it too real. It was impossible to miss the pictures on the bedroom wall, though. The boy's name in splodges of blue finger paint:

Joshua.

I knelt beside the bed and pressed my face into Charlie's hair. Inhaled him. Even at ten years old, I could still detect the faintest trace of milk and talcum powder. My baby boy. He stirred slightly as I pressed a kiss into his warm cheek, before I moved to the other end of the bed where Amber was coddled tightly in the blankets. I placed my hand gently on her brow, swiping a damp mass of hair from her face. She felt hot and slick to the touch. Feverish. I hoped she wasn't coming down with something.

As I stooped to kiss her on the forehead, she jerked in her sleep, letting out a low whimper before her eyes flicked open.

'Hey,' I whispered. 'It's okay. It's me. It's Mum.'

Amber couldn't see me, though. She wasn't awake. Not really. Even before her world had collapsed in on itself, she'd occasionally suffered from night terrors, waking up screaming in the dark, sending us thundering along the landing to her bedroom in the early hours of the morning. I'd felt guilty, of course. As if I was failing her in some fundamental way that was seeping out in her subconscious. In the end, we'd taken her to a doctor. Back then he'd assured us it was nothing but a symptom of an intelligent girl with an overactive imagination. She'd grow out of it, we were promised. Somehow I doubted it. Especially now.

Amber let out another moan, her eyes darting around wildly. I wondered what she was seeing. Could it really be worse than the reality we were stuck in now?

I felt her hand flutter up towards my arm, grasping my wrist. And suddenly she was awake, gasping for air, like a drowning girl plucked from the water. 'Mummy? MUMMY?'

'It's okay,' I said again. 'It's all just a bad dream. It's all just a bad dream.'

And for once, I felt like I was telling her the truth.

FIFTEEN

BY THE TIME I reached the old church I could hardly breathe. Though it wasn't yet seven, the sun was already a furnace, the sky overhead the colour of a slapped cheek. Inside my suit, I felt like I was being slowly boiled alive. Traipsing across the city, I'd noticed the outside of my mask was dirtier than usual, a fine layer of pink dust powdered across the visor. I'd seen this before, back in the old world. Every few years or so, a storm in the Sahara Desert would whip fine sand up into the atmosphere which then travelled across continents, choking the occupants of the towns and cities below. Sometimes it would mix with rain clouds, streaking the cars and pavements rusty red, a phenomenon that early civilisations called 'blood rain'. It was seen as a bad omen back then. A sign of impending death.

Though I wasn't usually one for superstitions, the sight of the dust spooked me. I felt exposed out there. I expected the screech of police sirens any moment. Tasers and handcuffs and questions I couldn't answer. Or else, something worse than the police. Something powerful and hungry crouched in the undergrowth. Watching my every move. Waiting for the right time to strike.

In an effort to calm my anxiety, I ran through the plan again. If you could call it a plan. In truth, I hadn't thought much further than tracking down Jazz and confronting him for tricking me. Though by now I'd more or less given up on retrieving my camera; maybe I would be able to find out a little more about him to include in my report to the police.

Or perhaps I was lying to myself. Perhaps I just wanted to see him again. To prove to myself that I hadn't imagined the whole thing. That I wasn't crazy.

I'd decided that of the two schools I'd narrowed it down to, he was more likely to be staying at the one closest to the church. As I approached the railings of what had once been a small junior and infants' school, however, I realised with disappointment that my hunch was wrong. There was no way anyone could be living there.

While the playground was still in surprisingly good condition, the painted lines that had once designated various sports pitches still just about visible between the cracks and patches of moss, the buildings themselves had not been as lucky. Of the two main blocks, one was little more than a shell, having been completely burnt out. On the opposite side of the playground, the other building wasn't much better off. Though it looked to have escaped the fire, its windows were shattered, its roof sunken. It was utterly uninhabitable.

With a sigh, I got ready to move on. The other school I'd identified was a good twenty-minute walk away. As I started to leave, however, something caught my eye on the far side of the playground. A flash of something silver peeking out from behind the building. Pressing my mask to the railings, I saw what looked like the rim of a bicycle wheel.

As I scrambled over the rusted railings, three or four birds erupted with a squawk from the ruins of the nearest building. I hurried across the playground as quickly as I could, conscious of the slap of my feet on the tarmac.

Even before I'd reached the far block, I could see it was Jazz's bike, although there was no sign of the trailer. The door it stood beside looked like it had been forced, the wood splintered around the lock. Sure enough, when I tugged at the handle, it creaked open. I took a step inside, pausing in the doorway to survey the scene.

To my surprise, the structure was in better condition than it had looked from the outside. Stretching out before me was a long corridor, with various doors leading off to classrooms. At one time, it looked like the floor had been covered in blue carpet tiles, most of which had now rotted away, revealing the wooden floorboards beneath. Though much of the paint had flaked from the walls, I could still make out the artwork of young children stapled to display boards, the paper yellow, the writing indecipherable.

Above me, several ceiling tiles had fallen away, revealing the slate roof above. Sunlight flooded in, illuminating a billion particles of dust suspended in the air. If Jazz really was living here, he was crazier than I thought.

Years ago, I remember reading that the dust in our houses was primarily made up of human skin. The millions of cells we shed from our body every day. Of course, after the outbreak I learned – we all learned – far more than I ever thought there was to know about skin. That it is our largest organ, covering almost two square metres of our body. That the thinnest skin is found on our eyelids and that the thickest is on the soles of our feet. I also learned the dust thing was a misconception. An urban myth. Skin cells only made up a fraction of household dust, which actually contained all manner of other substances. Pollen, animal hairs, carpet fibres, soil. Saharan sand.

Even so, the sight of so much dust in the air made me feel uneasy. Myth or not, I had no doubt there would still be traces of schoolchildren swirling around. Teachers. Parents. All ghosts now. A deadly cloud, hanging around me. Inside my suit, my skin began to itch.

With a deep breath, I forced myself to keep walking down the corridor, peeking into each classroom I passed. Like most places, the school had been abandoned suddenly. Mid-lesson from the look of it. Coats and umbrellas still hung on pegs, with brightly coloured lunchboxes stacked neatly in one corner. Educational posters crowded the walls, while displays of children's work had been strung from each corner of the room, dangling from the ceiling like Christmas streamers. On one chalkboard I could still make out faint writing, a question paused mid-word, never to be answered:

What happened to the dino…

If it wasn't for the layers of dust and cobwebs that coated everything, you could almost believe the kids had just popped out for morning break. That any moment they would be back, filling the corridor with a high-pitched clamour. Laughing. Squealing. Everything still ahead of them.

Just then, a loud thump rang out. Metal on wood.

Jazz.

I kept walking.

At the end of the corridor there was a set of double doors. I pushed them open and the hammering grew instantly louder. I was standing in the school hall. Nearest to the door, rows of PE equipment were lined up against the wall. Cones and bats and bibs and balls, all of them covered in a thick layer of dust. On the other side of the room was a raised stage, presumably once used for school plays and assemblies.

I didn't pay any attention to that stuff, though. No. Rather, I was too busy staring at the large wooden sailboat that lay in the middle of the hall, its mast almost touching the ceiling. On the side of it, a name had been painted in bright green paint:

HMS *Vagabond*

As I stood there, the hammering abruptly stopped and a man's face appeared from behind the wooden structure. 'I wondered when you'd show up,' Jazz grinned. 'I suppose you're looking for this, are you?'

Squinting, I looked up to see him waving a small black rectangle in his hand.

It was the camera.

SIXTEEN

FOR THE LONGEST time, there was nothing but darkness. There were no street lights, and with no moon to guide the way, I struggled to see anything as I nudged the steering wheel around the bumpy country roads. After what felt like hours, I came to a small hamlet, a few houses strung loosely around a church. I touched the brake, squinting into the murky night, until at last I spotted a huge country mansion peeking between the trees, a driveway the length of a football pitch stretching out before it. Pulling over to the side of the road, I stared up at the thick iron gates, above which a pair of marble lions eyed me from the top of tall stone pillars. Beside them was a white flagpole, a tatty Union Jack slumped at half-mast. From the bottom of the drive, there seemed to be no lights on in the house. There was no sign of life at all.

I had no doubt there'd be food in a house like this. Hell, they probably had a fully stocked wine cellar. A separate pantry just for cheese and dried meats. I could be in and out in a matter of minutes. Just as long as no one was home.

I killed the engine. Reached for my handbag. Opened the door.

By now it was freezing outside, and as I crossed the road my breath billowed out before me in grey clouds. As I approached the driveway, the gates seemed impossibly high. I had no idea how I was going to climb them, but as I got closer, I saw the padlock was open. I could just walk right in.

The cold metal bolt slid back easily. I slipped past the lion sentries, ivory stone chips crunching below my feet. As I neared the house, I began to feel more confident. A house this big would normally have its own security guard. A pack of dogs. I heard nothing, though. There were no cars in the drive and still no sign of any lights in any of the buildings. I figured the occupants had probably fled by private helicopter years ago. Or else they'd got sick. Either way, with each step I grew more and more certain that the place was definitely abandoned.

I was a hundred or so feet from the main building when I spotted something lying in the drive. At first I thought it was a piece of rubbish, some scrap that had blown in from the main road. Drawing closer, though, I saw it was a child's shoe. I froze. For some reason I'd imagined an elderly couple living there. Octogenarian landowners, swaddled in their ancestral wealth. I hadn't thought about children. Not that it really changed things. If anything, it seemed to support my theory that no one was home. Like us, they'd probably had to pack in a hurry, clothes and shoes spilling from sloppily stuffed suitcases as they bolted for their chauffeured limousine.

I stooped to pick up the shoe. As I did, I thought I noticed a glimmer of movement in my peripheral vision. I straightened up sharply and stared at the house. The windows remained dark. Unknowable. Was there someone standing there, just behind the glass? I stared at the building for a while, until I was satisfied that it was just the shadows playing tricks on me. Of course, there was no one there. The place was empty.

I glanced down at the shoe I was holding. As I did, I noticed for the first time a dark streak smeared across my palm. Mud? I held my hand up to my face to inspect it. In the moonless night, it was difficult to tell, but I thought I could make out a trace of red.

In an instant, I dropped the shoe and began backing up

the drive towards the car. Something wasn't right about this place. I didn't care how the blood had got there, or if there was an innocent explanation for it. All I knew is that I wanted to leave. Right now.

As I scrambled back into the car, I checked my hand again in the yellow interior light. It was definitely blood. And if it was still wet, it meant it was fresh. I slammed the door and turned the key, tearing away into the night, not daring to look in the rear-view mirror until the mansion was definitely out of sight.

FOR THE NEXT *forty minutes or so, I passed nothing that looked even vaguely promising. The road was one of those gut-pummelling country lanes, blind hairpin turns and bone-juddering potholes. Though I was aware I was near the coast, there was no sign of the sea. On either side of the road, a thick mesh of trees bore down on me. The remains of ancient woodland that had once covered the entire country. Glancing through the window, I had the feeling something was out there, watching me from the gloom. Even back then, I had a sense of some balance tipping in the world. Of nature returning. After centuries of cowering on the fringes, the forgotten beasts were stepping back out from the shadows, preparing to reclaim what was rightfully theirs.*

I had a feeling they wouldn't have to wait too long.

As before, there was no one else on the road. It was strange. I'd assumed that at the very least I'd see the occasional car as people fled the carnage of the city for the countryside. It was as if everyone else had got a message we'd missed.

Either that or they were already dead.

I kept driving. Now and then I passed the high walls of country estates like the one I'd stopped at earlier. There was money in this part of the world. Lords and ladies. Dukes and duchesses. If anyone was going to survive the end of the world, it was these people. I thought of the blood-stained shoe again. This time I didn't bother slowing as I passed them.

Eventually, the road led me to a larger village. Abandoned vehicles littered the road. A few houses had been obviously vandalised, their windows smashed or boarded up. Others, though, looked like they might still be occupied. Their curtains drawn. Doors closed. I wondered how many people were in there. Holed up and starving. Or else huddled in their bed, like the people we found in our cottage. Like Joshua and his mum.

I was about to push on to the next village when I passed a small parade of shops. A post office, a hairdresser's, a newsagent's. I slowed the car to a crawl. Of the three, only the newsagent's didn't have its shutter down. Though the windows were plastered with advertisements for groceries, making it difficult to see inside, they nevertheless looked intact. It was definitely worth investigating. I nudged the car to the side of the road. More than anything, I didn't want to get out again. I wanted to go home. To my old home, in the city. To a place where we could simply tap our screens if we were hungry. Where I didn't have to drive through the night in order to break into abandoned shops, or carry a carving knife around with me for fear of being attacked. But that home had gone now, along with the world it had existed in. And so, thinking of my sleeping children back at the cottage, I grabbed my handbag and forced myself to get out of the car.

Though the streets were deserted, I approached the shop cautiously, unable to escape the feeling I was being watched. Again, I found myself thinking about the abandoned shoe I'd found on the driveway, and the child whom it had belonged to. Instinctively, my hand moved to my handbag, pulling the strap tight across my shoulders.

As I approached the newsagent's, I realised I had no idea how I was going to get inside if it turned out to be locked. In books, it always sounded so easy. The protagonist simply shouldered the door and it burst open. Or else they produced a bent hairpin and picked the lock. I wondered if I could kick this one open, as I had at the cottage. But that had been a flimsy domestic door. This was a triple-glazed slab of glass, specifically designed to deter break-ins. In the event, however, the door flew open before I reached it. I watched in terror as a pair of hooded figures bundled out into the street, each of them heaving an overstuffed bin bag across their shoulder.

At the sight of me, they froze.

For a second, nobody spoke. Then the taller of the two figures snarled at me.

'Get out of the way.'

The voice was higher than I'd been expecting. I peered closer, startled to see a smooth face hiding beneath the hood. It was a boy, not much older than Amber. Behind him was another boy, this one even younger. Though their faces were set in sneers, their eyes were filled with panic. They looked terrified.

'I said move,' the boy repeated, his voice breaking slightly. 'I mean it.'

Although they were blocking the doorway, the boys were so short I was able to see over their heads into the shop. It looked like the shelves had been swept clean. I suddenly guessed what was in the bin bags.

'Wait a minute. I just want to talk to you. Where are you going? Do your parents know you're out here?'

'We don't have to tell you anything,' the first boy said, before turning to his friend. 'Come on, let's go.'

He went to step forward, but as he did, I moved to block him. 'Hey, not so fast.'

The boy's eyes opened wide as he stared at my hand. To my surprise, I looked down to see that I was holding the knife.

In an instant, the boy's demeanour changed. The scowl evaporated. His bottom lip began to tremble. 'Please let us go. My mum's not well. She sent us out to—'

'Hand over the bags.'

It was strange. Inside, I felt terrible. I was stealing food from desperate kids. Yet it seemed as though some other *person was speaking through me. Someone cold and mean, who didn't have space in her heart to care for two strangers. Not when her own children were starving.*

'Please...'

'The bags,' I said again, this time punctuating my point by thrusting the knife in their direction.

After that, everything happened so quickly I hardly knew what was going on. The older boy decided to make a break for it, barging past me. As he did, I managed to turn and grab hold of his bag. We tussled for a moment before the black polythene split open, scattering his haul of chocolate bars, crisps and fizzy drinks across the pavement. He took a step towards a can of Coke, but I lunged at him with the knife and he let out a squeal, scampering off down the street empty-handed.

That just left the younger boy. As I turned to confront him, he too tried to bolt. He was too slow, though. I threw myself at him, pinning him against the shop window by the lapel of his coat. Up close I saw how young he really was. He couldn't be more than ten years old. He looked terrified, silent tears streaming down his cheeks. A sour, vinegary smell filled the air as a trickle of urine soaked through his jeans. Still I didn't let him go.

'Please... Please don't kill me.'

'The bag,' said the psychotic woman who appeared to have inhabited my body. 'Drop the bag.'

He didn't move.

The woman took the blade and pressed it to the boy's throat, just below the tiny bob of his Adam's apple.

A speck of blood appeared, red against white.

The speck became a trickle.

All it would take was a little more pressure and...

I snapped out of it, lowering the knife and stepping back.

'I'm sorry,' I began. 'I didn't mean...'

The boy didn't wait for me to finish. With a whimper, he took the bag and ran to join his friend down the street.

'You bitch!' the older boy called back to me when his friend reached him. 'You crazy fucking bitch!'

I tried to say something. To apologise again.

When I opened my mouth to speak, though, I realised I was crying.

DRIVING BACK TOWARDS the cottage, I kept glancing over at the small mound of junk food that was piled up on the passenger seat. After the boys had left, I'd salvaged what I could from the road, hurriedly stuffing the food into my pockets and handbag, before I'd given up and fled to the car. What an idiot I'd been. There was hardly enough there to last us a week. I hadn't even gone back to search the shop. There might have been fresh food there. Stuff with actual nutritional value, rather than this pile of crap. But no, I'd panicked, too jacked up on adrenaline and drowning in shame to think clearly. I shook my head, trying to clear the image of the petrified boy from my mind. Was this who I was now? The kind of woman who'd threaten to stab a child over a couple of kilos of artificial colours and sweeteners? Or was this just the price of survival in the new world?

By the time I spotted the little cottage perched on the cliff edge, I was consumed with self-pity. Moments later, though, I forgot all about the boys at the shop.

Because as I pulled onto the driveway, I discovered there was a new car parked in front of the cottage.

But that wasn't all.

As I killed the engine and got out of the car, I noticed the front door to the cottage was wide open.

It was hanging off its hinges.

As if it had been kicked.

135

SEVENTEEN

THE BOAT WASN'T functional. At least, it wasn't functional yet. This was the first thing Jazz told me as he led me into the school hall. He was still wearing the white collar he'd found in the priest's quarters, though as he came out to greet me I saw he'd dispensed with the black robes, instead tucking the white card into the neck of a gaudy Hawaiian shirt, which was speckled with paint and sawdust. As he spoke, he waved his hands around excitedly, pointing to the boat as he explained that he had nothing to treat the timbers with.

'She wouldn't last more than a few minutes on the water, even if I could figure out how to tow her there. Which, of course, I can't.'

I nodded along gamely, though in truth I was so taken aback by the absurdity of the situation I was having trouble focusing on what he was saying. Night after night I had spent restless hours poring over satellite imagery of the school, trying to guess what his home might look like inside. I guess in a way I'd romanticised Jazz as a sort of desperate fugitive. And while I hadn't exactly expected a hidden cave complex and a cache of guns and explosives, I certainly wasn't prepared for this. Not that the boat wasn't impressive. It must have taken hundreds of hours to complete. A month, at the very least. Even so, I was utterly bemused by its presence in the hall. 'But what's the *point*?' I asked, almost before I could stop myself. 'If you're not planning on sailing it, why spend all this time on it?'

Jazz's face fell slightly. 'Well, for one thing it gives me something to do. A sense of purpose. That's important, you know? Three of my grandparents died in the first year of their retirement. You've got to keep busy. That's apocalypse 101, right?'

'I guess. But this? I mean, surely you've got enough on your plate with just trying to… you know?'

'Stay alive? Sure. But this is fun. I was training to be a carpenter when everything fell apart, so this helps me keep my hand in. And who knows, maybe some day I'll work out a way to get her onto the water? Either way, you have to admit she's a beauty.'

It was tough to argue with him. Functional or not, the boat was a work of art. I pictured Jazz crafting it from scratch, scouring the city for the right pieces of wood, as if pulling together a jigsaw puzzle, then fitting it together, sanding it down. As I admired it, I found myself reassessing this strange, feral man. It took dedication to build something like this. Vision. Sensitivity. Sure, he might be a little rough around the edges, but the person who built this boat couldn't be all bad. Could he?

Then I remembered the reason I was there. Because he'd tricked me. Stolen from me. Any warm feelings I had for him evaporated instantly. 'So about my camera…'

Jazz frowned. 'Ah. That. I'm afraid not. Sorry.'

'So what, you're just going to steal it? You know, it doesn't even belong to me, right? I got in a lot of trouble because of you. And that's without even getting into the fact you *touched* me to get it.'

'Oh come on. Don't make it sound creepier than it was. All I did was give you a hug. And it didn't hurt you, did it? You're not staggering around clutching your throat, are you? Anyway, you've got your funky space suit. Isn't that supposed to protect you?'

'That's not the point. You violated my personal space. You could have killed me.'

'Yes, well, I'm sorry about that. But you didn't leave me with much of a choice. You were filming me without permission. So if you want to talk about stealing and violating, let's go there.'

'That's different.'

'Is it? And what about putting *my* life in danger? Because you know that's what would happen if that footage got into the wrong hands. Not that I'm accusing you of anything. I know you wouldn't deliberately spill the SpaghettiOs. You're no snitch.'

I felt my cheeks redden. 'No... I mean... Of course not. It's just... It's just that I could really do with getting that camera back.'

Jazz smirked. 'And I could really do with a tin of lacquer and an electric sander, but sometimes we've got to work with what God's given us.'

We were each silent for a moment, the air between us thick with hostility, along with however many deadly pathogens.

'You know what, forget it,' I said at last. 'I'm leaving. You can keep the stupid camera.'

To my surprise Jazz looked genuinely hurt. 'You're going?'

'Yes. I shouldn't have even come here. I don't know why I thought you might act like a reasonable human being.'

'Well that's harsh. I was going to show you the boat first, but if you've got to go...'

I didn't answer for a moment. Having come all this way, it seemed stupid to leave without some sort of evidence. Perhaps if I hung around for a while I'd get a chance to slip the camera away from him.

'Fine. I'll stay ten minutes. But after that, I'm gone. Understand?'

Jazz frowned, cupping his hand to his ear. 'Huh? What was that? You know, if you're going to insist on wearing that mask, you're going to have to speak up. I can't understand a word you're saying.'

I took a deep breath, raising my voice as I tried again. 'I said—'

'I'm *kidding*,' he laughed, before turning back to the boat. 'Now, follow me. And please keep your arms and legs inside the vehicle at all times. The tour is about to begin.'

●●●

'IS IT SAFE?' I asked, as I clambered uncertainly up the ladder after Jazz.

Standing on the deck, I could see the boat was appropriately named. The structure was far more ramshackle than it had appeared on the ground, the wooden planks that lined the floor evidently salvaged from dozens of different sources. Here and there were repurposed items I vaguely recognised. A sandwich board had been sawn into strips and nailed to the side to create a railing. The mast appeared to be fashioned from a wooden telegraph pole. The sails made from old duvet covers. The entire thing was stitched together from rubbish.

'Safe? It's a hand-built boat standing in the middle of a crumbling school hall in the midst of a post-apocalyptic nightmare. But if you're asking if she'll take your weight, then the answer is I don't know. I guess we're going to find out, eh?'

Tiptoeing uneasily across the deck, I followed Jazz to a small wooden hatch. With a sharp tug, he pulled it open, revealing a set of rickety stairs.

'After you.'

I hesitated. If he was planning on hurting me, this would be a perfect opportunity. No one knew I was here. I'd never be found. I wondered how long it would take my family to realise I was gone. Weeks? Months? On the other hand, Jazz didn't strike me as a murderer. Mixed up, sure. And occasionally infuriating. But not a killer. Well, unless you counted his penchant for close physical contact. Either way, I found myself stepping forwards into the darkness, feeling for a banister to help keep myself steady.

As I reached the belly of the boat. I looked around in amazement. The lower deck had been converted into a sumptuous bedroom. A soft glow spilled from coils of fairy lights that hung from the ceiling, which I later discovered were powered by an old car battery. The walls had been painted a dark purple, while red velvet curtains had been draped across most of the surfaces. On the floor, no less than three sheepskin rugs covered the floorboards, while in the centre of the room was a plump double bed, covered in silk bedding. I had to stifle a laugh. It was so tacky. The kind of crassly erotic décor a teenage boy might design for a low-budget porn shoot. A cross between *Arabian Nights* and a Parisian brothel.

Jazz looked hurt. 'You don't like it?'

'No. It's not that. It's just… It's just that I wasn't expecting it, is all. It's unbelievable. Do you actually sleep down here?'

He nodded. 'I tried sleeping in the classrooms at first, but I couldn't take it. All those kids' work staring down at me from the walls? It was too creepy.'

We both lapsed into silence for a moment, thinking about the children who not so long ago would have filled the hall.

'Anyway, that's enough of that. Let's get out of here shall we? I've still got so much cool stuff to show you.'

'Really, I should be going—'

'Come on. Just five more minutes,' he pleaded, and again I was reminded of Charlie. The same whiny tone he'd use to beg for more screen time when he was a child.

'Seriously. I really need to…'

Before I could finish, though, Jazz turned around and disappeared back up the stairs.

'Come on!' he called. 'I'll race you!'

The next stop on the tour was the school bathrooms, an area that Jazz seemed especially proud of. The water had stopped working years ago, but in one of the cubicles he'd managed to rig up a basic shower using a pipe connected to a tank of rainwater he'd set up on the roof. He'd even managed to get one of the toilets flushing. At the sight of it, I became acutely aware of the needling pressure building in my own bladder.

'You know, I really do have to be getting home,' I said, crossing my legs as Jazz took me through the intricacies of the flushing mechanism.

'Okay. Sure. No worries. But before you go, at least let me show you the kitchen. It's the coolest thing here. Then you can go, I swear.'

With a weary sigh, I allowed myself to be led through the hall. The whole time we were walking, Jazz jabbered away, proudly pointing out improvements that he'd made to the place. I hardly listened. Instead, I stayed focused on the bulge of the camera in the back pocket of his jeans. More than once, I thought about simply reaching out and snatching it. Would he chase me if I ran? And what would he do if he caught me?

Before I could find out, we arrived at a large industrial kitchen at the back of the old school canteen.

'Now most of the time I have to make do with what I can scavenge.' Jazz pointed towards a huge saucepan that was sitting on top of a stainless steel hob. 'And let me tell you, that's getting less and less. Even some of the tinned stuff is starting to go bad now, though I've got a fair stock of dried bits. Rice and oats and the rest of it. When I got here, though, I found they had a little garden out the back and, well, take a look for yourself.'

He lifted the lid on the pot with a flourish, revealing a vat of bubbling brown liquid.

'What is it?'

'French onion soup. My mum taught me how to make it. Back before…'

At the mention of his family, he paused. For the first time since I'd met him, he seemed less sure of himself. Vulnerable, even. I wanted to find out more, but something told me not to push it. Instead I steered the conversation back towards the food.

'Don't tell me you grew these onions yourself?'

Jazz grinned, and without answering he reached under the counter and threw something at me. A small purple ball, still caked in soil. I looked down and saw a bristle of roots still attached at one end.

'When's the last time you saw a fresh vegetable?'

I shook my head. 'Not recently.'

'You can eat them raw, too. They're full of vitamins and minerals and all the rest of it.' To illustrate his point, he reached under the counter for another onion, taking a big bite out of the side of it, skin and all. He grimaced. 'Although I have to admit, they taste better in soup. You want some?'

'Tempting as it is, I think I'll pass,' I said, noticing the smear of dirt the onion had left on my glove.

'Suit yourself,' he said, taking a wooden spoon off the counter and dipping it into the pan.

As he turned, I saw the bulge in his back pocket had disappeared. He must have moved the camera when I wasn't looking. Sure enough, when he faced me again I saw the silver rectangle poking from the front of his shirt pocket. My heart sank as I realised I'd missed my chance. I decided to call it a day.

'You know, I really am going to have to head off now. It's getting late. And also, if I don't pee soon, I'm in serious danger of wetting myself.'

'You need the toilet? You can just use…' he paused. 'Oh, right. The suit. You don't think you could risk it? I mean, look at me. If there was something here to catch, I reckon I'd have caught it now.'

'Unless you can't catch it. Unless you're immune.'

Jazz shrugged. 'Who knows? It's a mystery, huh?'

I decided to go for broke. 'Yeah, but that's the point. Don't you *want* to know? You should be dead. But you're not. You're out here, surviving. Thriving, even. Have you ever stopped to consider how crazy that is? And you know if there is something special about you, well, you could be the key to stopping all this madness once and for all. Don't you think you've got a, I don't know, a duty to tell people about it?'

'A duty?' Jazz's face darkened. 'To what? Turn myself in to the government? To become a fucking lab rat?'

'No. Wait. I just mean—'

'I know what you mean. That's why you were so bothered about the camera. That's why you were filming me in the first place.'

'All I was saying—'

'You know what? You can *have* it if it means so much to you.'

With that, Jazz dug around in his shirt and held up the small silver camera. For a moment I thought he was going to throw it to me. I even put up my hands to catch it.

Instead, I watched in horror as he once again lifted the enormous lid off the saucepan.

And let the camera drop with a soft plop into the soup.

EIGHTEEN

I STARED AT the mysterious car that was parked in front of the cottage. It was a wreck. An old-fashioned, fossil-fuelled 4x4. Every panel dented or dinged. The paintwork scratched. The windows frosted with filth. This wasn't a city car. No. This was a working vehicle, designed to drag logs from the road. To transport sick sheep to the vets. To plough its way across bogs and beaches. This car belonged to a local.

I tried to stay calm. To rationalise. To breathe. Perhaps this unexpected visitor might actually be there to help us? Maybe the car was owned by some kindly village doctor, who'd taken it on himself to check we were settling in okay? Or else an enterprising local farmer had called round to sell his wares.

Only, why would they kick the door down?

I started to run then, reaching for my handbag only to realise I'd left both it and the knife it contained in the car. I kept going anyway, skidding into the hallway as I called out to my family, unable to hide the panic in my voice.

'Colin? Charlie? Amber?'

There was no response.

As I entered the living room, I saw the place had been destroyed. The television was on its side, the screen shattered. The floor covered in broken glass. By now I was near hysterical, my breath coming in dry, irregular gasps.

They had been attacked while I was out and now they were

all dead and I was alive and I never should have left them and oh God the killers were probably still in the house and here I was shouting my head off and oh God oh God oh...

When I turned into the kitchen, however, I was greeted by a sight so unexpected that it stopped me in my tracks.

Perched on the table were Charlie and Amber. Still in their pyjamas, their faces were creased, their hair sticking up. They looked tired, but oddly serene. Most importantly, they were unhurt. Beside them was Colin. He too looked surprisingly calm, if thoroughly dishevelled. His T-shirt was torn around the neck, exposing his shoulder. In his hands was a baseball bat. As he turned to greet me, I saw he was sporting a split lip and rapidly swelling black eye.

Before I could say anything, he shifted his weight, and for the first time I saw the bruised and bloody figure tied to a kitchen chair behind him.

'We had a bit of trouble,' Colin said.

COLIN HAD BEEN *dozing off on the sofa when he'd heard the car pull up. In his sleepy state, he'd assumed it was me returning from the food run. But something about the timbre of the engine was off. The speed it was travelling. The violent churn of gravel. He was up and on his feet before the first thump at the front door, scrambling for a weapon, when Amber had come through from the bedroom, rubbing her eyes.*

'Daddy, what's that noise? Where's Mummy?'

Thump.

'Go back in there and shut the door and don't come out until I say so.'

Thump.

Before she could argue, there was a loud crack as the front door gave way.

'Go!' he'd yelled, reaching for the nearest implement to defend himself with, which turned out to be a plastic spatula.

Seconds later he heard heavy boots in the hallway, a gruff voice calling out. 'Sarah? Joshy?'

Colin just had time to register the bedroom door slamming behind Amber, and then the man was in the living room, a baseball bat gripped tightly in his fist.

Looking at the man now, unconscious and tied to the chair, I found it was difficult to see what he looked like. His face was too swollen to make out his features. Colin said that he thought he was younger than us. Twenty-five? Thirty? At the sight of Colin, he'd frozen. His lip curled.

Then he started yelling.

'Where are they? What the hell have you done with them?'

'Listen, I know what this looks like. But you need to calm down. I've got my kids in the house,' Colin had said, eyeing the bat. 'Let's just sit down and talk about this.'

The man only snarled, though. 'Your kids? What about my nephew? And my sister? What have you done with them?'

'I haven't done anything. Now if we could just calm down and…'

The first swing of the bat swept a clock and vase from the mantelpiece. The second smashed the TV screen. 'Where are they?' the man screamed. 'Where the FUCK are they?'

Colin tried to explain that they were already dead when we'd got there, but it was hopeless. The man wasn't listening. He didn't want answers. He wanted revenge. He swung the bat again, this time connecting with a large antique mirror. It was then Colin dived at him.

Unused to physical violence, Colin had quickly found himself pinned to the floor by the younger man, his fingers pressed around his throat. He was about to pass out when a small voice sounded somewhere above him.

'Are you okay, Daddy?'

It was Charlie, wide-eyed and pale.

The unexpected interruption made both the men look up. It was then Colin took his chance, overturning the man and pummelling his face until he stopped moving.

He'd been unconscious ever since.

As Colin was telling me this, I occasionally glanced over at the kids, who were still sitting silently nearby. Amber avoided eye contact, her knees drawn up to her chest protectively. Charlie on the other hand looked utterly nonplussed by the situation. Bored even. He stared at the bloody intruder, stifling a yawn.

'So what do we do with him now?' I asked.

Nobody answered.

...

IT WAS MORNING before the man came around. With no better plan, we'd simply left him tied to the kitchen chair while we tucked the kids back up in bed and then crawled off to the sofa to sleep. Not that I managed to get more than an hour or so. Most of the night I lay there awake, tossing and turning while I thought about the man in the other room. I felt bad for him. How easily the roles could be reversed. It could have been Colin's brother crossing the city to look for us, only to find another family squatting in our apartment. And how would he have reacted? Probably much like this man, I imagined. Confused. Scared. Furious. Still, I hoped he might at least wake up in a more reasonable mood. We would explain to him the sad news about the mother and child, and that we were staying here temporarily in order to protect our own children. Surely he'd understand that?

The tone of his cries in the morning told me otherwise. We scrambled into the kitchen only to find Charlie already standing there, staring at the deranged man with the detached expression he'd worn the night before. While Colin tried to explain to him what had happened, I ushered Charlie back to his bedroom, where Amber was huddled on the bed, her eyes wide with terror.

'Everything's fine honey,' I said, throwing my arm around

her shoulder and giving her a squeeze. 'That man is upset, but Daddy is sorting it all out now.'

'Is Daddy going to kill him?' Charlie asked, a little too eagerly for my liking.

'Don't be silly.'

'Because I read that the quickest way to do it is to sever the carotid artery with a really sharp—'

'That's enough, Charlie,' I snapped. 'Nobody is going to kill anybody.'

When I got back into the kitchen, however, I wasn't so sure. While the man continued to scream obscenities, Colin stood nearby, a murderous look in his eye.

'He fucking bit me.' He held up his hand to reveal a deep gash. 'Nearly had my finger off.'

'Here, let me try.'

The second I approached the man, though, he started hollering again, rocking his body against the chair so hard I was worried he'd tip himself over. 'Murderer! You fucking people are all murderers!'

'Calm down. Please. Just listen. We haven't murdered anyone. We're here because—'

'Liar! You lying bitch! You'd better let me go before I call the police on the lot of you. Help! HELP!'

It was hopeless. I returned to Colin, leading him through to the living room and shutting the door so we could hear ourselves over the man's cries.

'What are we going to do?'

'Well we can't let him go,' Colin said, holding up his bloody hand again. 'The guy's a cannibal.'

'You don't think we could convince him to leave quietly?'

'Not without him attempting to kill us first.'

I pursed my lips. 'Well he can't stay here. Amber's freaked out enough as it is. Besides, there's hardly enough food to feed ourselves, let alone a stranger.'

Colin stared at me, shocked. 'You don't mean…?'

'No. God, no. I don't want to hurt him. He just needs to be somewhere that's... not here.'

We stood silently for a moment while the man continued to holler obscenities at us, his voice cracking with the force of his cries.

'Look, why don't we put him outside?' Colin said at last. 'Just for now. Just until we figure out what to do with him.'

It was a terrible idea. But it was the only one we had.

IT TOOK US almost half an hour to drag the man out of the house and into the garden. The first time we tried to move him, he screamed and thrashed so violently it was impossible to hold on. In the end, Colin had to threaten him with the baseball bat just to get him to stay still. It was strange seeing Colin like that, flecks of spit exploding from his mouth, the veins pumping in his neck as he thrust the tip of the bat into the man's face. I'd always thought of my husband as gentle. Meek, even. Yet now he seemed to be able to tap into violence at will, as if something dark and primal was rising in him. I thought back to the children I'd met at the shop. My knife at the boy's neck. It seemed our capacity for brutality was far closer to the surface than I'd ever imagined. Unlike me, however, Colin didn't seem to be in any danger of backing down. In fact, if I didn't know better, I'd have almost said he was enjoying himself, his rage like a physical release after months of tension. Or perhaps he just liked the sense of power the bat gave him.

By the time Colin had finished shouting, the man was subdued enough to get him outside, where we proceeded to position him as far as we could from the house, propping him against the fence at the very end of the garden. Once he realised we were serious about leaving him out there, he sagged forward in the chair, his voice dropping to a hoarse whisper.

'It doesn't make any difference anyway.'

I tried to nudge Colin towards the house, but he shook me off him. 'What doesn't make a difference?'

'Anything. It's all fucked. We'll all be dead soon anyway. You. Me. Your children.'

'Bullshit,' Colin growled. 'They'll work out whatever it is that's making people sick and they'll roll out a vaccine and—'

The man made a noise like a broken engine, his black eyes bulging, his swollen cheeks growing redder and redder. For a moment I thought he was choking on something, until I realised he was laughing. 'A vaccine? What are they going to vaccinate us against? Each other?'

We stared at him, confused.

'You mean you haven't heard? They're saying there's a virus that makes you allergic to other people. Something in the air. Now isn't that about the funniest thing you've ever heard. You people going on and on about protecting your family, when it's your precious family who are gonna end up killing you.'

'The air?' Colin growled. 'What do you mean there's something in the air?'

'Why should I tell you shit?'

Colin raised the bat again, the same dark look clouding his face. 'Because if you don't, you'll be sorry. That's a promise, my friend.'

'Colin, there's no need to…' I began, but he shook me off him.

'No, Angela. There is a need. This guy turns up here and starts smashing up the place and then threatens my wife and children? He's lucky to still be alive. Now I want him to tell me everything he knows about this so-called virus before I—'

He didn't get to finish his sentence. At that exact moment, the man chose to try and make his escape, springing up from the chair and lunging towards me.

Later I would realise what had happened. While we'd been talking, he'd somehow managed to work his legs and arms free from the ropes. At the time, though, it was all just an explosion of movement. One minute he was tied to the chair, the next he was screaming in my face, teeth bared, hands outstretched to throttle me. To scratch and tear and pull and punch.

To kill me.

Only he never got that far.

Because as he dived forwards, Colin fumbled for the baseball bat he'd kept tucked under his arm and swung it through the air. Straight into the man's skull.

The sound was sickening. Like a melon dropped onto concrete and splitting open.

And then the man was toppling in slow motion, his torso wilting while his legs remained stubbornly planted to the ground, until at last gravity caught up with him and he crashed backwards onto the lawn. He twitched a couple of times, and then lay still.

I didn't speak. Didn't scream. I was too shocked to make a sound. Colin, on the other hand, remained calm. He took a step forward and prodded the man's chest with the tip of his boot. He could have been kicking the tyres of a car for all the emotion he showed. By now a fresh trickle of blood was streaming from the man's ear, a dark pool forming on the grass.

Colin shrugged. 'It was him or you,' was all he said, before he turned away and walked slowly back towards the house. 'It was him or you.'

NINETEEN

ALL THE WAY back to the apartment, I seethed. I stewed.
I simmered. The absolute *nerve* of that man. And the look
on his face after he'd dropped the camera. The self-satisfied
smirk. And the fact he didn't even *attempt* to apologise. Not
that I'd have heard him if he had, so quickly had I turned
and stormed from the school, a string of curses reverberating
from my mask. Well, one thing was for certain, that was the
last time I'd ever see Jazz again. I'd been an idiot to think
that a man like that was ever capable of behaving civilly. I
wouldn't make that mistake again. Oh no. As far as I was
concerned, the sooner the authorities caught up with him,
the better.

I was still in a foul mood by the time I eventually got back
to my room, something that wasn't helped when I slumped in
front of my computer to discover I had no fewer than twenty-
three missed calls, every single one of them from Colin. So
much for not being missed.

I let out a groan.

I knew I should call him back immediately and offer
some kind of excuse.

My alarm didn't go off and I slept in.

I was ill with a cold.

I had an important meeting at work.

Instead, I stood up again and walked over to the

kitchenette, procrastinating. Though the surfaces were already immaculately clean, I dug around under the sink and then attacked them with antibacterial spray, buffing them until the laminate gleamed and my arms ached. I remember reading a report online about the high rates of OCD amongst survivors. There were stories about people who showered five, ten, fifteen times a day. Or washed their hands over and over again until their skin was raw, their fingers cracked and bleeding. Though I wasn't at that stage yet, I certainly recognised the impulse. My own tolerance for dirt of any kind had steadily diminished over the years, to the point where even the sight of a coffee ring or a crumpled tissue was enough to quicken my pulse.

As I cleaned, I found my mind racing back to the haze of dust in the old school. The filth underfoot. The mud-caked surface of the onion. All that risk, and for what? In an effort to prevent myself from hyperventilating, I went to the fridge and grabbed a bottle of water. As I sipped at the cool, filtered liquid, I remembered I hadn't yet taken my medication that morning. I opened the cup board, and automatically began rattling the pills into my palm. Vitamin D. B12. Iron. Niacin and calcium. When I reached the last two, however, for some reason I paused. Picking up the tub for the green ones, the anti-depressants, I turned it around, reading the list of possible side effects on the back for the first time in years. *Drowsiness, nervousness, insomnia, dizziness, nausea, skin rash, headache, diarrhoea, constipation, decreased sex drive, dry mouth, weight loss...* The list went on.

Back in the old world, I remember obsessing over what I put in my body. I would scan food labels, conscientiously avoiding anything that contained anything I didn't recognise as 'natural'. Sodium benzoate, sulphur dioxide, potassium bromate. Aspartame and acesulfame-K. Sorbitol and saccharin. It seemed that half the contents of the chiller aisle were out to kill me and my family. But it wasn't just food I had to worry about. There were neurotoxins in our

Tupperware. Carcinogens leaking from our carpets. From air freshener to oven cleaner, it seemed our homes were nothing more than overpriced deathtraps.

Of course after the virus, most of my anxieties about that stuff evaporated overnight. It's hard to feel uptight about hand sanitiser once you've watched the charred remains of your neighbours blowing down the communal hallway. Besides, it wasn't like we had much of a choice any more. We ate and drank whatever arrived at the drop-off points. We took whatever medicine we were instructed to take. Yet as I stared at the warning signs on the medicine label, I felt the old concerns stirring in me. How long had I been taking them now? Four years? Even the kids were on them. And what benefit were they really having? It wasn't like any of us seemed remotely happy.

Very quickly, before I had chance to talk myself out of it, I took both tubs and emptied their contents directly into the waste disposal unit, listening as they disappeared down the sides of the steel chute with a satisfying clatter.

The second they'd gone, I felt a shudder of regret. Of panic. What if I got sick? Or had withdrawal symptoms. But behind those worries, I also felt a slither of pride at my tiny act of rebellion. Who was a do-gooder now, huh?

Invigorated, I returned to my computer, finally ready to face Colin. Ready to lie.

In the event, however, there was no need. For when Colin finally answered, he didn't ask where I'd been. Rather, I was greeted by the unusual sight of my husband in a state of absolute hysteria.

'It's a disaster,' he gasped. 'I'm ruined.'

I was confused. This was not the Colin I knew. Calm. Pragmatic. He looked like a mad man, his hair wild, his tie hanging to one side, his eyes manic.

'Wait. Slow down. What's happened? What's ruined?'

'Everything!' Colin was practically shouting now. 'It's that fucking boy again. I know it. He's gone too far this time. I swear, if I find out it's him, I'll... I'll...'

'Colin, stop. Get a grip. Breathe.'

He looked directly at the camera then. His eyes were red around the rims. He took a couple of deep, juddering breaths and then nodded. 'Sorry,'

'It's fine. What's going on?'

'I don't know where to begin.' He let out a groan, taking another of those huge, shivery breaths, like a boxer getting ready before a big fight. 'Okay. So you know the latest project I've been working on?'

'The beach thing? The magic gloves?'

He rolled his eyes. 'The application of kinaesthetic technology in a virtual environment.'

'Fine. Sure.'

'So, for the last few months we've been beta testing the product with a select group of clients, inviting them on short mini-breaks to the island. Just a few hours here and there so we can iron out any bugs in the program. And it's been going well. Better than well. The response from the clients has been incredible. Almost too good. We can't get them to log off. They want to stay there forever. Of course, my manager is delighted. Everyone is. In fact, things have been looking so good that we've been thinking about bringing the launch forward by a few months. And then this morning... This morning I got a phone call...' His voice cracked, his words dissolving into a string of unintelligible sobs.

'Come on, Col. Hold it together. What happened this morning?'

'So this morning I got a call from Xan.' He took another deep breath. 'As in Xan fucking Brinkley. My manager's manager. The guy at the top of the food chain. And it seems that last night... Last night someone broke into our system and leaked footage of the tests online.'

'You were hacked?'

'Yes, we were hacked. And it's bad Angela. Really bad.'

'But why would someone do that? Surely no one's going to be interested in a bunch of people sunbathing?'

Colin let out a hollow cluck. 'Sunbathing? You think that's why people come to the island? The most immersive VR experience ever devised and you think people waste it lying around on a beach?'

I paused, trying to digest what he was saying. 'Okay, so there are a few images of people having a virtual bonk. That doesn't sound that bad? Even if Charlie was somehow involved, I don't think—'

'If? *Of course* the little shit was involved! Who else?'

'Hey, watch it. I know you're upset, but that's a pretty big accusation.'

'Is it? I mean first Amber, and now me? You think that's a coincidence?'

'Now wait a minute. You were the one who said there was no evidence it was him who hacked Amber.' I stumbled, finding myself in the novel position of trying to defend our son. I didn't know what to think. Yes, I knew Charlie was troubled. And yes, it did seem like an unlikely coincidence. But even so, surely as his parents we had a duty to give him the benefit of the doubt?

On the screen, Colin's head was in his hands, tugging at the remaining hair on his scalp.

'Well, have you at least tried talking to him about it?' I asked.

Colin sat up then, a crazed look in his eye. 'Ha! Yeah. Right. I must have sent him a hundred messages this morning, but he's not answering. He's not even online. I've got a good mind to put my suit on and go and knock on his door. I mean, obviously I'm not going to do that. But I don't know *what* to do, Angela. I feel like we've lost control. He won't listen. He won't talk. We have to do something. I mean, he needs professional help.'

'Look, you need to calm down. You still don't know for certain it was him who leaked your footage. So, why don't we all just—'

'Just what, Angela? This is the worst day of my entire life and you want me to calm down? Do you have any inkling of what's at stake here? This could be the end of everything. My whole career down the drain. Which means no money. And then what? You think we're going to be able to keep this place going on the peanuts *you* bring in each month?'

'Hey! I know you're upset right now, but there's no need to—'

'And you know what the worst thing is? It's that you don't even have the faintest idea what it is I do. Three years I've been working on this thing, and you treat it like it's some kind of fancy 3D porno website I'm building. You don't respect me.'

'That's not fair, Colin.'

'Isn't it? Because you clearly don't understand how important this stuff is. This is life and death shit, Angela. Right now, there is compromising footage of A-list clients trending on every video site on the web. What, you think we'd let just anyone test this stuff? We're talking CEOs. Film stars. Foreign heads of state. Powerful people facing public ridicule and ruin and who want nothing more than a punching bag. Well guess who they're looking at, Ange? And that's before they've put two and two together and worked out that it's none other than my own son, the fucking *deviant* in the next room, who is the source of this whole nightmare.'

'Colin. I know you're under pressure now, but you need to—'

'Don't tell me what I need to do. You don't know anything. Now, if you'll excuse me, I've got to go and attempt to extinguish the fucking *forest fire* that is my career right now.'

'Colin, wait...'

Before I could finish, though, the screen went black. He'd gone.

I tried calling Charlie. Then Amber.

There was no answer from either of them. Amber wasn't even showing as online.

I sat there for a while, motionless. It was past midday and I still hadn't logged on for work. I couldn't seem to make myself move. In the blank screen in front of me, I could make out my reflection. I looked like a ghost. Tired. Sick. Older than I'd ever looked before.

And totally alone.

●●●

DAYS PASSED. I spoke to no one. Colin wouldn't answer my calls. Neither would the kids. I felt adrift in my room. In all the years I'd spent by myself, I'd still never been more than a text message or a phone call from my family. Now nobody was talking. I couldn't even hear them through the walls. There was no Amber on her treadmill. No Charlie blasting away at his computer games. No Colin, yelling or gnashing or wailing. If I closed my eyes and listened, all I could hear was my own pulse. Blood in my ears, like the swell of a dark and endless ocean.

In the evenings I ate my dinner alone in front of the computer. As much as I'd privately mocked Colin for his 'family meals', I nevertheless dutifully turned on my webcam at the usual time each day, hopeful that I might find another member of my family online. There was only ever my own face, though, the other three squares as black as bottomless pits. I sat and watched myself chewing away at whatever irradiated mush I happened to have defrosted that night. And after that, I sat there watching myself watching myself.

For the first time in five years, I began to feel the crushing weight of claustrophobia. The walls were too close together. The ceiling bearing down on me, the floor pushing up. I was being squeezed. Squashed. Ground out of existence.

It was the pills, I decided. I'd been a fool to throw them out. What had I been thinking? Of course I needed medication to keep me level. Who wouldn't? Life was fucking intolerable without them. I craved booze. Dope. Anything to take me away from my thoughts. To numb me to the interminable present. But of course I had nothing. Nothing, that is, but the thought of Jazz fucking Freeman taunting me. This was all his fault. Everything had been fine until I'd first spotted his stupid orange T-shirt that early summer morning. Not perfect, but fine. We got by. And now? Now everything was ruined.

In an attempt to escape my spiralling thoughts, I threw my attention into work, spending fourteen, sixteen hours at my desk. Whenever my attention wandered, I found my fingers moving on autopilot, opening new windows on my desktop. Gossip columns. Social media. Stupid pictures of animals. Empty-calorie ephemera. Or else I'd find myself hunched over a search engine, tapping in the same rhetorical questions over and over again. *Why am I so sad? When will it be safe to go outside again? Is it too late to start again?*

At night, though, there were no such distractions. I lay there in bed, the darkness closing in on me, like a pillow over my face. In my desperation to escape my memories, I tried everything. Meditation. Counting sheep. I even tried masturbating, though of course I found it impossible. As much as I deride Colin for his use of pornography, perhaps part of me is simply jealous. Even before the outbreak, I'd never enjoyed the sight of strangers' flesh smeared across the screen. It always reminded me of American wrestling. The impossible anatomy of porn stars. Their tits, teeth and tan as fake as their orgasms. The terrible acting. The brutish, pantomime patriarchy. It turned my stomach. Added to the fact that most of the people starring in these pre-virus clips were in all likelihood long dead, and I tended to view porn as the digital equivalent of a cold shower.

That left me with only my fantasies for company. They were equally hopeless, though. My half-hearted attempts at constructing a vaguely plausible scenario were always sabotaged by the nagging reality that physical intimacy would inevitably result in sickness and death. Or else I'd be hijacked by memories from the past. Time and time again, I was visited by the image of the boy I'd threatened at knifepoint, the terror in his eyes, the dark trickle of blood on his pale neck. Or else I'd recall that dark day in the cottage when we dragged the man into the garden. The damp crack of the bat opening up his skull. Not exactly the most erotic material.

Giving up on the operation altogether, I'd eventually fall into a fitful sleep. But even then, I couldn't escape the past. One of my recurring nightmares involved the boy at the shop again, only this time I didn't stop when he dropped the bag. Instead, I kept hacking away at his neck in a frenzy, stabbing him over and over until his head tore away altogether, leaving nothing but the gristle of his windpipe and spine, a geyser of blood erupting from the stump of his neck.

Other times, I'd see visions of Jazz standing topless on the deck of his boat, his muscles straining as he knelt to saw a length of wood. Or else I'd see him beneath the gaudy silk sheets in his cabin below deck, a look in his eyes that was equally terrifying and exciting. In a strange way, these dreams were even more disturbing than the ones about the boy. By the time dawn broke, I'd be wide awake, drenched in sweat, furious with him all over again.

After three or four days and nights of this torture, I decided the only way I was ever going to regain my sanity was to visit the school again. I needed to confront Jazz and tell him exactly what I thought of him and his pathetic attempt to live outside of the system. Couldn't he see how selfish he was being? This was a man who might very possibly hold the key to saving the human race, and yet there he was living on a diet of onion soup and building boats that would never sail. If only I could convince him to hand himself in, then they could use him to develop a vaccine and I could get out of this godforsaken room for good. Not that he'd ever go for it. Oh no. He was far too self-righteous for that.

Thankfully, though, I had another plan.

AND SO, ONCE again, I found myself climbing into my hazmat suit before sunrise. Without a camera, I decided to take my mobile phone instead. I wouldn't be able to film him with it, but I hoped I could at least use it to record audio. There was a small Velcro flap on the front of my suit and I stuffed the phone inside. It wasn't ideal, as the sound was likely to be muffled, but I figured that as long as I had some record of our conversations, at least my story would be believed.

As I crept down the hallway, I stared at each of the three closed doors. Charlie's, Colin's and finally Amber's. I pictured each member of my family, asleep in their individual beds in their individual rooms. It seemed impossible that I could be standing so close to each of them and yet be so far away. For a moment, I fought the urge to hurl myself at the doors. To kick them open. To let in the light. The air. To hell with the danger. Just so the four of us could be together one last time. So I could talk to Amber, to see if she was okay. To Charlie, too, and hear his side of the story. Instead, I continued down the hallway, being as quiet as possible as I set off into another forbidden morning.

The walk was easier than it had been the last time. Or perhaps it was simply that I knew precisely where I was going. Though the day was bright, the sun was cooler, and I found myself shivering as I trudged down the centre of the deserted streets. As ever, there were no police. No soldiers. Maybe they didn't bother with this part of the city? Or maybe there weren't any to begin with? Maybe they were just invented by the government to keep people from doing something as stupid and reckless as the thing I was doing now. Either way, I reached the rusting school gates without incident. I paused for a moment to retrieve my phone, setting it to record before I stowed it away again in my secret pouch. Then I hopped over the railings and set off across the playground.

As I approached the door, I felt a building sense of anticipation. At least I did until I noticed that Jazz's bike was no longer leaning up against the wall outside. Was I too late? Had I missed him? I tried to stay calm. He'd probably just parked it round the back out of sight. There was nothing to worry about.

When I reached the door, however, I was less sure.

The door handle was smeared with something that wasn't there before. Something dark and red.

For a moment I scrambled for a reasonable explanation. Hadn't Jazz talked about painting his boat?

But then I opened the door.

And saw the footprints leading down the hall.

There was no mistaking it then.

It was blood.

And lots of it.

PART FOUR

TWENTY

I KNEW RIGHT away that I should turn and run and not look back. That would be the sensible thing to do. Something terrible and violent had happened there, and the longer I stayed around, the more likely something terrible and violent would happen to me.

Yet for all my survival instincts told me to get out, I kept going, following the trail of blood down the hall. It wasn't hard. There was a lot of it. A footprint here. A smeared handprint there. I wondered whether Jazz might have injured himself while working on the boat. Hammers, saws, axes, nails. All it would take was a slip of the hand. As I edged closer to the hall though another, darker explanation occurred to me. That perhaps it was not Jazz's blood at all. That maybe it belonged to someone else. Someone Jazz had hurt.

Someone like me.

I swallowed down my fear. Jazz might have been intolerably rude, but he didn't seem violent. Even so, it took all of my courage to keep going once I reached the swing doors that led to the hall.

'Hello?' I whispered.

There was no answer. I tried again, a little louder this time. 'Is there anybody here?'

The trail continued across the scratched wooden floor, leading off around the side of the boat. While I've never been especially squeamish, the sight of so much blood made me itch. Even with my suit and mask, I couldn't help but think about the toxic cells lurking in each red streak. Enough to infect my entire family. To wipe out half the city. Again the urge to run was almost overwhelming.

'Hello?' I tried again.

This time, I thought I heard a noise in response, though it was difficult to tell with the swish of my suit in my ears. I kept walking, preparing myself to sprint for cover at the first sign of danger.

As I reached the edge of the boat, however, I was greeted not by the hostage situation that had been playing out in my mind, but by a pile of crumpled blankets. I was about to step over them and move on, when the blankets let out a groan. Then they sat up, and I saw that huddled under the layers of stained fabric was Jazz.

He attempted a smile, but it came out as more of a grimace. 'Okay, so don't freak out, but I've had a bit of an accident.'

He didn't look well. His skin deathly pale. His forehead puckered with sweat. Very gently, he pulled back the sheet to reveal his leg.

Or at least, what remained of his leg.

●●●

IT WAS A dog that did it. Though he swore it looked more like a wolf. Or a mutant. Its face deformed. More teeth than he'd ever thought possible. He'd been out exploring again and found a hardware store a couple of miles from the school. The jackpot, he called it. Completely untouched. He was just finishing loading up his trailer with supplies, when out of nowhere he heard a snarling behind him. He turned in time to see a flash of black fur. And then it was on him. For a moment he thought it was all over. But then he'd grabbed a piece of wood from the trailer and somehow managed to fight the thing off, until eventually it scurried away, whimpering back to the shadows.

For a while he hadn't even realised he'd been bitten, the shock protecting him from any pain. It was only when he started pedalling that he looked down and saw his trousers were saturated with blood. After a few minutes he was forced to abandon the bike altogether and hobble back to the school. That was yesterday afternoon, and he'd been lying here ever since.

Swallowing down my fear of contamination, I cleaned up his leg as best I could, while at the same time attempting to minimise my contact with the wound. 'You need to get to a hospital,' I said once I'd finished. 'That dog could have had anything in his saliva.'

Jazz laughed weakly. 'Good point. I guess I'd better go to hospital. I'll call an ambulance, shall I?'

'You know what I mean. There're still doctors you know. I could call one for you. You have to do something or you could lose your leg. Or worse.'

I glanced down again at the wound. Jazz didn't have a first aid kit, so I'd used water from the kitchen to clean it up, boiling it on the stove first and adding a few spoonfuls of salt for good measure. Once I'd washed the dried blood off, I saw the leg wasn't as bad as I'd initially thought. That's not to say it looked good. There were puncture marks all along his calf, running from his ankle to his knee from where the dog had attacked him. Some of them looked deep. More alarming than the cuts was the red line tracking up his thigh.

'I mean it. You need to call someone. If you won't, I will.'

'No.' For the first time I saw the fear in his eyes. 'You know what will happen to me if you call for a doctor. If it's a choice between that and dying, I'd rather just stay here.'

I looked again at the red line. It seemed to be growing by the second. 'Fine. But you can't just leave it like that. I'm pretty sure I've got some antibiotics in my first aid kit at home. At the very least I've got some cream we can use to clean the cuts up properly. When's the last time you had a tetanus shot?'

Jazz shrugged. 'Hey, there's no need to make a big deal out of this thing. I'm just tired. I'll get some sleep and I'll be fine.

'Don't sleep.' I stood up, getting ready to leave. 'You need to try and stay awake if you can. I can be back here in…' I paused. I'd forgotten about the time I needed to spend in decontamination. 'I can be back here later today. This afternoon latest. Just stay here until then, okay?'

'It's not like I'm going to run off anywhere is it?'

•••

SLUMPED INSIDE THE quarantine tent, every second seemed to last a week. While I waited, I stared unblinkingly at the red light, willing it to turn green.

'Come on,' I whispered under my breath. 'Come the fuck on.'

My biggest fear was that I would be too late. That I would arrive at the school and find the infection had spread and that Jazz was in a coma. Or worse.

Then there was the question of the antibiotics themselves. Even if I did manage to find them and make it back to the school in time, there was no guarantee they would work. Like most people, the first thing we did when we returned to the city was stock up on as much medication as we could get our hands on. Though the official pharmacies had long since either been raided or closed, a thriving black market had quickly sprung up in their place. This was before the authorities had shut down the dark web, and for a brief window of time, there was no end to the bargains that could be delivered by a bio-suited mercenary. For a vastly inflated price, naturally. Back then the demand for Tamiflu was off the charts, and just like everyone else, we gobbled it down religiously twice a day, despite the warnings from the authorities that it provided no protection from the virus. We didn't care, though. We were willing to try anything if it meant not getting sick. Along with the Tamiflu, we had dozens of packets of antihistamines delivered to our door. Blue Ventolin inhalers. Benadryl. Claritin. Colin even managed to get his hands on a couple of EpiPens, though again these were later proved to be utterly ineffective against the virus. We also had a range of antibiotics, just in case. It was those I was relying on to help Jazz, though whether I had the right ones, or whether they were even still in date, I had no idea.

When the light finally turned green, I sprinted back to my room. I didn't even bother taking my suit off before I began raiding the first aid box, stuffing anything that looked vaguely useful into a small bag. Once I'd finished, I looked frantically around for anything I might have missed. There was an unopened bottle of water on the side, so I put that in the bag, too, along with a couple of energy bars. At least he could have a break from onion soup.

The clock on the wall read midday. I couldn't believe it was so late already. Again I wondered if it wouldn't be better to simply call a doctor. They could probably be with him within minutes if I explained the situation to them. Although that would mean I'd also have to explain how I knew he was there, which would be a tricky conversation. And then there was the fact I'd made him a promise. I thought about the fear in his eyes. The panic in his voice. While I was still angry about the camera, I couldn't bring myself to simply turn him in. Not in the state he was in. No, I decided to stick to the plan and bring him the drugs. There'd be time later to try and convince him to talk to the authorities. For now I just needed to make sure he didn't die.

Forcing down a chocolate bar, I quickly logged on to my computer where I found several messages from clients already waiting for me. With no time to answer them properly, I tapped out a generic email to my manager, once again feigning illness. As I swallowed down the last of the chocolate, I suddenly remembered my mobile phone. Reaching into my pocket, I saw it was still recording, though the battery was almost dead. I hit 'Stop' and saved the file, before I spotted I'd received a new message. This one was from Colin.

Shall we talk?

I stared at the screen, trying to think of an appropriate response, until eventually the phone beeped and the battery died altogether. I put it down next to my computer. I'd reply later. There was no time now. I picked up my mask, swung the bag of drugs over my shoulder and headed for the door.

I HARDLY REMEMBER the journey back to the school. Gone was the illicit pleasure of being outside. I felt detached from everything. Trapped in a bubble, with only the endless rasp of my respirator and the fog inside my mask for company. For all I could see, I might as well have been Amber on her treadmill, the cracked concrete churning endlessly beneath me, step after step after step...

Somehow, I found myself back at the school gates. Without stopping, I launched myself at them, swinging one leg over the railings. As I attempted to pivot round, however, my other leg seemed to get caught in something, and the next thing I knew I was lying in a tangled heap on the floor of the playground. Though slightly winded, I forced myself to my feet and dusted myself down. There was no time to be hurt. I picked up the bag from the mossy concrete and limped on towards the school.

As soon as I was back inside the hall, I began calling his name.

This time there was no answer.

I hurried across the wooden floor until I reached the boat.

For a moment I thought he'd gone. But then I saw him, still huddled beneath the blankets where I'd left him.

Stooping over him, I saw how pale he was, his lips almost blue. I wasn't sure he was conscious, but then suddenly he twisted his head towards me. 'Hey,' his voice no more than a croak. 'You came back.'

I went to work cleaning his leg, spraying it with antiseptic and applying a light bandage. It was awkward working with the thin material, especially in my bulky gloves, and several times I knocked his leg, causing him to cry out in pain. Once I'd finished, I dug through the bag to find the most likely box of antibiotics.

'The packet says you need to take two every six hours for a week.'

He punched two of the small white capsules out into his open palm, swallowing them down with a sip of water before slumping backwards, his eyes closed. 'Why are you being so nice to me?' he asked, his voice a cracked slur.

'Shush. Just try and get some sleep. You need to save your strength.'

'I mean it. You could have just left but you didn't. You came back. I bet you're a great Mum too... I bet you...' He trailed off as he fell out of consciousness.

There was nothing else to do but wait and hope the drugs worked.

'I've got to go now,' I said quietly. 'People will miss me. I'll try to come back tomorrow and check how you are.' I bent down and placed a couple of energy bars next to him. 'Try and eat something if you can. You need to keep your strength up.'

He didn't answer.

As I turned to leave, however, there was a rustle of movement. I looked down and saw he'd propped himself up again. 'Hey, what did you do to your leg? Are you hurt?'

I shook my head. He wasn't making sense. He was probably delirious. 'No, silly. It's your leg that's hurt, remember? Just try and get some rest and I'll see you tomorrow.'

Jazz was adamant, though. 'Look,' he pointed. 'Look.'

I smiled sadly, glancing down all the same.

That's when I saw the streak of red on my own leg from where I'd fallen in the playground.

It wasn't the blood that bothered me, though.

Rather, it was the gaping hole in my suit.

And through the hole, my bare skin.

Raw and open.

Exposed.

TWENTY-ONE

IN THE END, we decided against burying the man. It just didn't seem worth the effort. We simply declared the garden out of bounds and slipped back into our routine. We played board games. We did chores. Washed clothes. Swept the floor. And, on the odd occasion the kids did ask about the strange man who attacked Daddy, we shrugged our shoulders and furrowed our brows.

'What man?' we said.

Food was still a problem, of course. After a few days of living on little but chocolate bars and fizzy drinks I'd developed a pulsing headache behind my eyes, my stomach cramping on the empty calories. Though I felt physically exhausted, I struggled to sleep at night, my thoughts wild and jittery. The kids too seemed strung out on sugar, their moods see-sawing between laughter and tears, Amber even more sensitive than usual, Charlie quick to bicker or whine.

It was Colin, though, who seemed most affected, becoming more withdrawn and morose with each passing day. I suspected this wasn't just down to the deterioration of our diet. Several times I caught him making painstaking examinations of the bite on his hand, holding it up to the light to look at it, dressing and re-dressing the wound, smearing it with antiseptic ointment. One night, as we lay on the sofa, he finally confided his fears to me.

'I've been thinking. Maybe we should start sleeping separately.'

I smiled, made a joke. 'If this is your way of asking for a divorce, you really need to work on your timing. It's not like there's a whole bunch of dating options out there.'

'I'm serious. And I'm not just talking about us either. The kids. There's space for a room each if I take the garage. We could ration out the food so we don't have to eat together. Keep contact to a minimum.'

'What are you talking about? Is this about what that man said? About the virus being in the air? You do know he was crazy, right?'

'I'm not talking forever. Just for now. As a precaution, until we get to the bottom of things. What harm could it do?'

I sat up then, anger rising in me. 'Harm? You're talking about isolating our children on a whim. You've seen Amber. You really think she'd cope with being locked up on her own? And what about Charlie? He'd eat his rations on the first day and then starve. It's utter madness. We've been cooped up together in this house for a fortnight. If we were allergic to one another, we'd be dead already.'

Colin glanced down again at his hand.

'Oh, come on. The bite? Now you're just being paranoid.'

Now it was Colin's turn to get angry. 'You know I think, just this once, I might be entitled to a bit of paranoia. A fortnight ago I buried a mother and child in the garden. Earlier this week I beat a man to death with a baseball bat. This is not business as usual, Angela. In case you hadn't noticed, things are utterly fucked up. So when I make a suggestion that could potentially keep our family safe, the least you could do is take me seriously.'

He rolled over, furious. The conversation was over. Though we were under the same sheet, our bodies didn't touch. We might as well have been in different rooms.

At some point in the night, I managed to drift off to sleep. When I woke again, it was still dark. Something was different, though. *Something was wrong. That's when I realised Colin was gone.*

I was up in a flash, fumbling for the light switch. He wasn't in the living room. Nor the bathroom. I staggered through to the kitchen, then into the children's bedroom, where Charlie and Amber were still fast asleep. There was no sign of Colin anywhere.

I tore back through the house, working myself into a frenzy. What if he'd actually cracked and walked out on us? Or worse. What if he'd decided he couldn't take it any more? He wouldn't be the first. In the immediate aftermath of the virus, suicide rates had rocketed. I tried to imagine my life without him. How I'd explain it to the kids. How I'd carry on.

By the time I'd searched every room in the house I was shaking. I went outside, calling his name as loudly as I dared, my voice small and shaky in the night. There was no response. It was the first time I'd been out of the house since we'd dragged the man to the bottom of the garden, and though it was thankfully too dark to see anything, the thought of his body lying out there made my skin crawl.

I moved around to the front of the cottage to look in the garage. As I did, I passed the car. Sure enough, when I pressed my face to the glass I could make out the shape of my sleeping husband, squashed up on the back seat. For a moment I thought about waking him. Of hammering the glass and screaming at him for being so selfish. For scaring me like that.

Instead, I simply returned to the living room and curled up on the cushions, cold and alone beneath the thin blanket.

The next morning, I woke to find Colin in the kitchen, preparing a breakfast of Sprite and Kinder Egg. I waited for him to apologise for leaving me in the night, but when he didn't mention it I didn't push. We were all under pressure. It was hardly surprising if one of us lost it once in a while.

Only it wasn't once in a while. Over the next few days, I

watched as Colin steadily withdrew from the rest of us. He'd eat alone, or find excuses to be in the garage, tinkering with the generator or solar panels. In the evening he would get ready for bed, then make his way to the car. When I finally questioned him about it, he muttered something about not wanting to take any 'unnecessary risks'.

Consciously or not, his behaviour seemed to trigger a reflective response in the children, who also retreated to distant corners of the house. Gone were the long afternoons playing Monopoly. The fun and the games and the laughter that up until that point made things just about bearable. Instead, we became four independent beings living under one roof.

Still, as distressing as this new development was, I had more pressing matters to worry about. Our food supplies were running dangerously low. One of us would have to go out and hunt for food again. It was either that or starve. Yet, as desperate as our situation was, I couldn't seem to motivate myself to do anything about it. In fact, I could hardly bring myself to do anything full stop. I found it was getting harder and harder to get up off the sofa each morning, my limbs heavy, my head fuzzy. I found myself slumped for hours in the living room in a sort of trance. Neither awake nor asleep. Not seeing. Not thinking. Just sitting.

The next day, as I lay motionless on the sofa, I looked up to see Charlie standing nearby. He was holding something in his hand.

'Someone keeps trying to ring you,' he said, handing me my phone.

I took it from him. I hadn't seen my phone in days. Weeks even. We'd all long since given up trying to get a signal, and I was amazed to see it still had some charge.

Swiping the screen, I saw that Charlie was mistaken. There were no missed call notifications. I was about to hand it back to him when I noticed the small red alert sign on the screen. It was a text message.

Half convinced I was hallucinating, I opened it up and read it. Then I read it again.

Charlie peered over my shoulder, trying to see what I was looking at. 'Who's it from Mummy? What does it say?'

It took me a moment to answer. When I did, my voice sounded strange and distant, as if someone else were speaking. Someone who didn't believe the words that were coming from their mouth. 'It's from the government. It says… Well. I think it's saying that we can go home.'

TWENTY-TWO

IT'S A FUNNY thing to know you're dying. I don't mean that in an abstract sense. Technically, we're all dying. Even you, my poor sweet Egg. Or at least you will be if and when you are ever conceived. Sorry to break it to you, but from the moment you meet Mr Sperm, the clock starts ticking. But no, I'm talking about dying imminently. In months rather than years. In days rather than weeks. When it's close enough that you can count the hours.

Back in the old world, I never really gave my own death much thought. Sure, it was there in the background. Something unpleasant but inevitable, like renegotiating my car insurance, or going for a smear test. There was no point in fighting these things, but equally there was no need to dwell on them until they were actually happening.

Then, of course, everything went insane and death was everywhere. Colleagues. Friends. Family. These weren't the nice, neat sanitised deaths I'd pictured on the rare occasion I'd actually considered my own demise. Everything tied up in a neat bow. An old woman tucked up in bed, thumbing through her photo album one last time before quietly slipping off into an eternal slumber, surrounded by three or four generations of smiling relatives. These were violent, messy, abrupt deaths. People ripped from the world in their prime. Or sooner. Before their lives had even really had a chance to begin.

But even after the virus hit, my real concern was always the children. That was my biggest fear. Whether fleeing the city, or camping out in that damn cottage, I was always convinced the children would get sick. I never considered that it might be me who fell ill. It never occurred to me that I might be the one falling backwards from my chair, clawing at my throat as if choking on a sandwich. That it might be me weeping and rocking and tugging my hair, praying to a God I actively didn't believe in to give me one more shot at living. Or at the very least, one more chance to see my family and make things right.

And yet, here we are, Egg. Here we are.

•••

THE FIRST FEW hours after I realised I'd been exposed are a bit of a blur. My initial instinct had been to run. Leaving Jazz sprawled on the wooden floor, I sprinted for the double doors and down the hall. I stopped before I got to the playground, though. Where was I going to go? Outside was even more dangerous than in the school. And it wasn't as if I could risk going back home and infecting the house. No. I had little hope but to sit there and wait it out. Maybe I'd get lucky? After all, Jazz had managed to stay healthy all this time. If I wasn't showing symptoms in three days then I could assume I'd dodged the bullet. Until then, there was nothing for it but to sit tight.

By the time I shuffled back into the hallway, I was convinced I could already feel the virus working its way through my bloodstream. My breath was short. My heart was hammering. My skin prickling. This is how it begins, I thought. Within hours I'll be feverish. By tonight my eyes and nose will be streaming. By the morning I'll be struggling for air. After that, it will only be a matter of time.

Jazz was still on the floor where I'd left him. By now he was totally unconscious. Part of me had an urge to kick him.

To take out my fury and frustration on his ribcage. In truth, though, it was hard to see any of this as his fault. Not really. I had been the one who had followed him here. I knew how dangerous it was, and yet I kept coming back again and again. No, if anyone deserved to be kicked, it was me.

All at once, I felt anger slide towards self-pity. I wanted to curl into a ball and weep. I even thought about lying down next to Jazz. If I was going to die anyway, wouldn't it be better to feel the warmth of another human one last time? Of course, I kept my distance, unable to stomach the thought of being found like that. Entwined with a stranger. That was assuming we were found at all. I pictured archaeologists millennia from now, digging down through layers of sediment to find our last moments preserved in stone. Tagging our bones. Shipping us off to museums. What would they make of the scene? Two bodies beside a boat inside a school. I imagined scholars arguing over the circumstances of our death. Were we castaways? Had we drowned?

I shook my head. Who was I kidding? Museums and archaeologists were relics of the old world. No one would ever find us here. Our vanishing would go unmarked by the world at large, like so many millions before us. Only my family would notice I was gone. One more misery to add to all the others. And that was if they noticed at all.

Still, I decided to keep my distance from Jazz. The less exposure, the better my chances. I needed to be alone. For a moment I thought about barricading myself in one of the classrooms. One look through the dusty windows made me change my mind. The spidery handwriting of a lost generation. All those faded hopes and dreams captured in crayon.

This is my family…
This is my house…
When I grow up I want to be…
It was too much to take.

I had to find somewhere, though. With every passing

minute, my symptoms were getting worse. My chest wheezy, my throat raw. I hardly had the strength to keep standing up.

With nowhere else to go, I found myself clambering up the side of the boat and descending the stairs into the dim glow of Jazz's secret bedroom.

And there, curled up amongst the dusty silk sheets, I lay down and waited for the end.

'YOU SHOULD EAT something.'

I woke with a start, unsure for a moment of where I was. Then it all came rushing back to me with sickening clarity. The school. Jazz. My torn suit. I sat up too fast and the room began to spin, my vision speckled with a detonation of stars. When I finally managed to focus again, I saw with a start that Jazz was sitting at the end of the bed. Though still pale, he looked slightly brighter than earlier. In his hands was a bowl, wisps of steam curling from the top.

I shook my head. 'I'm not hungry.'

'I know. But you told me to eat earlier and it made me feel better. Now it's your turn.'

All I'd eaten since last night was a lone chocolate bar. I was starving. Only I didn't dare to eat. Even with my suit ripped, taking my mask off seemed unthinkably reckless. Especially in this room, with Jazz so close I'd probably be able to smell him.

I shook my head again.

'Look, if it's me you're worried about I can just leave it here,' Jazz said, reading my mind. 'Just promise me you'll eat something, or you really will get sick.'

With that he placed the bowl down on an upturned crate that doubled as a bedside table and disappeared back up the stairs.

I don't know how many hours passed while I lay there, writhing under Jazz's shiny sheets. By then I was in too

181

much pain to sleep. My stomach cramped with hunger and my bladder was ready to burst. Every so often I would glance over at the bowl of pale brown soup that Jazz had left for me. By now, a thick skin had congealed over the surface. Even so, the sight of the liquid nearly pushed me over the edge. My tongue felt swollen and heavy in my mouth, like an old piece of meat. It occurred to me that even if I somehow managed to avoid the virus, I might end up dying of thirst.

I rolled over and pulled back the sheets. The wound was nowhere near as serious as I'd initially thought. It was more of a graze than a cut. In the old world it would hardly have warranted a plaster. On the other hand, the tear in the suit was pretty bad, the material flapping open, exposing nearly my entire knee. I tried to think back to what I knew about the virus. It was strange. In the first months after we returned to our apartment, the news was full of almost nothing else. There were flash reports with each new discovery, confident scientists explaining the exact mechanism that helped the virus to spread. Like most infectious diseases, it was transferred from person to person through contact. A cough or a sneeze. An unwashed hand. A kiss. Once contracted, it worked its way down through the respiratory tract, binding to the surface of healthy cells, reprogramming them and replicating itself, killing the host cells in the process. 'Like a killer cuckoo,' I remember one jovial scientist chuckling. Once infected, you were rendered allergic to human skin particles. Dander. Dust. The problem was, there was no reliable test to find out if you were sick, until you keeled over. Hence the safest option was to assume everyone was infected and avoid all direct human contact. At least in the short term.

Back then, the breakthroughs came thick and fast. It seemed a vaccine was only ever a few weeks away. Until then, it was a case of hanging on. Of sitting tight and keeping a stiff upper lip. We shall overcome and all that patriotic nonsense they tend to roll out in times of national disaster. As the months became years, however, the idea of a cure seemed to drop out of the news. Whenever it was mentioned, the scientists seemed less optimistic. They'd purse their lips and puff out their cheeks, muttering about mutating genetic codes. Impossible working conditions. The death of key colleagues. The loss of vital research. The focus now seemed to be on making the present more palatable. Advances in streaming services and VR technology. The ever-broadening range of rations available to us. The stabilisation of electricity and water supplies. The way they made it sound, there was no reason to *want* to leave the comfort of our homes, even if it should one day become safe to do so.

Lying there on Jazz's bed, I began to do some calculations. The way I saw it, there were three possible scenarios I was facing. The first was the bleakest: I'd contracted the virus years ago, and up until now I had successfully avoided exposure to enough foreign skin cells to trigger symptoms. If that was the case, then the game was up. I was already a dead woman. The rip in the suit saw to that. Whether or not I took off my mask and ate the soup, it made no difference. I had three days.

In the second scenario, I still hadn't contracted the virus, but Jazz was a carrier, who had somehow managed to remain asymptomatic up until now. Presuming he hadn't infected me yet, the dust wouldn't affect me. I should leave the mask on, wait for three days to rule out scenario one, and then leave. Simple. The only problem was that I'd probably die of dehydration before then.

Finally, there was a chance that neither of us was infected. That would explain how Jazz had managed to stay alive so long. In this scenario, there was again no need for the mask. So long as it was just the two of us here, I was safe to eat the soup.

The more I puzzled over these three outcomes, the more I realised I didn't have a choice. All my options were taken away the moment I tore my suit. Now all I had was maths. And the maths was telling me that my very best chance of survival was to get some liquid into my body.

Willing my terror away, my shaking fingers worked the zip on my suit until I managed to lower my hood. And then, with a final gasp of filtered air, I undid the loops around the back of my head. And lifted off my mask.

I blinked.

Looked around.

Everything seemed brighter. More real. It was like moving from 2D to 3D. Though I knew it was irrational, I could almost *see* the virus in the air, suspended like second-hand smoke. I held my breath for as long as I could, but in the end I had no choice. I exhaled, then breathed in deeply, filling my lungs.

Then again.

And again.

The air smelled thick. Heavy. I was so used to the sterile, climate-controlled environment of my room, that it took me a moment to place certain scents. Damp. Mould. Freshly cut wood. And, strongest of all, onion soup.

I reached for the bowl, the brown liquid slopping over the sides. The first spoonful was a severe test for my gag reflex, the contents like cold mucus. I persevered, forcing the salty broth down my throat. By the time I got to the last spoonful, it was almost palatable. Once I'd finished, I finally dragged myself out of bed. My legs felt weak and shaky, the floor seeming to lurch violently away from me. This was the virus getting to work on my nervous system, I told myself. It wouldn't be long before I couldn't stand at all. Before my breath became a rasp. At the thought of this, my head began to spin even faster, anxiety setting my fingers and toes tingling. For a second it felt like my airwaves were closing up then and there. I collapsed back onto the bed. Grabbed my throat. Gasped for air.

Then I remembered Amber, all those years ago, back at the cottage.

'*In-through-your-nose-two-three-four…*'

'Out-through-your mouth-two-three-four...'

After a minute or two, the room swam back into focus. I wasn't dead. Not yet. With a Herculean effort, I forced myself back to my feet. And then, very slowly, I made my way up the stairs and out onto the deck.

It was lighter up there than I'd been expecting, crisp dawn sunshine filtering through the windows and the cracks in the roof. Peering over the edge of the railing, I spotted Jazz standing in the centre of the hall, his back turned away from me. I called out to him.

'Hey, I'm up. Thanks for the soup. How's the leg?'

He didn't respond.

'Hey!' I tried again.

Still he didn't move.

I was about to call out a third time when I noticed that, for some reason, Jazz was holding the axe aloft, the handle gripped tightly in his fist. I gave an involuntary shiver as the spectre of a hundred horror movies flashed through my mind. Was this the part of the film where the laid-back loner suddenly reveals himself to be a bloodthirsty psychopath? Was I about to be slashed and dismembered like so many B-movie extras?

I was about to turn and run when something stirred on the far side of the hall. I didn't move. Crouched in the far corner of the room, half hidden in the shadows, was some kind of animal. Instantly, I knew it was a dog. The same dog that had bitten Jazz. It must have picked up his scent and was back to finish him off. Any moment now, it would stalk into the room. An ear torn off. An eye gouged out. Its jaw split open on one side to reveal blood-red gums and two rows of terrible teeth. A childhood nightmare made flesh and fur. A living, breathing monster.

'Come out,' Jazz called into the shadows, gripping the axe tighter. 'Come out now or you'll be sorry.'

The dog shifted its weight again. Pacing. Prowling.

And then it spoke.

'Please don't hurt me.'

The dog took a step forwards.

I blinked. Tried to understand what I was seeing.

As the dog padded out into the light, I saw it wasn't a dog at all.

It was a person, dressed in a white protective suit and mask.

A person I knew.

'Please don't hurt me,' the person said again.

And this time I recognised the voice.

And nothing made sense. Nothing.

Because the person standing in the hall was Amber.

TWENTY-THREE

EVEN WITH THE *text message from the government, Colin wasn't convinced it was safe to return to the city.*

'Maybe we should wait?'

'Wait? For how long?' I asked that evening, once I'd finally managed to pin him down for long enough to talk about it. 'Days? Months? We haven't got enough food to sit around twiddling our thumbs, hoping the authorities come to our rescue. We're stuck out here in the middle of nowhere. They're going to deal with the cities first. That's where the infrastructure is. It could be years before they get around to helping people out here. That's if they even bother helping us at all.'

Colin crossed his arms defensively. He was standing on the far side of the living room, with his back against the wall. About as far as he could get from me without actually leaving the cottage. 'But the text said we need to stay indoors and avoid physical contact. Shouldn't we start doing that now? I mean, squashing into the car and recycling the same air for the next few hours seems a little risky, doesn't it?'

'Oh for God's sake. It's not like you're about to go hitchhiking with a bunch of strangers. It's us, Colin. Your family. The same people you've been living with for weeks. And no one's got sick yet, have they?'

'No. But the man said—'

'The man who's currently dead in the garden. The man whom we killed? And while we're at it, don't you think that's another reason for us to leave? Even if by some miracle someone does turn up to rescue us, how do you think it's going to look when they stumble across a corpse laid out on the lawn? Not to mention the other two buried under the flower bed…'

'That's not fair. We had nothing to do with them, and you know it.'

Still, my point seemed to have got through to him. Several times over the course of the day, I caught him lingering by the window, peering out anxiously at the back garden. That evening, as we each sat in our separate part of the house having eaten our miserable excuse for a dinner, Colin suddenly called us all through to the kitchen. 'I've made a decision,' he said. 'It's time to pack. We're going home.'

We would leave for the city first thing in the morning.

●●●

I GUESS I'D expected the kids to be excited to be going back to the city. Strangely, this wasn't the case. As we loaded up the car the next morning, a sense of gloom seemed to settle over them. Swinging the boot shut, I tried my best to be upbeat.

'I bet you're excited to see your bedroom again?' I said to Charlie. 'You'll have your books. Your toys.'

Charlie only shrugged, though. 'I'll probably have to burn them anyway.'

'What are you talking about? Why on earth would you have to burn your things?'

'That's what Amber told me. She said the virus would be all over everything and we'd have to burn them or we'd catch it and die like everybody else.'

'Well that's just ridiculous. Why would she say something like that?' I turned back to the house and called Amber's name.

A minute later she trudged out, every inch the disaffected teen.

'Listen. I want you to come over here and say sorry to your brother for scaring him. Telling him he'd have to burn his toys. What absolute rubbish.'

For a moment I thought she was going to challenge me, but then she gave a defeated shrug, looking at her feet. 'Sorry.'

'You could at least pretend you mean it. And you can give him a hug while you're at it.'

Still scowling, she shuffled forwards, snagging Charlie in a half-hearted embrace. As the two of them came together, Colin emerged from the cottage, a bundle of blankets in his arms. At the sight of the kids hugging, he dropped them and ran forwards, waving his arms as if attempting to put out a fire.

'Stop! Jesus! Let him go! What did I tell you two about not touching each other? I'm not joking. This stuff is serious.'

At the sound of his voice, Amber and Charlie broke apart immediately.

'Colin…' I began, then stopped. There was no point.

Ten minutes later we were leaving the cottage for the final time. Earlier, with the kids out of earshot, Colin and I had discussed covering our tracks, just in case on the off-chance someone came to investigate. We talked about untying the man and burying him. Hiding his car. Staging an accident. Scrubbing the place to make sure we hadn't left any fingerprints or DNA. Hell, maybe we should just burn the whole place to the ground?

In the end, though, we simply walked out, the broken front door flapping open behind us. There just didn't seem any point in trying to clean up. I doubted very much the people who'd been here before us would be missed. There probably wasn't anyone left to miss them.

Climbing into the car, I was again struck by the children's reluctance to leave.

'Couldn't we stay just one more day,' Charlie whined.

'Or a week,' Amber said hopefully.

I shook my head. 'What is it with you guys? I thought you'd be over the moon. Anyone would think you didn't want to go home.'

Neither of them answered.

Once we were all in, Colin undid each of the windows. I didn't protest. It was a bright day and the fresh air was welcome after weeks stuck inside the stuffy cottage. As we reversed down the drive I watched as the small white cottage receded into the distance. I thanked it silently for saving our lives.

WE WERE AROUND an hour from the city when we saw the first car. Though we were beginning to get sketchy Internet reception, the GPS was still out, and at the sight of the other vehicle, Colin nearly swerved off the road in surprise. I guess, like me, he'd forgotten there was anyone else left in the world beyond our little family. Within a few minutes, though, we spotted another car, then another. Dozens. Then hundreds. It was like an exodus in reverse. All of them heading in the same direction. All of them heading towards the city.

As we turned onto the motorway, Colin suddenly hit the brakes, slowing us to a crawl, then to a total stop. My heart sank. Stretching out as far as I could see was the longest line of traffic I have ever seen. All three lanes were totally gridlocked.

With so many vehicles around us, even Charlie and Amber began to take an interest. 'Where did all these people come from?' Charlie asked. 'Amber told me everyone was dead.'

'I did not.'

'Did too.'

I didn't answer. I too was shocked by the sheer volume of people. It would take hours to get back at this rate. If not days.

In the back seat, Charlie stuck his head out of the window. 'Stop that,' Colin snapped. 'It's dangerous. You could—'

Before he could finish, Charlie began shouting. 'Daddy!

Mummy! Who's that? Over there. On the other side of the road. Can you see them?'

I shifted in my seat, trying to see whatever it was he was pointing at.

There were just cars, though. Thousands and thousands of cars.

And then suddenly I saw what he was pointing at. Or rather whom he was pointing at; stalking through the traffic was a man dressed in a hazardous materials suit.

All at once, everyone started talking, our words tumbling over each other.

'Who is that?'

'Why is he wearing…?'

'I'm sure it's nothing to do with us.'

'Is that a…?'

Abruptly we all fell silent.

For at the same time, we saw what the man was holding in his hands:

A gun.

And he was aiming it straight at us.

TWENTY-FOUR

'JAZZ! STOP! WAIT! Let her go. I know her. She's my…'

As I sprinted across the school hall towards the spot where Jazz was now grappling with Amber, I felt reality wheeling away from me. Surely, I was still asleep. Fever-dreaming under Jazz's sheets. How else to explain Amber's presence here? In this crumbling hall, in this secret place, on the wrong side of the city. How else to make sense of any of this?

'… daughter,' I gasped as I finally reached them. 'She's my daughter.'

They both froze for a second, staring at me. Then Jazz let go of Amber and lowered the axe. He took a couple of steps backwards.

Amber was the first to speak, her voice high-pitched and panicky, as if she was struggling to prevent herself from screaming. 'Mum? What's going on? Who is this guy? Is that a boat? Why are you—'

'Stop right there,' I shouted, cutting her dead. 'You don't get to ask questions. Not yet. Now, you've got about thirty seconds to explain what the *hell* you're doing here. And don't even think about—'

'Me explain?' Amber's eyes flashed furiously behind her mask. 'I don't think I'm the one who needs to explain anything here, *Mother*. Like, who even is this creep? And where's your mask? What's going on? Oh my God, is he your…? Are you and Dad *splitting up*?'

As Amber's tone grew increasingly hysterical, Jazz began to back away. 'You know, it sounds like you guys have got some family stuff to work through, so if you don't mind I'm just going to—'

'Freeze,' I growled. 'We need to get this thing straightened out. Now, Amber, I want you to listen to me carefully. This is Jazz. He's my *friend*. I met him while I was out on patrol. He needed help. Medicine.'

Amber's eyes widened, and she began brushing frantically at her suit, swiping away at invisible dust particles. 'Oh my God. Is he sick? Has he got…?'

'It's nothing like that. He just got a nasty bite and he needed some antibiotics, that's all. He's on the mend now.'

On cue, Jazz held up his bandaged leg. Already the angry red streaks had begun to recede, the antibiotics doing their work. 'You should have seen the dog. It was like something out of a horror movie. It had great big—'

'Yes. That's quite enough, thank you, Jazz. So, as I was saying, I'd come here to drop some medicine off when, unfortunately, I had a little accident of my own. Nothing bad. Just a small rip in my suit. But as a precaution, I thought it better to stay here for a few days just to make sure I didn't bring anything home.'

As I talked, Amber eyed me suspiciously. She looked like she had more questions she wanted to ask.

'That's what *I'm* doing here,' I pressed on before she had a chance to speak. 'Now it's your turn. What possible reason could you have to deliberately disobey me *again* and put yourself in danger like this? And how on earth did you even find me?'

Behind her mask, Amber looked pale. Utterly exhausted. For a moment I thought she was going to try arguing with me. But then she took a deep, juddering breath and the fight seemed to drain out of her. 'I'm… I'm sorry. I was awake yesterday morning and I heard your door open. I came out to see what you were doing, but by the time I got my suit on you'd left the house so I… I followed you.'

I stared at her in disbelief. 'Yesterday morning? But where have you been until then?'

'I just kind of… hid. In the corridor out there. I looked through the window and I couldn't see you and I… I got scared. I wanted to go home but I wasn't sure of the way back and…' Amber kept talking, but the rest of her story was indecipherable, swallowed by a wave of sobs.

At the sight of her tears, I felt myself soften. 'I just can't believe you'd do something so stupid. Did you sleep at all? Have you eaten anything?'

She shook her head.

'There's plenty of soup,' Jazz said. 'I can heat you some up if you like.'

I shot him an angry look. 'No, Jazz. There is not soup for Amber because Amber is not taking her mask off. Do you understand me?'

Jazz shrugged. 'All I was saying—'

'Well don't,' I snapped, before turning back to Amber. 'Okay. Look, here's what we're going to do. You can be back home in just over an hour if you head off right now. I can draw you a map showing you the quickest way. You've got pens and paper here haven't you Jazz?'

A look of confusion clouded Amber's face. 'You mean… You mean you're not coming with me?'

'No. I just told you. I have to wait here for two more days. After that, I'll be right back.'

'But why can't I just stay here with you and then we can go back together?'

'Because it's not safe. Don't you understand? I'm not hanging out here for fun. I've been exposed. You haven't. Now I need you to go home. Jazz, have you got that pen?'

'And what if I don't go?' said Amber, the hysteria creeping back into her voice. 'You can't make me.'

Behind us, Jazz piped up again. 'To be fair there's plenty of room here if she—'

'*Enough*. No one is talking to you, Jazz. Now go and fetch me those damn pens. Amber's leaving in a moment.'

As Jazz hobbled off, Amber scowled. Muttered something under her breath.

'What was that?'

'Nothing.'

'No, come on. Spit it out. You've obviously got something you want to say.'

Her lips pursed, as if chewing on something foul. 'Just forget it,' she mumbled

After that, we stood facing each other in silence. Five feet away. It might as well have been five hundred.

While we waited for Jazz to return, it occurred to me that if I was sick, then this might be the last time I saw her. I didn't want it to be like this, her last memory of me an argument. I tried to think of something to say. To comfort her. Some wisdom I could impart. In the end, though, all I could think about were the cold practicalities of her journey home. 'Listen, I want you to go straight home, do you understand? Stick to the main roads and don't stop anywhere. Are you listening?'

Nothing.

'And when you're back, I'd rather you didn't say anything to anyone. About me I mean. If Dad asks if you've seen me, don't... Just tell him you don't know anything. Can you do that for me, Amber? Amber?'

'Whatever.'

'Whatever? What does that mean? This is important. I could get in a lot of trouble if anyone finds out I'm here. Serious trouble. As in police trouble, Amber. As in prison. Do you hear me?'

Before she could answer, Jazz returned, a thick permanent marker in his hand. 'You know, I was just thinking. I don't mind walking your daughter home. I'd have to go slowly with my leg, but I could take you as far as the city?'

'For God's sake, Jazz, how many times do I have to tell you to stay out of this? It's dangerous enough her being here in the first place without her getting up close and personal with Father McNoMask over here.'

'Oh, but it's okay for *you* to hang out with him?' Amber interrupted. 'You're such a *hypocrite*, Mother. It's always one rule for you and one rule for everyone else.'

'That's not fair. Can't you see I'm trying to protect you here? That's all I've ever done.'

'Oh really? So, you came all the way out here to keep us safe? Is that it? When you were running around playing medicine woman, ripping your suit, it was us you were thinking about? Really?'

'Hey… No. That's not…' I floundered, the moral high ground crumbling beneath me.

'You know, Amber. What your mum did was a very brave thing,' Jazz said gently. 'If it wasn't for her then I'd probably be dead right now.'

'Well, gee. I'm so happy to hear that,' Amber hissed, turning on him. 'Good old Mum. Running around the city, rescuing random dudes from dog bites. Isn't she just the best? What a hero.'

'Amber. Honey. Please. You need to calm down—'

'Funny how I don't see her running to rescue *me* when I need help. Nope, there's no sign of Supermum when *my* life's falling apart. Do you even have any idea what the last few weeks have been like for me? Having my private life violated? Becoming a laughing stock at school? Having every last one of my friends abandon me and call me a slut? To become a fucking *meme*?'

'Amber, please. I tried to reach out to you—'

'Oh please. You tried to reach out? Really? How hard did you try? Did you cross a city and put your life in danger to help me? Maybe if I was an indie boy with a six-pack and surfer hair you'd have tried a bit harder.'

'Amber. You're not being—'

'You know sometimes I think it would be easier if I did just disappear for good. If I just walked out of this place and kept walking. Anything's better than going back to that prison we all call home.'

Behind me, Jazz cleared his throat. 'You know, Amber, we're all in prison. It's just some of us have bigger cells than others.'

I swivelled round, spitting through tightly clenched teeth. 'I said to keep *out* of this, Jazz. If I need pop philosophy quotes I'll buy a goddamn fridge magnet. Now if you don't mind, this is between...'

Before I could finish, there was a clatter of footsteps, and I turned to see Amber storming off towards the double doors. 'Wait,' I yelled. 'Amber. Stop. Where are you going? I haven't even drawn you a map yet...'

I chased after her. I tried to catch her. I really did.

But as I reached the corridor, I was just in time to see the door to the playground closing behind her. I was too late.

She was gone.

TWENTY-FIVE

'CAN YOU SEE his gun?' Charlie squealed, jumping around in the back seat. 'It's a semi-automatic MP5. It can shoot 900 rounds a minute!'

Amber groaned. 'Oh my God. You are such a geek. How do you even know that?'

'Because it's awesome.' He held up an imaginary sub-machine gun and began blasting his sister in the chest. 'Uh-huh-huh-huh-huh-huh-huh…'

'Both of you, shut up,' Colin growled, eyeing the soldier, who to my horror did indeed seem to be grasping a semi-automatic weapon of some kind.

A weapon that he seemed to be levelling directly at us as he approached our car.

'Hello there, sir,' Colin began as the soldier stopped a few yards from our open window. 'How can I help you?'

'OUT NOW,' the soldier yelled, jabbing his weapon at Colin. 'Get out of the vehicle.'

'What?'

'Get out,' the soldier repeated. 'All of you.'

Without another word, the four of us clambered from the car, out onto the motorway. Amber looked terrified, silent tears already streaking her face. Even Charlie had fallen quiet, apparently no longer excited by the sight of the gun. In the gridlocked queue of traffic that surrounded us, I sensed strangers pushing their faces to their windows. Watching the drama unfold. Grateful it wasn't happening to them.

I glanced over at Colin, willing him to try and reason with the soldier. When I saw he was staring at his feet, I spoke up instead. 'Listen, do you mind telling us what this is all about?'

'QUIET,' the soldier barked. 'You'll speak when spoken to. Now, we've had reports of a vehicle matching this description carrying infected persons towards the city.'

I shook my head in disbelief. 'Infected persons? You must be mistaken. I mean, look at us. We're just a normal family trying to get home. Now if you'll just—'

Before I could finish, though, Charlie let out a cry. 'Mum! Look, it's Amber. She can't breathe again.'

I swivelled round to see Amber was indeed bent double, gasping for breath.

In an instant, the soldier began barking into his radio. 'Live incident in Sector Five. I repeat, live incident. Containment unit required.'

'No!' I shouted. 'She's not sick. This has happened before. It's a panic attack. She's just scared, that's all. It's hardly a surprise with you waving that bloody gun around.'

Colin was by Amber's side now, his hand on her back. 'Come on, breathe for me. In and out. That's it, you remember. Good girl…'

'Get back,' the soldier yelled. 'I repeat, step back from the target.'

Amber was puce by this point, her eyes bulging in her head.

'Target? She's not a target. She's my daughter, and she's terrified. What the hell is wrong with you?'

'Get back,' the soldier screamed, thrusting his gun in Amber's direction, his finger pulsing against the trigger. 'I won't tell you again.'

'Stop!' I cried. 'Please. She's just a child. She's just a frightened child.'

Colin looked up, still trying to reason with the man. 'Just

give us a minute, will you? Just give us one minute and we'll get this ironed out. It's just a mistake, can't you see that? A silly mix-up. If you'll just listen...'

But the soldier wouldn't listen.

Instead he took another step towards them, his gun still raised. 'This is your last warning. Three... Two...'

One.

A shot rang out.

TWENTY-SIX

FOR THE NEXT two days, I hardly left the boat. I wasn't sick. My nose was dry. My chest was clear. And, while occasionally I would get strange symptoms – shooting pains in my arms and legs, headaches, pins and needles, dry mouth – I put them down to anxiety. As for the virus, I was almost certain I had escaped it. For whatever reason, I'd been spared. I would return home unscathed. I'd been given a second chance.

But strangely enough, none of this made me feel any better.

Mentally, I was a wreck. I couldn't stop my thoughts from spinning of control, especially at night. I kept recycling the same dark fantasies over and over again, Amber's last words to me echoing in my ears:

Sometimes I think it would be easier if I just disappeared for good.

I couldn't believe I'd let her leave. That I hadn't tried harder to stop her. That I hadn't chased her out of the school and into the playground. At the time, I'd told myself I didn't have a choice. While being inside the school without a mask was dangerous, going outside was out of the question. As the days passed, though, I knew I was wrong. I should have gone after her, to hell with the consequences. That's what a good mum would do.

Time and time again, I found myself thinking back to the

first days after Amber was born. After we'd brought her home from the hospital. There was elation, yes. Relief that we had both made it through the grizzly trauma of birth. But that relief was underpinned by a clammy-skinned, sleep-stealing, gut-shredding terror. I was paralysed by the enormity of motherhood. You'd think I'd have been prepared. I'd had nine months after all. I had checklists telling me what to expect and when. I had mummy-to-be yoga manuals and self-hypnosis DVDs. I was a member of online forums where I'd swap war stories about haemorrhoids and acid reflux with other expectant mothers. But pregnancy is such an abstract state that it was easy to forget all those hospital visits and scans and check-ups were actually building up to something.

Perhaps that's why, when I found myself back at home with an actual living, breathing baby to care for, I found it so hard to adjust. In an instant, all of my needs and desires, everything I'd spent my life working to achieve, was rendered utterly insignificant by this tiny pink screaming machine. I had a sense of duty that went far beyond anything I'd ever felt towards my career, or even my marriage. It was utterly terrifying. If I didn't feed her, she'd die. If she got too hot, or too cold, she'd die. If I dropped her, she'd die. She was utterly dependent on me for survival. It was all on me. I had to keep her alive. That was my job. And I was good at it. Sure I might have failed in some areas, but she kept on breathing. And even when the world went insane in a way that I could never have predicted, I'd still always put her first. Her and Charlie. All of the terrible things I'd done. The people I'd hurt. I did it all for them. To keep them safe.

And now I'd wrecked it all.

Amber was gone, and it was all my fault.

Well, almost all my fault. For when I wasn't mentally berating myself, I reserved some resentment for Jazz. After all, if I'd never set eyes on him, none of this would have happened. If he hadn't invited me to the school. If he hadn't been bitten by a dog. If he never fucking existed.

If, if, if…

As if sensing my anger, Jazz made an effort to tiptoe around me. By then he was more or less back to his old self, the colour back in his cheeks, the limp gone from his walk. During the day, I heard him hammering on the deck above me. The only time it stopped was when he crept down to the cabin with a bowl of food. Each time, I'd refuse to speak to him, rolling over and mumbling something ambiguous at the wall. Sometimes he'd try and initiate conversation.

'How are you feeling today?'

'Did you sleep okay?'

'Are you still worried about Amber?'

I remained silent, staring stubbornly at the wall until I eventually heard him go, after which I'd begrudgingly swallow down whatever tepid muck he'd brought me to eat.

Of course, when it came to the bathroom, I had no choice but to leave the boat. The extended run of hot weather had dried up Jazz's reserves of rainwater, and with no flushing toilet, he'd instructed me to go outside and dig a hole. Each time I went out there, I made sure to get dressed into my mask and suit, even though I had to take it off all over again to pee. Squatting in the dirt, I'd look over the little allotment, trying to take my mind off the toxins that were probably leaching into my skin while I was out there.

Alongside onions, there was wild salad, kale, broccoli, along with a bunch of other things I couldn't name, everything pegged out neatly with twine and covered with a fine mesh to deter birds. I had to admit it was an impressive set-up. I remember wondering where the hell he'd learned this stuff. I couldn't believe he'd been an avid gardener before coming here. But then again, I still knew hardly anything about him. Where he'd come from, what he was doing here – in other words, all the things I'd first come here to try and find out – were still a total mystery to me. As preoccupied as I was about Amber, I decided I still wanted to find out more about him.

IT WASN'T UNTIL the next afternoon that I had a chance to talk to him. I was out in the allotment again when a long shadow fell over me.

'I think the salad's seen better days. Slugs, I think. Or mice maybe?'

I looked up, shocked to see Jazz standing in the entrance to the garden. I still hadn't clambered back into my suit yet, and all I was wearing underneath was my vest and shorts, which were starting to look and smell a little grimy. I pulled up my hands to my chest in an awkward effort to cover myself.

'Oh, come on,' Jazz laughed. 'You think I'm going to judge you? I've been wearing the same shirt for about a month now!'

It was true. Jazz was still dressed in the same Hawaiian shirt he'd worn the first time I'd visited the school, though he'd long since dispensed with the dog collar. Now, he mostly wore the shirt unbuttoned, flashing his muscular stomach every time he moved.

'Look, I know I've been a little... tetchy.'

'It's fine. I get it. You're worried about your daughter. And that's totally natural. But I honestly believe she'll be fine. She seems smart. Besides, she made it all the way out here by herself didn't she? I'm sure she'll get home okay.'

At the mention of Amber, I felt a familiar tightening in my chest, my words coming in a breathy tremble. 'I know but... but she said... about just disappearing...'

'She was just angry. People say things they don't mean when they're angry.'

'I know... but... but what if she's not just saying it. I mean, look at you. You disappeared, didn't you? I mean, you must have lived somewhere before you came here?'

Jazz looked pained. 'It's complicated. With my parents it was... it was difficult.'

'Hey, look. I'm sorry. I didn't mean to pry. I lost people, too. I know how tough it can be to lose someone you love.'

Jazz shot me a grim smile. 'Lose someone? Nah, my parents aren't dead. They live about thirty miles from here. At least as far as I know.'

I stared at him, confused. 'So what? You ran away?'

'I didn't have a choice. It was unbearable there. They treated me like a kid. The whole fucking species is dying out and they wanted to make sure I was up to date with my coursework. I couldn't take it. You know they tried to put cameras in my room so they could spy on me?'

I thought of Amber again.

Anything's better than going back to that prison we all call home.

For a moment, I thought I was going to vomit. 'So, what? You just walked out?'

'And I've never looked back,' he said, before noticing the look on my face. 'But hey, don't worry. Your daughter's not going to do that. My situation was completely different. I couldn't have stayed any longer. It would have killed me.'

'But going outside without a suit could have killed you, too. *Should* have killed you. Did you ever think about that?' I found myself getting angry. 'Sure, things might have been tough at home, but maybe your parents were trying to protect you? Keep you safe. Did that ever cross your mind? Or were you too busy thinking about yourself? And what about them now? They must be sick with worry. Not knowing if you're alive or dead. You have to call them. You have to let them know.'

'Jesus, give it a rest.' His face clouded over. 'I know you're worried about your daughter, but there's no need for you to project that stuff on me. I already told you that our situations are completely different. I did what was right for me at the time. Amber's going to do what's right for her. Which I'm sure is going to be heading back home.'

'I'm sorry,' I said quietly. 'I'm just worried.'

'It's fine.'

We lapsed into silence after that. Though it was still hot

out, a shiver ran through me, as I once again became acutely aware I was standing there semi-naked.

'So, if you don't mind, I'm going to get dressed.'

'Oh, hey, that reminds me. The reason I came out here was to see if you wanted me to have a look at your suit?'

I frowned.

'Your suit. You're going home tomorrow, right? I thought I could patch it for you. I've got some thread and stuff. It won't be perfect, but it'll be better than it is now.'

I looked down at the crumpled material in my hands. It seemed silly to worry about a little rip, especially as I was standing around outside in little more than my underwear. Yet at the same time, repairing it would provide some protection if I did happen to bump into anyone on the way back. 'That would be very kind of you.'

'No problem-o.' Jazz reached out to take the suit.

'Woah,' I cried, cowering to conceal my exposed body. 'Not, like, right now. Let me get dressed first and get back to the boat and then you can collect it.'

'Really?'

'Yes *really*,' I blushed. 'I mean… I don't want… I…'

Jazz laughed. 'It's cool. I'll come and grab it in a bit. Now you'd better run along. The last thing you need on top of everything is to catch a cold, right?'

TWENTY-SEVEN

ANOTHER SHOT RANG out, and for a second I was too stunned to scream.

She was dead.

Amber was dead.

But then there was another shot, this one further away, and I realised it was someone else who had fired. All of us, including the soldier, turned towards the direction of the gunfire. There was some sort of disturbance taking place further on along the motorway, a man weaving in and out of the stationary lanes of traffic and out of view, followed by what looked like half the army in pursuit.

The soldier turned back to us. By some miracle, Amber seemed to have recovered slightly, her breathing starting to return to normal while Colin stroked her back.

In the distance, another trill of gunfire sounded, and the soldier's radio crackled something indecipherable. He looked torn. 'Right, you lot,' he barked at last. 'Back to your vehicle.'

None of us moved.

'I said go. That's an order.' And with that he sprinted off in the direction of the melee down the road.

We didn't have to be told again. The four of us climbed back into the car as quickly as we could, slamming our doors behind us before he could change his mind.

IT TOOK MORE *than seven hours to get off the motorway. It wasn't just the sheer volume of people returning that had clogged the city's arteries, though later we would read reports that close to a million people had been on the roads that day. Rather, it was the improvised checkpoints that had been set up between each junction that made it impossible to drive for more than a minute or two without having to stop again. At each of these points, military vehicles were parked sideways across the lanes to create an artificial bottleneck, a militia of bio-suited soldiers ready to stop and inspect each and every vehicle entering the city.*

It was almost two hours before we reached the first of these checkpoints. While we waited, more soldiers patrolled the lines of cars, playing the same distorted message through megaphones, over and over again:

'Please remain inside your vehicle and ensure all doors and windows are closed. We will be with you shortly. Thank you for your patience.'

When the first of the soldiers reached our car, he pointed at us. For a second, we all froze, bracing ourselves to be dragged outside again. But then the soldier spoke.

'Windows. You need to do up your windows.'

Colin hesitated for a moment, mumbling in protest.

'But the text message said...'

The soldier jabbed his finger again and Colin hit the button, sealing us in together.

'Well I guess that's that,' he grimaced.

'It'll be fine.' I reached for his hand, but he pulled away sharply, fumbling in the side pocket for a squirt of hand sanitiser instead.

'Mummy, do you think we're going to get shot?' Charlie asked from the back.

'We've been through this. No one's getting shot, honey. Isn't that right, Dad?'

I turned to Colin for support, but he wasn't paying attention. Instead, he had pulled the front of his T-shirt up over his mouth and nose, using it as an improvised face mask. With a sigh, I turned to my phone instead, refreshing and re-refreshing the browser in an attempt to get an update on the traffic, the Internet crawling as slowly as the vehicles that surrounded us.

TWENTY-EIGHT

IT WAS EVENING by the time Jazz finally called down the stairs to tell me my suit was ready. While I'd waited, I'd examined my body in the dim light of the cabin. It had felt like years since I'd really looked at myself. As a teenager, I remember being permanently perched on the bathroom sink, staring intensely at my reflection. Back then, I'd spend hours agonising over my bad skin, my greasy hair, doing my best with my mother's make-up to patch myself up. And then there were photos. Parties, concerts, restaurants – even just hanging around at people's houses – there was the constant threat of being snapped everywhere we went. I remember only too well the agony of waking up after a bleary night out and desperately scanning various social media sites, untagging pictures of myself, begging and bargaining with friends to delete the least flattering offenders, lest they permanently tarnish my carefully cultivated online brand. Thankfully those days are long gone now. I can go weeks without looking in the mirror. It's not like there's anything to get dressed up for any more. Photos and video are obviously still important currency, but for the most part they are confined to headshots and can be easily manipulated with the right combination of complimentary lighting, cosmetics and photo-editing software. These days, with the webcam angled exclusively above the shoulders, it's almost possible to forget you have a body at all.

Down in Jazz's secret bedroom, though, I was painfully aware of how old I looked. Even in the drab light I could decipher signs of ageing everywhere. The spidery purple veins that lined my inner thighs. The dimpled sag of my bottom. The downward slump of my breasts. The stretch marks on my belly, the skin loose where it had once been as taut as a snare drum. I felt repulsive. After all those hours I'd spent grooming and primping and dabbing and spraying, I'd still been betrayed by biology.

Jazz's voice called out from somewhere above me. 'Hey, I'm all done.'

'Just leave it up there. I'll come up and get it when you're gone.'

'I'll throw it down. Get dressed. I've got a surprise for you.'

Before I could reply, there was a soft slap as my suit appeared at the bottom of the stairs. Holding it up to the light, I saw Jazz had done a good job with the repair. Indeed, unless you were looking for the rip, you wouldn't know it was there at all. Again, I was surprised by how able he seemed. Colin couldn't so much as reattach a button. Yet this kid was practically self-sufficient. It was amazing.

Once I was dressed, I made my way up the stairs onto the deck, where I was shocked to find Jazz had set out a small table and chairs for dinner. My heart sank. The last thing I felt like doing was sitting down and socialising. In truth, all I wanted to do was to curl up and pass the hours until it was time to leave. On the other hand, it looked like he'd made a real effort. The table was laid with an old curtain to act as a tablecloth, with a tea candle burning in a little dish in the centre. There was even a vase filled with a few stringy dandelions from the garden.

I took a seat, staring down at the steaming bowl of unidentified mush in front of me. 'Looks good,' I said, forcing a smile as I reached for my spoon.

'Hang on. Close your eyes a minute. I've got a surprise for you.'

'You mean this isn't the surprise?' Still, I did as I was told.

'Okay, you can open them now.'

I looked up to see Jazz grinning. In his hands was a large glass bottle.

'Is that…?'

'Vodka. I found it in a house a few months ago now. It's still sealed. I've been waiting for the right occasion to crack it.'

I watched as he pulled out the stopper and took a hit straight from the bottle, before handing it to me. I hesitated. 'You know, I think I'm going to sit this one out if it's all the same to you. I'm not exactly in the mood to party.'

'Oh come on! Don't be such a killjoy. Do you know how rare this stuff is? For all we know, this could be the last bottle on the planet.'

It was true. Back when the dark web was still active, you could get alcohol delivered to your door, as long as you were willing to pay the eye-wateringly inflated prices. But once that closed and supplies ran dry, there was nothing to replace it with. Of course I'd heard stories online of people making home brew, taking canned fruit and mixing it with water and sugar before leaving it to ferment into moonshine. It didn't exactly sound like an appealing process, though, and as a result, I hadn't touched a drop for over four years. Seeing the fresh bottle of vodka made me nostalgic for simpler times. Still, as tempted as I was to escape from reality for a few hours, the sight of Jazz's lips wrapped around the bottle were enough to put me off. 'No really, I shouldn't.'

'Look, if it's germs you're worried about, don't,' Jazz said with his uncanny ability to read my mind. 'If I had anything you'd have caught it by now. Besides, the alcohol is a disinfectant. It'll kill any bugs. Trust me.'

I snorted. 'You know, when I was growing up, it was generally considered good sense to run like hell in the opposite direction from any man who asked you to trust him while handing you an open bottle of spirits.'

All the same, I took the vodka from him and lifted it to my lips, spluttering as it scorched my chest. 'Jesus!'

'It's good, right?' Jazz laughed, taking the bottle back from me.

'I don't suppose you have any lime or soda?'

'Sorry, we're fresh out,' he said, taking another sip. 'You want some more?'

'No. Definitely not. That's enough for me.'

But then I took the bottle anyway. And I drank. And I drank.

And then I drank some more.

•••

IN THE OLD world, I'd always been a fairly good drunk, careful to stay on the right side of tipsy, laughing loudly without descending into slurred words and self-pity. That night with Jazz, though, the booze hit me hard. Maybe that's what I wanted. Certainly, it felt good to relax for once, the anxiety of the last few days melting away with each hit from the bottle. As the hours passed, the two of us settled into a long, rambling conversation.

'So tell me about your family,' Jazz asked me at one point. 'I mean, I've met Amber. But what about the others. You've got another kid, right?'

'Oh come *on*,' I slurred. 'You don't want to hear about this stuff. You give me my first drink in half a decade and you want to talk about those guys. Really?'

'I'm serious. It's interesting. You know, it's crazy. I find it hard to picture you as a mum. You just don't seem that... What's the word?'

'Maternal? Gee, thanks.'

'No. I was going to say you don't seem old enough.'

'Oh shut up. Now I know you're drunk. I'm old enough to be your mother. How old are you anyway?'

'Twenty-four? I mean, I've kind of lost track of the months. Where are we now? I'm twenty-five in December.'

'Twenty-four. Jesus, what was I doing at your age? Probably too much of this,' I said, pointing at the bottle. 'And here you are, building ships at the end of the world. Which begs the question, how the hell did you learn to do all this stuff? You said you were a carpenter. But the gardening. The cooking. I mean, I could hardly make a cup of coffee at your age.'

'Well it's not like I had much choice. It was either this or... Hey! Stop trying to change the subject. We were talking about your family. So, do you guys get on or what?'

I made a face. 'You saw how Amber was with me. That was a fairly good representation of my relationship with my family. They despise me. Or at least, I assume they despise me. They don't actually speak to me, so it's hard to be sure.'

'I don't think Amber hates you. I think she's just frustrated. And who can blame her, right? I mean, it's not easy growing up like that.'

'Like what? Alive?'

'You know what I mean. So anyway, what about your husband?'

'Colin? Yeah, I'm pretty sure the kids hate him, too.'

'No. I mean, what's he like? What does he do?'

'Colin's fine. He's a computer programmer. He's been working on some big secret project recently that's been stressing him out. His company have designed this, I don't know how to describe it, this virtual desert island or something. It's a place where rich people pay a load of money to go and hang out. It sounds kind of silly, but he insists it's a big deal. What's the phrase he keeps using? *Game-changing*. Apparently it's going to be game-changing.'

'Well that sounds... depressing.'

'Depressing?'

'No, I mean, I get why he's doing it. It'll probably make him very rich. It's just that if all the rich people start spending all their time on a virtual beach, I guess that means they've given up for good on trying to find a safe way for the rest of us to hang out on an actual beach.'

'Well... I... I hadn't thought about it like that before,' I admitted.

We were both silent for a moment.

'So do you guys get on?' Jazz asked. 'You and Colin?'

I shrugged. Took another swig from the bottle. 'Who knows? We used to, when we were younger. Things were simpler then. Fun. And then we got married and had babies. And for a while, that was fun, too. Not all the time. But we were still essentially on the same page. Even when everything went to shit and people started getting sick, we were still a team. We went through so much stuff together. It was us versus everyone else. But once we sealed ourselves away...'

'He changed?'

'Or maybe we both changed? Never mind the same page, we weren't even reading the same book any more. It was like he just wilted. Gave up. No, that's not right. It was more than that. He *embraced* the new world. If I'm honest, I think he secretly prefers it. Living alone? All that time and space to do whatever he wants? I don't think he'd move back in with us even if it was safe.'

'And what about you? You don't like living alone?'

'Are you kidding? All I ever wanted when I was growing up was a proper family. Sure, I had my mum and dad, but they hated each other. My brother and I weren't close. Not really. I wanted the real thing. Or at least the idealised, sitcom version. To wake up next to the same person and go to bed with them at the end of the day. To eat breakfast together around a table. In-jokes. Traditions. Trust. And now... now I'm just so fucking lonely all the time...' To my surprise, I found I was crying. 'Oh God, I'm sorry. I don't know how we got into all this. I'm drunk. I should be grateful for what I've got, right? I'm still alive. I've got my health. A nice house.'

'Hey. Don't be sorry. It's cool. It's good to open up. I mean, look at me. You think I don't feel lonely sometimes?'

We were silent for a moment, his words hanging in the air, mingling with the vodka fumes. And then, as if it were the most natural thing in the world, he reached out and brushed the hair from my cheek, before letting his hand drop lower, his fingers coming to a rest against my bare neck.

I let out an involuntary gasp, a flutter of electricity shooting through my body as I pictured my whole throat turning pink, a deep warmth radiating out from the place where his fingers lay.

'Stop,' I murmured.

'Stop what? I'm not doing anything.'

All the same, he left his hand there, caressing my collarbone with a surprising tenderness, his movements heavy with intent..

Later, I would ask myself why I didn't tell him to stop. Why I didn't just stand up and take myself off to bed. Walk away. Was it simply because I was drunk? Or on some level, had I been hoping this would happen all along? Ever since I'd first spotted that speck of orange on my computer screen. After all, it had been me who'd stalked him through the city. Me who'd returned to the school again and again. What did I think was going to happen?

In that moment, though, there was no space for analytical thought. There was only instinct. The primal sensation of touch. Warmth.

Skin on skin.

Even now, I'm still not sure who kissed whom. Only that somehow our mouths found each other in that quiet school hall, and that suddenly the world crumbled away beneath me, leaving only a few smudged vignettes to cling to in the darkness. My teeth at his throat. His hand in my hair. The desperation with which we both tore at our clothes. Sweat. Saliva.

And then he was lifting me. Hoisting me up, as if I was the

child and he was the parent, before carrying me down, down, down, into the dark glow of his secret bedroom and laying me out on the bed.

After that, there was only pure sensation. The churn and shudder of our bodies as they locked together. The unbearable building of friction, every nerve ending snapping and crackling, like metal grinding metal, the sparks building to a fire so hot and intense that it tore through my foundations and melted my core. And then I was falling. Erupting. Dissolving.

When it was over, we lay clutching one another like two spent boxers, the fairy lights flickering overhead like a cartoon concussion. I tried to speak, but there was nothing to say. No words that could make it make sense. Not then. Not ever.

And so I simply crushed myself closer to him, the room already lurching away from me, rocking me towards an uneasy sleep, as if the boat was lost at sea, tossed and tussled, at the mercy of some violent and terrible storm.

PART FIVE

TWENTY-NINE

I CLUTCHED AT my throat, gasping and spluttering. I was soaked in sweat, drenched from dreams of drowning. Once I realised I wasn't underwater, I glanced around, confused for a second as to why I appeared to be lying on the set of a 1970s porno shoot. Then I felt a sharp pain in my head, and the night before came flooding back to me in one nauseous gush. I sat up, the room threatening to wheel away from me. The bed was empty. I couldn't decide if that was a good thing or not. All I knew was that I had to leave. I had to get out of this place. I had to get back to Amber.

With my head still spinning, I scrabbled around on the floor for my underwear, before my eyes settled on the patched suit and mask folded neatly on a chair in the corner of the room. When I'd finished getting ready, I slumped down onto the edge of the mattress, sweaty from the exertion of getting into my suit. Before I had caught my breath, I was startled by a depressingly enthusiastic thunder of footsteps, as moments later Jazz appeared in the doorway.

'Oh, hey. You're awake. Jeez, it smells like an oil refinery down here. Hope you're not feeling too seasick'?

His laugh set my teeth on edge.

I looked away. Muttered something non-committal.

'Yeah, it was a pretty heavy night, wasn't it? Still, we had fun… Right?'

I didn't say anything.

'Okay. Well, anyway, I've made some breakfast upstairs. It's out on the deck if you're hungry?'

When I finally spoke, my voice was a dehydrated rasp. 'Give me a second, will you?'

Once he was gone, I sat motionless, willing myself not to vomit. Waves of shame and regret crested and crashed over me. How could I have been so stupid? I was a grown woman for God's sake, not some hormone-addled teenager. More than anything in the world, I wanted to disappear. To evaporate into the atmosphere. Or at the very least, to creep off the damn boat without the obligatory awkward conversation I was about to have. But there was no other way out. And so, with a sigh so deep and flammable it felt like a part of my soul was leaking out along with it, I headed up the stairs after Jazz.

By the time I reached the deck, my hangover was in full voice, my hands shaking, my stomach sour. Every step I took sent my booze-pickled brain ricocheting around my skull. Still, I felt slightly better now that I was wearing my suit and mask. It felt good to have something between me and the world. Between me and Jazz.

At the sight of me in my suit and mask, Jazz's smile faltered slightly. He was sitting at the table, two bowls of congealed baked beans before him. The candle from the night before had melted away, while the dandelions drooped pathetically in their vase. 'I hope you're hungry', he said, gesturing hopefully towards the beans.

'You know, if it's all the same to you I think I'm going to head off.'

Jazz looked wounded, his eyes as big and wet as a scolded puppy. 'Really? You know what they say about breakfast being the most important meal of the day, right?' He laughed unconvincingly.

I shook my head. Swallowed hard. 'Listen, about last night—'

'It's fine. I mean, I get it.'

222

'You do?'

'Of course. You got what you wanted and now you're leaving.'

'Jazz. Come on. Don't be like that.'

'Like what? It's true isn't it? And it's fine. We're both consenting adults after all. Nobody got hurt.' His eyes narrowed. 'Now hadn't you better run along? Calvin's probably waiting for you.'

'*Colin*.'

'Whatever.'

'Jazz…'

For a horrible moment I thought he was going to cry. For the first time since I'd met him, I saw how young he really was. Under the hair and the dirt and the sunburn. He was just a kid. 'I'm sorry,' I mumbled, ducking past him and heading towards the ladder.

As I did, he hissed something at me, the words buried beneath his breath.

I should have kept walking. I'd had enough fights with Amber to know not to take the bait. Instead I stopped. Turned. 'What?'

'I said, you're just like my mother.'

'And what the hell is that supposed to mean?'

'Just that she was a real bitch, too.'

'Oh great. So we're doing name-calling now? Grow up, will you.'

'Well how would you describe yourself? Last night you said you loved me. That you'd never been happier—'

'Last night I was *drunk*. I didn't know what I was saying. And maybe I was happy. I don't know. All I know is that this morning I've got more important things to worry about than happiness. Namely making sure my daughter is okay. And if you had any sense, you'd go and find your parents, too. Before your luck runs out and you end up getting sick.'

Jazz laughed at this. 'Luck? And you want *me* to grow up.'

'What do you mean by that?'

'Well look at you. You're not exactly on your deathbed, are you? And you think that's just down to good old-fashioned luck? Yeah right. Maybe we're both *magically* immune? Like that wouldn't be the most insane coincidence in the world.'

'What are you saying?'

'Oh come on, Angela, isn't it obvious? There is no virus. Or at least there isn't one any more. Maybe there was once, but it died out years ago. Now it's just an excuse.'

'An excuse?'

'To keep us in our place. To keep us tucked safely away in our rooms.'

I shook my head. Snorted. 'Really? That's the best you've got? I'm too hungover for conspiracy theories, Jazz. I've got to make sure Amber's safe. I'm sorry. I really am. But that's all that matters now. I'll see you around.'

With that, I hauled myself over the railings and shimmied down the ladder.

'Fine,' Jazz yelled at me as I dashed across the school hall. 'Go. Leave me. Just don't blame me when you end up all on your own.'

I didn't respond. Didn't break stride. I was already gone.

●●●

STAGGERING THROUGH THE city, I felt sick to my stomach, my mask fogged with stale alcohol. Lurid scenes from the night before came flashing back to me. Hair. Sweat. Teeth. Flesh. I shook my head, trying to shake the images away and focus on Amber instead, her name seeming to chime with each echoing footstep:

Am-ber.

Am-ber.

Am-ber.

As I drew closer to the apartment, I attempted to tap into some long-buried maternal telepathy. As ridiculous as it sounds, I'd always imagined I was connected to the kids by some sort of psychic umbilical cord; a pure, magical bond that could traverse any locked door or solid wall. But lumbering through the deserted streets, I realised I felt nothing at all. I'd been wrong all along. The only thing that had ever connected us was Wi-Fi.

When I finally made it back, the decontamination tent seemed to take even longer than usual, the red light taunting me for what felt like centuries. Millennia. I crouched there, ready with the zip the moment it eventually turned green. When it did, I fought my way through the canvas, blundering into the hallway, my heart hammering, head spinning.

And then I stopped.

For echoing off the hallway was the familiar motorised clunk of the treadmill.

Amber.

She was safe.

She was home.

Relief flooded through me. After all the days of worry, I felt like I could finally breathe again. I stood there in the hall, listening for a moment. She sounded as if she was moving more gently than usual, her signature thud missing, replaced with the simple whir of the belt, as if she were only walking. Trudging on the spot. Who could blame her after everything she'd been through? The poor girl was probably exhausted. I stared at her bedroom door longingly. I wanted to break it down. To see her one last time in person. To apologise for letting her go. To promise I'd never leave her again.

But I didn't do that. It wasn't worth the risk.

And so, returning to my bedroom, I decided to text her instead.

As I rushed to retrieve my phone from its charger, I saw random medical supplies from the first-aid box were still scattered across my bed. The sight of them instantly brought back memories of Jazz. Of the night before. I took a deep breath. While Amber might be safe, I still had a world of trouble ahead of me. I still had to explain to Colin where I'd been for the last four days.

Amongst the supplies, I spied a box of aspirin. I didn't take one, though. I didn't deserve pain relief. I needed to suffer. Instead, I reached for my phone, punching my PIN in with shaking fingers, then tapped out a quick message to Amber.

Hey. Are you all right? Glad you got back okay X

I felt like I was going to hyperventilate.

While I waited for her response, I scrolled through my other messages and missed calls. To my surprise, there were hardly any. A single sentence from my boss, hoping that I felt better soon. A few from clients. Nothing that mattered. Nothing from the kids, obviously. Amber was probably still angry with me. And I wasn't exactly expecting Charlie to reach out. But to hear *nothing* from Colin? That was strange. I suddenly had a terrible thought. What if Amber had made it back and told him where I'd been? It was the only explanation. He'd probably been online and arranged a divorce by now. Or else gone straight ahead and contacted the police. I had to find out.

I hovered over Colin's last message to me:

Shall we talk?

I pressed his name, feeling like a condemned woman.

As his phone rang, I realised I was holding my breath. He wasn't going to answer. He knew where I'd been. What I'd done.

And then suddenly, just like that, he picked up.

'Hello, love.'

It was a trap. It had to be.

'Um, hi,' I said, my voice little more than a whisper. 'I mean, hello. I'm sorry it's taken me so long to get back to you.'

Pause.

'To get back to me?'

'Yes. You said you wanted to talk?'

'Oh right. That. Sorry. I've just been so busy with everything I guess I lost track.'

'With work?'

'Of course. I mean, you've seen the news. It's been insane here. Hey, are you okay? You sound kind of strange?'

'Actually, I've been under the weather for the last few days. Out of the loop. So I haven't seen—'

'The news? Probably for the best. It's been a bit of a roller coaster. The press have been like hyenas, of course. Calling constantly. Looking for a quote. *VR company in major security breach*. The sort of headlines you never want to wake up to. We took the videos down immediately, but the word still got out. Our tech guys still haven't managed to trace the culprit yet by the way.'

'So Charlie…'

'Well. Like I say. They haven't pinned it on anyone yet.'

'Have you talked to him?'

'I think Charlie still needs a little more time. I've decided the best thing to do is to be hands-off and let him come to me when he's ready. Anyway, if I'm honest I should probably thank him.'

'Thank him?'

'Yeah. Funny thing, publicity. Since reports of the attack started leaking out, things have kind of *mushroomed* here. We've had more enquiries than we know what to do with. Our share price has rocketed. It turns out you can't buy this kind of coverage. My boss is delighted…'

Colin babbled on for a while. As he did, I felt the events of the past four days receding like a bad dream. I was safe. And, while she still hadn't responded yet, Amber was safe, too. Maybe everything really could just slot back to the way it was before? And yet, despite my relief, I couldn't help feeling a pang of disappointment. How could Colin have failed to notice I'd been gone for all this time? It was ridiculous. Was he really that preoccupied with work? Or was it more than that? Perhaps not being able to physically see me any more made it easier to forget about me? Had I just become one more open tab on his browser? Interchangeable with his other Internet girls at the click of a mouse, the swipe of a screen.

'So what do you think?' Colin asked.

I hadn't been listening. 'About what?'

'About tonight? Like I just said, we've got a closed demo session running later this evening. The system's still in beta at the moment, so it's entry by invite only. It tends to be a pretty exclusive list, but I think I can probably get you in. If you want that is? You're always saying you want to find out more about what I do at work.'

I closed my eyes. I still felt wretched. I needed to eat. To wash. To sleep. The last thing I wanted to do was spend the evening playing computer games with a bunch of geeks. Nevertheless, I felt an overwhelming urge to make amends for my actions the previous night. It looked like this was to be my penance. 'That sounds lovely.'

'Great. I've got a spare headset and gloves here. I can drop them over to the quarantine tent now and you can pick them up later. The session starts at eight-thirty, but I'll send you over all the details. You're going to *love* it.'

'Well thanks. I guess.'

'You know, I think it's really great that you're showing an interest in this. I know things have been tough lately with the kids and everything, but it's nice to know that when it comes down to it we're still a team. We still… Oh shit, that's my boss on the other line. I'll catch you later tonight?'

'I can't wait,' I croaked. 'I literally can't wait.'

THIRTY

BY THE TIME *we had endured our fourth interrogation in less than three hours, we had long since stopped protesting about the repetition of details. We knew the drill by then. ID and driving licence. Names, addresses, vehicle registration. Were we carrying any firearms, explosives, weapons, drugs or live animals with us? Had we experienced fevers, chills, sore throats or sensitivity to light in the last fourteen days? In return for our answers, we were each examined by a masked soldier with the word Medic stencilled on the back of their white hazmat suit. A torch was shone in our eyes, our temperatures taken, our cheeks swabbed, before we were at last permitted to drive on. The first time it happened, Amber burst into tears, prompting the medic to confer with her colleague, as if Amber's distress might be symptomatic of some underlying pathological condition. At last she begrudgingly waved us on. We were free to go. At least until we reached the next checkpoint, when the whole miserable routine would start all over again.*

Others weren't so lucky. More than once we saw cars being filtered away from the main road, the soldiers evidently unhappy with one or more of the passengers' answers or vital signs. From my restricted view, it looked like these cars were simply parked up on the side of the road and abandoned, while the occupants were led away towards a waiting military truck, to be taken God only knows where.

Even when we eventually turned off the motorway, the military presence didn't end there. When we'd fled the city, the streets had been empty. There hadn't been another vehicle on the road. Now the city was hardly recognisable. The streets churned with military personnel, searching cars, setting up barricades, directing traffic. Though most of the buildings we passed still looked abandoned, large white tents had been erected in public areas, marked Aid or Medicine or Relocation or Missing Persons.

Colin, who had opened the windows again the moment we were off the motorway, seemed delighted by the activity. 'You see, guys?' he said, turning to the children in the back seat. 'Everything's going to be okay. The army are here to look after us.'

While Charlie shared his father's enthusiasm, marvelling at each armoured vehicle and automatic weapon he spotted, the sight of more soldiers only seemed to increase Amber's anxiety.

'Is the virus still here?' She grasped my hand, squeezing it so tight I stopped being able to feel my fingers. 'I thought they'd found a cure. Why is everyone wearing masks?'

It was true. Not only was every soldier clad in the same white hazardous materials suits and masks as the ones on the motorway, but the civilians also had their faces covered, some with simple surgical masks, others with full respirators that looked like they'd been bought from hardware shops.

'Try not to worry, sweetheart. It's probably just a precaution. I'm sure—'

Before I could finish, the car lurched forwards. I looked up to see a soldier had stepped out in front of us, his palm outstretched.

Colin scowled, his enthusiasm for the heavy military presence suddenly evaporating. 'Not another bloody checkpoint,' he said, before leaning his head out of the window. 'Is there a problem here?'

The soldier didn't answer, though. Instead, he gestured for us to join yet another long queue. This one, however, didn't look like another checkpoint. Rather, it led towards a colossal white tent that had been set up in the car park of what used to be a supermarket, this one perhaps ten times bigger than the other tents we'd already passed. I squinted at the sign in the distance, red letters sprayed hastily above its entrance:

DECONTAMINATION ZONE.

THIRTY-ONE

SITTING AT MY computer later that evening, I wanted to cry. My hangover hadn't slackened at all. If anything, it had got worse, no matter how many energy bars I crammed down my throat. Still, I tried my best to be upbeat, reminding myself how lucky I was. After all the time I'd spent in the school, the only symptoms I'd come away with were fuzzy head and stomach cramps. I was a walking bloody miracle. It was no good, though. I didn't feel lucky. I felt rotten. And not just physically. The more I puzzled over the fact I hadn't got sick, the more confused I felt about the whole thing. Why hadn't I got sick? Was it really just a fluke? Or was it a sign of something else? I thought about what Jazz had said. About the virus being dead. I remembered reading somewhere that flu viruses were only capable of living outside of the human body for around twenty-four hours or so. Was it possible then that, without anyone left to feed on, this virus had simply fizzled out on its own? And if that was the case, then why on earth were we still living like this? Divided. Alone. Miserable. Why hadn't anybody told us it was safe to go outside again?

I shook my head, trying my best to stop dwelling on questions for which I knew there were no answers. I was alive. That was all that really mattered. And, while I still hadn't heard from my children, I knew they were safe, too, the whirr of Amber's treadmill still just about audible through the walls.

Now, the important thing was focusing on the present. I had a job to do. A marriage to save.

As I caught a glimpse of my reflection in the monitor, though, I didn't feel like I was about to save anyone. I felt like an idiot. In addition to the ungainly virtual reality headset that was perched on my forehead, I was wearing a pair of futuristic-looking gloves, a tangle of wires snaking down my arms. To complete the look, I was squeezed into an unflattering outfit that can only be described as a full-body wetsuit, the inside of which was studded with an uncomfortable array of pads and sensors, each one digging painfully into my flesh. In his email, Colin had stressed that this was only a prototype suit, and that the finished product would be more refined. For his sake, I hoped he was right. I couldn't imagine clients actually *paying* to dress up like this.

Glancing at the clock, I saw it was already ten past eight. I was tempted to abandon the whole thing. I could simply turn my phone off and say I'd fallen asleep. Surely Colin would understand? One thought back to the night before was enough to change my mind, though. And so, with as much enthusiasm as I could muster, I plugged the trailing cable from my suit into my computer, clicked on the link Colin had sent me and lowered my headset.

•••

FOR A MOMENT I was blinded by a snowstorm of pixels. The disorientation was so violent I feared I would throw up. Seconds later, though, it settled. I blinked. Looked around. To my astonishment, I was no longer sitting in my room. Rather, I appeared to be sitting on a beach. A stretch of coastline so photogenic that no holiday brochure could ever do it justice. The sand as fine and white as powdered bone. The sky the colour of crushed sapphire. And sandwiched between the two, an infinite slash of turquoise water, stretching all the way to the sun. It was a vision of paradise.

I stood up. Looked around. The attention to detail was astonishing. I could actually feel the sand between my toes. The sun on my skin. I realised how much better I suddenly felt, the snarl of my hangover instantly soothed by the rhythmic lap of the tide.

'Hey! You made it!'

I turned to see Colin waving as he emerged from the water. At least, I thought it was Colin. As he drew closer, I wasn't so sure. He was too tall, his hair too thick. He looked trimmer, too, his pale paunch replaced with a flat stomach, the muscles in his arms defined. When he spoke again, though, he still had Colin's reedy voice. 'I was worried you weren't going to come.'

'Well here I am. And there you are. And just look at you. Been hitting the virtual gym?'

'Oh this?' Colin grinned sheepishly. 'One of the neat things about this version of TouchSpace is that you get to design your own avatar. It's just a bit of fun, really.'

I glanced down at my own body, noticing for the first time my cartoonish bosom, a pair of beach balls straining to escape a skintight swimsuit. 'And what about these? Are these just a bit of fun?'

Colin blushed. 'I mean… I didn't have much time to build anything for you so I just picked something off the peg. Is that okay? You can go back and choose something else if you like? Hair, ethnicity, body type. It's all customisable.'

I raised an eyebrow. 'It's fine. Let's just hope this thing isn't programmed to simulate back pain.'

'Great. That's settled then. So, do you want me to give you the guided tour? We've got half an hour or so before the other delegates log on.'

'Really? I thought you said it started at eight-thirty?'

'Ah. Yes. I just thought it might be nice for us to have the place to ourselves for a while. In a few months' time this place will be crawling with virtual tourists. But now… Well now it's just us. We could go for a swim if you like?'

'*You* want to *swim*?'

This was not the Colin I knew. On our family holidays in the old world, I had known him to sit on the beach, rather than get in the water, his back the colour of raw bacon, his face buried in some godawful sci-fi novel. He'd claim he was happy to watch our things while we swam, but I knew the truth. He was scared. The sea terrified him. Even on our honeymoon in Barcelona, we spent our days apart, him traipsing around museums and football stadiums, me nursing a jug of sangria on Icària Beach. No, poor Colin has never been much of a swimmer. At least, not in the real world.

Here, though, he was different. In fact, this steroid-buff version of my husband appeared to be practically amphibious. Bobbing there in the perfectly rendered digital ocean, the water as clear as champagne and as warm as a bubble bath, I watched as he dived beneath the waves, his bronzed legs kicking like a synchronised swimmer. Periodically he came up for air, having retrieved some treasure from the seabed. A starfish, a conch shell, a crab claw.

'It's incredible, isn't it?' he said. 'Even now, I keep finding things I've never seen before.'

'It's certainly very realistic. How does it work? Like a virtual holiday? People log on and hang out at the beach?'

'That's one option. But to be honest, you'd be wasting your time and money if that's all you came for. The beach isn't much more than garnish. The real action happens in the city. That's where the parties and clubs and bars and all the rest of it are.'

I looked back at the deserted beach, stretching out as far as I could see. 'There's a city here?'

'Well, it's more of a town at the moment. But the team have got huge plans. There's talk of historical recreations. San Francisco in the sixties. Berlin in the thirties. Ancient Rome. Egypt. Greece. The only limit is the client's imagination. And, of course, how much they're willing to pay. Speaking of which, it's probably time we were going. People are going to start arriving soon.'

I followed Colin out of the water, glancing around for a towel. Within seconds, though I was completely dry. 'Hey, have you got anything I can change into? I'm not sure I want to meet your fancy clients dressed like Baywatch Barbie.'

Colin grinned. 'Of course. I've actually got something lined up. Wait there one second?'

The whole world seemed to shimmer and warp for a moment. And then he disappeared.

'Colin? I called. 'Colin?' I stepped forward into the spot of sand he'd last occupied, my temples beginning to tighten, my heart racing as I realised I'd been abandoned.

A second later, however, he reappeared. Only now he was no longer wearing swimming trunks. Instead he was dressed in a white tuxedo, complete with a red bow and sash. 'I hope that's okay? It's off the peg again.'

I looked and saw my own swimming costume had been replaced by a sequinned black dress. On my feet were a pair of stiletto heels.

'Not exactly beachwear,' I said, reaching down to unhook my shoes.

When I straightened up, Colin looked worried.

'I'm joking. It's perfect. Thank you.'

He whistled with relief, before reaching for my hand.

I hesitated, fighting away visions of Jazz from the night before.

Flesh on flesh.

Skin on skin.

'It's perfectly safe. Trust me. There's nothing to be scared of here.'

I smiled. Swallowed down the visions. Slipped my hand into his. It was fine.

Together, we began to walk.

Hand in hand.

Husband and wife.

THOSE FEW MINUTES together on the beach might just rank as the happiest moments of our entire marriage. Certainly, they were the best in the last five years. Strolling along that perfect slice of virtual shore, it was possible to forget that I was actually alone in my bedroom, hooked up to a sophisticated computer. Everything just felt so *real*. There was a light breeze blowing as we walked, and I burrowed into Colin's side for warmth. This was much better than being with Jazz, I told myself. All the comfort of another human with none of the risk attached. Colin had been right. This thing *was* a game-changer. If this was what the future looked like, I decided, then perhaps things weren't quite so bleak after all.

We'd been walking for maybe ten minutes when I detected a sound in the distance. The muted throb of a bassline. We kept going, the music swelling louder and louder, until eventually we came to the source. A huge, glass-fronted nightclub, backing directly onto the beach. Inside, a wild party sounded like it was in full swing.

I frowned. 'You're meeting your clients in here?'

'This is one of the most popular spots in the whole town. Why, is there a problem?'

I looked over towards the pair of menacing security guards who were looming either side of the entrance. 'No. I'm just surprised. This doesn't really seem like our kind of place, that's all.'

Colin squeezed my hand. 'You're going to love it in here. Trust me.'

And then he was leading me towards the doors, nodding at the security as though they were his best friends.

'Nice to see you again, Mr Allen,' they boomed in unison as we slipped through the doors.

Inside, the music was intimidatingly loud, a seamless mix of commercial dance, each song indistinguishable from the last. It was like stepping into a live action perfume advert, an impression that was further compounded by the décor, a slightly corporate glaze of stainless steel and glossy black surfaces, everything bathed in soft, tasteful lighting.

'Isn't this awesome?' Colin yelled. 'We had some of the top DJs in the world contribute exclusive mixes for us. In later versions we're hoping to make it possible to integrate with your playlists. Imagine that. A nightclub that only ever plays the songs you want to hear.'

Again, I was struck by how different he was. In the real world, Colin had always despised places like this. Even when we were young, before the children came along, he would have done anything to avoid going into town, balking at the price of drinks, laughing at the hyper-groomed clientele. Now, however, he seemed utterly at home.

'Where is everyone?' I shouted back. 'This place is empty.'

It was true. Whereas from outside the club had appeared to be jumping, the only people I'd seen since arriving were the security guards at the front entrance. Though there was a long bar stocked with an artful display of craft beers and premium spirits, it was completely deserted. There weren't even any bar staff.

'Oh, they're here all right. There's a basement bar downstairs. People tend to congregate down there. It's *legendary*. Here, follow me.'

Again, I allowed myself to be led by the hand through a maze of polished glass. As we walked, the club seemed to get darker, the music so loud I could feel it reverberating in my ribcage, rattling my heart out of rhythm. I was feeling hungover again, wave after wave of anxiety crashing over me. More than anything, I wanted to return to the solitude of my room. But I couldn't. Not with Colin so happy. He was like a little boy showing off his homework project to a teacher. And so, when we finally reached a small unmarked doorway on the far side of the dance floor, I forced a smile and made my way down the stairs.

●●●

IT WAS QUIETER in the basement. Much quieter. Once the door had closed behind us, the thump of music from the club upstairs dropped away, leaving only a low murmur that I couldn't quite place. Broken pipes? A swarm of bees? It was too dark to see much of anything at all.

As I made my way down the stairs, however, strange shapes gradually began to emerge from the shadows, and I saw the room was crammed with people. I say people, but in truth none of them looked like anyone I'd ever seen before. Rather, they appeared to be strange, mutant beings, dressed in PVC hoods, tottering on vertiginous heels. Some of them had collars around their necks and crawled on the floor like dogs, while others were strapped into latex corsets, completely naked below the waist.

None of them turned around to greet us as we reached the bottom of the stairs. Instead, they stood in a loose circle with their backs to us, their attention utterly absorbed by whatever was happening on the other side of the room. I turned uncertainly to Colin, but he only smiled, gesturing for me to move deeper into the room.

The crowd shifted, creating a gap in the circle. It was then that I realised where the sound was coming from. Lying on the floor, surrounded by the crowd, was a writhing mass of tangled limbs, an abstract sculpture made of flesh. At first, nothing made sense. It was like an optical illusion, everything bent and splayed at impossible angles. But then the sculpture seemed to shift slightly and I realised what I was looking at.

In the centre of the circle, a woman lay moaning and writhing on the floor. Arranged around her, penetrating her from every angle, were three men, their faces contorted with a mixture of concentration and pleasure. I watched in horror as one of the men let out a whimper, shuddering violently into the woman's mouth, before collapsing backwards onto the floor. Almost instantly he was replaced by another member of the crowd, this time a leather-clad woman who grabbed the woman by the hair and pulled her face violently towards her crotch.

I'd seen enough. I took a step backwards from the circle, but as I did, I felt a pair of hands slip around my shoulders and begin roughly kneading at my oversized chest. I lashed out with my elbow, struggling to break free, only to feel a wet tongue sliding up my neck towards my ear.

'It's fucking *hot*, right?'

I turned around, shocked to find Colin bearing down on me. Or rather, Colin's avatar, for I knew now this wasn't really my husband. The quiet, sensitive, if slightly apologetic lover. No. This Colin was some sort of sex-crazed monster. This Colin was a stranger.

'I think I want to go home,' I said quietly.

Colin grabbed my wrist. 'Go? Are you crazy? Do you know the strings I pulled to get you in here tonight? You just need to relax a little. It's all totally anonymous. You can be anyone you want here. *Do* anything you want.'

I tried to pull my arm away, but he only gripped me harder. He seemed to be growing taller by the second. 'Really, Colin. I don't like it.'

'What the hell is wrong with you?' he snarled. 'You're embarrassing me.'

'You're hurting me.'

'Hurting you? How do you think I feel? It's been five years, Angela. Five years since we've been together, and you want to leave before we've even fucked? You're my wife. I have rights.'

'Please, Colin. I don't want it like this. Not here. Not with these… people.'

'These *people* are keeping a roof over our heads,' he growled, before softening slightly. 'Look, I get it. Really, I do. You've been locked away for so long that you've forgotten what it's like to interact like this. Face to face. It feels scary.

Wrong even. But I've already told you, none of this is really happening. You're still safe in your little room. No one can make you sick here. This is just a fantasy. And it's supposed to be fun! The only limits are your imagination. If you don't believe me, look at this.'

With that, Colin finally released my hand and took a step back. And then, with an ugly leer, he reached down and tore away his trousers, exposing himself. I gasped. I'd never given much thought to Colin's penis before. I mean, it was fine. Unremarkable. Neither especially big nor embarrassingly small. The thing between Colin's legs, however, was like no penis I'd ever seen before. As long and thick as my arm, it twitched menacingly in my direction, its tip glistening with a foul-looking fluid.

I did the only thing that came to mind.

I swung out my stiletto and kicked him as hard as I could between the legs.

Colin let out an agonised scream as he crumpled in two. 'Jesus, Angela! What the hell is…'

I didn't hear the end of his sentence. Instead, I tore off the VR headset and threw it as hard as I could across the room, Colin and the awful nightclub disappearing with it. My hands were shaking so much that it took me a while to get out of the gloves and wetsuit. Once I was free of them, I hurled them towards the furthest corner of the room.

And it wasn't until later, when I stood trembling under the shower, that I realised I was crying.

THIRTY-TWO

IT WAS DARK by the time we finally pulled up to the car port below our apartment block. There seemed to be some problem with the electric key fob, so Colin had to get out and manually force the gate open. Once we'd parked up, we found the lift wasn't working either, and so we took the stairs, Charlie skipping excitedly ahead, the temporary hazmat suit he'd been given at the Decontamination Zone swishing with each step. When he reached the double doors at the top of the stairs, though, he turned and ran back to us. Even behind the mask, I could see he was nervous.

As I pushed open the double doors on to the third floor, I could see why. The flickering lights overhead lent the trashed hallway a surreal, nightmarish quality. As Charlie stooped to pick up a discarded Action Man doll from the floor, Colin yelled at him. 'Leave it. Don't touch anything, do you hear me? It could be very dangerous.'

Charlie dropped the doll and the four of us picked our way quickly across the hallway and into the apartment, which to my relief looked exactly the same as we'd left it. Only now we were each viewing it through the reinforced polycarbonate visor of our respirator masks.

As Colin shut the door behind us, Amber tugged at the sleeve of my suit. 'Will you give me a hand with the straps, Mum,' she said, tugging at her mask. 'I can't get it off.'

I reached down to help her before Colin stepped between us, pulling us apart. 'What do you think you're doing? You heard what the man said to us earlier. It's important we leave our gear on while we're in the same room.'

'But Dad, I can't breathe.'

'You're being silly, Amber. I need you to be a big girl now. Look at your brother. He's not complaining, is he?'

As if on cue, Charlie picked up his imaginary machine gun and emptied an invisible chamber into Amber's chest. 'Look, Daddy. I'm a soldier!'

'You see, Amber?' Colin continued. 'You just need to stay positive. This isn't forever. It's just temporary until we can get our rooms converted properly. Besides, it probably won't even come to that. There'll be a vaccine soon enough and then things will go back to normal. You'll see. Now, let's work out where everyone's going to sleep, shall we?'

THIRTY-THREE

IT WAS LATE by the time I stumbled out of the apartment, the streets totally dark. It was raining, too, water running down my visor, making it hard to see. Not that it made a difference. I knew exactly where I was going.

As I splashed through dark puddles, it occurred to me that I'd never been out of the apartment at this time before. That was one of the first things they taught us at neighbourhood watch. Bad things happen at night. Not that I cared any more. Nothing could be as bad as Colin and his virtual sex club.

I couldn't stop thinking about how different he'd seemed there. Not just physically, but the things he'd said. The way he'd acted. He'd been unrecognisable. Or was he? The more I thought about it, the more I began to wonder if there'd been a different side to him lurking just below the surface all these decades. Just waiting for an excuse to present itself. I remembered the dismissive snort he gave in the cottage garden, right after he'd killed that man. The slight shrug of his shoulders, even as the man's brains were leaked onto the grass. And the expression on his face. It wasn't a smile exactly. More... satisfaction. As if he'd swatted an especially irritating fly. At the time I'd put it down to the stress of the situation we were in. The bravado was a coping mechanism. He was doing what he had to in order to protect his family. To survive. Now, though, I considered another explanation. What if Colin actually *enjoyed* exerting power over people? What if that's just the kind of man he was when the chips were down? Someone who could crush a man's skull without blinking. Who couldn't see anything wrong with trying to force himself onto someone who clearly wasn't interested. And without the pesky interference of the real world to keep him in check, maybe it was *that* Colin who had been free to fester and grow over the past five years. What was it he'd said about TouchSpace? That it allowed you to be whomever you wanted? Well if that was whom he wanted to be, we didn't have a future together. I didn't need someone like that. I needed someone kind. Funny. Tender.

In other words, I needed Jazz.

As I approached the school, I was distracted by a noise. A scratching in the shadows. The scrape of loose gravel. It was probably just a cat, I told myself. That, or my imagination playing tricks on me. There was nothing to be worried about.

Seconds later, however, I heard another sound. This time, there was no mistaking it. Footsteps. Heavy boots on concrete, followed by a burst of radio static.

Soldiers.

I scanned the street for somewhere to hide. A doorway I could duck into. An alley I could slip down. I was too late, though. Across the road I saw the flicker of a torch light, a cold beam swooping the pitted tarmac, until it caught me. I froze on the spot, shielding my eyes from the harsh halogen glare, before a hard voice called out.

'Hey! Hey you! Stop right there.'

For a moment, I thought about complying. Perhaps I'd be given a chance to explain. I'd tell him about neighbourhood watch. How I'd got my patrol rota mixed up. *Silly old Angela.* We'd work everything out and he'd let me go with a warning.

Then I thought back to the soldiers we'd met while trying to get back into the city all those years ago. Soldiers who didn't think twice about pointing an automatic weapon at a defenceless child.

No. There'd be no explaining. No letting me off with a

warning. They'd act first and ask questions later. If they asked them at all.

I pictured myself dropping to my knees, my hands in the air. A government issue boot prodding my face down into the road, settling briefly on the back of my neck. My hands wrenched behind my back and bound with cold metal cuffs before I was dragged screaming into a decontamination car.

At this point, I'd like to tell you I was thinking of Amber and Charlie. Or even you, my poor sweet Egg. But it's not true.

As embarrassed as I am to admit it, I was thinking of Jazz. I had to see him.

Even if it was just one more time.

And so, as the soldier screamed at me to stay put, I turned and sprinted, bracing myself for bullets that somehow never came.

I RAN AND I ran, the rain making it impossible to see where I was going. I hopped walls, scrambled over fences, squeezed down alleys, while the torch light lurched behind me. The radio crackled. The soldier barked expletives. Any moment, I expected an eruption of gunfire, as my pursuer finally lost patience.

'Hey! You! Stop!'

I kept running, slipping and sliding on the wet tarmac, yet somehow I managed to stay on my feet, until eventually the footsteps behind me grew fainter and fainter and I could no longer hear the soldier's cries or see his torch. As impossible as it seemed, I had got away.

Eventually, when I was quite sure I was no longer being followed, I came to a stop. As I gasped to catch my breath, I looked around. To my surprise, I realised I was only a few roads away from the school. Even in my panic, I'd run straight towards Jazz.

Sticking to the shadows, I splashed forwards until I caught sight of the familiar railings that surrounded the school. Before I reached them, however, I saw something was wrong. Very wrong. There were people in the playground. Vehicles. Lights.

More soldiers.

Creeping closer, I saw the school's front gate hung open, the metal posts lying twisted on the floor, as if rammed at high speed. As I reached the railings, I dropped to my knees, ducking out of sight. Sure enough, three military trucks were parked up in formation around the door of the main building, their engines still purring, lights flashing. Four suited figures stood nearby, automatic weapons levelled at the door.

My first instinct was to tear off my mask. I needed air. I couldn't breathe. I wiped the rain from my visor, trying to see. Perhaps Jazz had got away, I told myself. Maybe he'd heard them coming and escaped through the garden at the back. Seconds later, though, a cry went up from the playground. And then suddenly there he was, his limp body being dragged out through the door, a burly soldier on each arm. Was he alive? Dead? It was impossible to tell. Either way, he wasn't putting up a fight, his head lolling forward, his legs scraping along the tarmac. He reminded me of the roadkill we sometimes used to pass on the side of the road back in the old world. The secret majesty of a deer or fox transformed into a sorry sack of fur and blood and bone. One of the soldiers moved to roll open the door of the nearest van, as the others bundled Jazz inside, slamming the door.

Before I could react, a second cry rang out from the school. This time it was a female scream. I looked up just in time to see another figure being dragged towards the van. My head began to spin. What the hell was Jazz doing with another woman in there? A woman who, from the looks of it, was dressed only in gym shorts and a top. No mask. No suit. I peered closer trying to get a better look at her. I was too far away, though. All I could make out was a fuzz of dark hair, before she too was forced violently into the van.

The door slammed shut.

There was a squeal of tyres.

A blast of a siren, before the van disappeared into the night.

PART SIX

THIRTY-FOUR

FOR A WHILE, I thought about disappearing. Of just walking into the night and never going home. But then rational thoughts kicked in. What would I do? Where would I live? I didn't have any answers. And so, with nowhere else to go, I began the long trudge back towards the apartment.

All along the pitted street, stars smouldered in dark puddles. A world upside down. Heaven in reverse. I thought of Jazz's fairy lights. How long would it take for his boat to rot away now that there was no one to care for it? Years? Centuries? Or perhaps the school roof would simply collapse, burying it under a ton of rubble. Splintered wood. Concrete. Dust. Either way, it would never see the ocean now. Not that it was ever supposed to. No. The more I thought about it, the more I realised that the boat wasn't designed to sail. Rather, it was just something he'd built to impress naïve women. Like a peacock flexing his tail feathers, it was simply a brag. A boast. The towering mast only slightly subtler than Colin's digital cock. And hadn't it just worked a treat?

Oh, what a fool I'd been.

Of course there had been another woman with him there. There had probably been dozens of women. Hundreds. Every one of them led down the stairs to his gaudy little cabin. Every one of them hearing his sob story about the parents who didn't understand him. Every one of them drunk on vodka.

No, I realised. In the end, Jazz was no better than Colin. Different, yes. But not better. He only ever had one thing on his mind. I saw that now.

A breeze was blowing and I felt a chill on my leg. Looking down, I saw the stitching on my suit had come undone, and was now gaping open, revealing my pale thigh beneath. It didn't matter now. Nothing mattered.

I kept walking.

When the grey silhouette of my apartment block loomed into view an hour later, I almost turned and fled all over again. What was waiting there for me? Children who wouldn't speak to me? A husband who'd rather spend his nights immersed in a fantasy world? I pictured the years unravelling inside my room while I moved from my desk to the kitchen to the bathroom to my bed and then back again, shackled to a screen.

Work, eat, sleep, wash, repeat.

Surely there had to be more to life than that? Or perhaps I was just being greedy. I was one of the lucky ones, after all. I'd survived. I had food. Shelter. A high-speed Internet connection. I had access to the sum of human culture at the click of a mouse. Every book, every film, every song. I could speak to anyone, anywhere. I could shop to my heart's content. Hell, if I really wanted to, I could lose myself in a virtual world.

So why did I feel as if I'd been hollowed out? Why did I feel so utterly alone?

As I drew closer to my apartment, I slowed and then stopped. Parked outside the front of the building was a police van. Of course, it could have been there for any reason. Perhaps one of the other residents had reported a break-in? A domestic disturbance?

In my heart, though, I knew it was there for me.

This time, running didn't even cross my mind. I was so tired, handing myself in would almost be a relief. To defer all responsibility for good. To be told where to go. What to eat. When to sleep. Besides, I'd spent so long locked up by this point, how much worse could a real prison be?

As I crossed the dark courtyard, the front door creaked open, framing a figure in the light. I froze, my hands in the air, ready to comply with the police officer's commands. Ready to accept whatever punishment was coming my way.

To my surprise, however, it was not a police officer who came lumbering towards me. No. Even though they were dressed in a suit identical to my own, I recognised the figure instantly as Colin, something long and metallic gripped tightly in his fist.

Instantly, my mind flashed back to the nightclub. My stomach lurched. Was Colin out here in the real world to finish the job he'd started? Only this time he'd brought a weapon with him to make sure I didn't fight him off. For the first time, I realised how scared I was of the man I'd called my husband all these years.

I was about to turn and run when a light flashed on, and I saw it was a torch Colin was carrying. He called out to me then.

'Angela? Jesus. Where the hell have you been? I've been trying to call you.'

What could I say?

'Don't tell me you knew she was missing and didn't say anything?'

I stared at him, for a moment unable to make sense of either his presence there or of the scramble of words spilling out of him.

'Missing? Who's missing?'

'Amber! I presume that's why you're out here, isn't it? To look for her? Christ, the least you could have done is let me know. I've just spent the last hour upstairs talking to the police.'

'Wait…' I stalled, the pieces stubbornly refusing to fall into place. 'Amber is missing?'

'Of course Amber's missing,' he snapped. 'She's gone to meet up with that boy, Jamal. I just know it. I swear to God if I get my hands on him, I'll kill him. I'll actually kill him.'

'But how did you…? When did you…? Missing since when?'

'According to her computer logs, she's not been online for nearly thirty-six hours. Apparently she left her treadmill running to throw us off the scent. In fact, if Charlie hadn't accessed her system, we'd never have found out. He called me just after you... after you logged off. When you didn't answer, I called the police. I thought you'd both... Never mind. There's an officer still up there now, going through her things.' Colin paused, as if something was only just occurring to him. 'Wait a minute. So if you didn't know about Amber, what *are* you doing out here.'

'I, er...' I floundered. 'I had a bad feeling. Mother's intuition.'

Colin eyed me suspiciously. 'Whatever. There's no time to lose. I suggest we split up and start looking. If only we had an address for that fucking Jamal character.'

I hesitated. 'But the police... Have they said it's okay for us to look for her? Won't we be in trouble?'

Colin glared at me, his scorn visible even through his clouded visor. 'My daughter is out here alone. If they want to arrest me, then good luck to them. Otherwise, I'm going to find her and bring her back home. Now are you coming or not?'

And with that, he turned and stalked off across the courtyard, shouting Amber's name.

WE STAYED OUT there for an hour or so, walking in circles until a suited policewoman eventually came down from the apartment. While Colin continued to search, she led me towards her van. Apparently she had a few questions she wanted to ask me. The officer took out her tablet to read her notes.

'We understand this is a difficult time, Mrs Allen, but there are a few things we need to run through with you if that's okay?

I nodded.

'The first thing to mention is that we found Amber's hazardous materials suit and her respirator mask in her bedroom. As there's no sign of a struggle, I'm sorry to say that we're working on the presumption your daughter has left the residence unprotected, most likely of her own volition. Now is there any information you could give us that you think might be relevant? How were things at home? Was she happy?'

Before I could say anything, a cry went up from nearby. A girl's scream. Seconds later, Colin came stumbling back into the courtyard. Only this time, he wasn't alone. He was dragging someone with him. A girl.

Amber.

He'd found her.

By the time I reached them, she'd stopped fighting and gone limp. Colin had her arms pinned tightly behind her back, and her head flopped forwards. She looked like a person who'd given up.

I don't know what I was expecting.

That's not true.

I know exactly what I was expecting.

I was expecting fireworks.

I was expecting screaming and crying and joy and relief and anger and promises and forgiveness and redemption.

I was expecting a new start.

A glimmer of hope.

A happy ending as the credits began to roll.

But Colin only shook his head.

'It's not her,' he said.

'What?'

Somewhere behind us the policewoman was shouting at us to step away from the suspect.

'It's not her,' he repeated.

The policewoman was on her radio now. She was calling for back-up. For a decontamination team. For a quarantine zone to be set up.

'I don't understand,' I said.

Colin started to say something, but Amber looked up.

And then I did understand.

Because Colin was right. It wasn't Amber. It was some other teenage girl. Some other runaway. Somebody else's daughter.

'I found her curled up in the doorway of an old shop,' Colin said. 'I can't believe she's out here without a suit. She must be mentally ill or something…'

I stopped listening then. I was numb. So that even when the girl started thrashing again, kicking so violently that the policewoman had to step in to help Colin restrain her, all I could do was stand there and stare.

My daughter was gone.

I'd lost her.

I watched as the policewoman led the girl to her van, forcing her into the holding cell in the back. I thought back to Jazz and the girl in the school. Where were they now? I wondered. Hospital? Prison? Or would they just quietly disappear? Their records deleted. Another problem solved.

I watched as the policewoman slammed the door. And then she froze. She put her glove to her helmet and began speaking into her radio.

'… Yes. That's right. Amber Allen. Okay, I'll pass it on. Over.'

She came to me then. Smiling behind her mask. Although as she drew closer, I saw there was a look in her eye. Something less comforting. Something almost accusatory.

'Mrs Allen. We've had a report come in that we've located your daughter.'

'Amber? You've found her?'

'It's still unconfirmed at the moment, but yes, it looks like it. Apparently she was picked up by a decontamination team on the other side of town. She was hiding in an old school building, along with another male suspect.'

THIRTY-FIVE

AS COLIN DISAPPEARED into the bedroom, Charlie ninja rolling behind him, I turned to Amber. Even with the mask on, I could see her eyes were puffy and red, her cheeks wet, a bright bubble of snot around her nose.

'Hey. Come on now. Don't cry into your mask. You'll drown.'

She didn't laugh at my joke.

Though she was almost as tall as me, I knelt down beside her and gave her a hug. To hell with Colin. 'I know it's not much fun wearing the mask, but you'll get used to it. And you heard what Dad said. It won't be for long.'

'It's not about the stupid mask,' she said, shaking my arms from her shoulders. 'It's everything. I just want things to go back to how they were. I want to go back to school. I want to see my friends.'

'And you will, honey. You will.'

Her face contorted. 'No I won't! Why do you keep saying that? Why do you and Dad keep telling me everything's going to go back to normal when it's clearly not going to? Of course I'm not going back to school. Mrs Andrews is dead. Mr Perkins is dead. The librarian, the dinner ladies. My friends. Everyone. They're all...'

She trailed off, her face a smear of tears and snot. She

rubbed a hand across her visor, forgetting for a moment about the mask, her frustration bringing even more tears.

I placed my hand on her back. She tried to shake me off again, but this time I kept it there, her warmth radiating through her suit. 'Hey. Listen to me. I know things seem bad now. And I know you're hurting. But Dad's right. You have to try and look at the positives. We're still alive. The four of us. Against all the odds, we made it. Can't you see how amazing that is? And after everything we've been through, things can only get better. Maybe not right away, but they will. Just as long as we stay positive, we can make the most of this situation. Together we can make it work. Do you believe that?'

Amber shrugged.

I held her tighter, pulling her to me so that our masks bumped together. 'I need you to believe that, honey. Really I do. Because we might still have a bit of a way to go on this journey. We might not even be halfway through it yet. All I know is that this, here.' I tapped my mask. 'This isn't how it ends. Say it with me. This isn't how it ends.'

Amber sniffed. Pulled a face. 'Stop, Mum. You're so embarrassing.'

'I know. It's silly. But just say it once. Just for me.'

She rolled her eyes. 'This isn't how it ends,' she mumbled.

'That's right, sweetie. It isn't. Not by a long shot. This isn't how it ends.'

PART SEVEN

THIRTY-SIX

SO THIS IS how it ends. Back at the beginning. Stuck in this room with just you for company. Just you and me, my sweet Egg.

And it really is just us now. Two months have passed since Amber was picked up by the police, and she still hasn't come home. Though technically still a minor, and as such unable to be charged as a criminal, it doesn't look like she'll be released anytime soon. If at all. Officially she is being held in isolation in a military hospital for 'observation'. For security reasons, we are not allowed any contact with her, or even to know her location. As a result, I still have no idea what she was doing back at the school. Whether she went there to look for me or to see Jazz or simply to escape her room, I can only guess. Perhaps I'll never know the truth. All I know for certain is that she's still alive. And that's got to be worth something.

Hasn't it?

As for Jazz, I don't know what has become of him. I presume he too is alive, though what kind of life he has ahead of him now I can't imagine. Perhaps he will be lucky and be released back to his parents' custody. Not that he'd consider that lucky. Or maybe he will turn out to be useful to the government after all. Maybe he will help them develop a vaccine, the secrets in his blood eventually unlocking the doors to all of our cages once and for all. Though I fear that is just wishful thinking on my part.

Either way, I doubt I'll ever find out. Naturally, I denied all knowledge of him and the school and everything else when we were formally interviewed by the police. As far as they are concerned, Colin and I are model parents. Even so, news of our family troubles evidently travelled fast. Within hours of the police leaving, Fatima was in touch to offer her condolences, as well as to suggest that, in light of everything that had happened, it might be best for everyone involved if I stepped down from my role with neighbourhood watch with immediate effect.

As for Colin, he's made it clear he doesn't have anything to say to me. Especially not in person. He's refused my calls, and the handful of messages we've exchanged since the police left have been terse to say the least. My questions answered with a single emoji. Thumb up or thumb down. Though he hasn't spelled it out, I suspect he blames me for Amber disappearing. Not that he can prove anything.

Although something tells me he will find out. And sooner rather than later. Especially if my darling son Charlie has anything to do with it.

Charlie.

I'm still not sure what happened to him. Where I went wrong. I still remember him as a baby so clearly. If I close my eyes I can still picture him the way he was. The way he *felt*. The exact weight of him on my lap. The clasp of his fingers around my neck as I carried him. The butterfly flutter of his eyelashes on my cheek when I stooped to kiss him. My funny, cheeky, sweet little boy.

But that boy has gone now. And he's not coming back.

The last time I spoke to Charlie was the day after we found out Amber had gone. Colin had insisted I call him to thank him for his 'heroic' work sounding the alarm. I thought about querying what he was doing snooping around on her computer in the first place, but in the end, I thought better of it. I was the adult, after all. Besides, there was a small chance Charlie was just as worried about his sister as we were.

To my surprise, he answered my video call immediately. He seemed to have grown even fatter since the last time we spoke, although this might have just been because he was topless, mounds of pale, gelatinous flesh filling the screen. At the sight of me, he grinned horribly, adding several chins to the thick roll around his neck. 'Mother. What a pleasant surprise.'

Fighting back my repulsion, I mumbled a brief thank you, and told him I hoped he was doing okay. Before I could log off, however, he leant forwards into the webcam, so close that I could make out the remnants of breakfast smeared around his lips.

'Actually, *Mummy*, there was one thing I wanted to ask you about before you go.'

I froze.

'It's probably nothing,' he continued. 'Only when I found out my poor big sis was missing, I decided I'd better check all of the computers in the house. Just in case there was anything *unusual*. You know? To help track her down. Dad's was clear, of course. Unless you count all the viruses from...' he smirked, 'well, whatever. When I got to yours, though, I couldn't help noticing something strange seemed to be going on with your phone. Of course, you're aware that it backs up automatically to your computer?'

I swallowed hard.

'Anyway, I hate to break this to you, but it looks like you've been hacked. I just don't know how else to explain it.'

'Explain what?' I asked suspiciously.

'Well, according to your location data, it looks like your phone travelled all the way across the city on a number of occasions. Looking at the map, it seems as if it visited a church one day. And then an old school after that. The same school that they found Amber at.' He snorted. Sneered. 'Isn't that just the most bizarre coincidence? And then there are these strange audio recordings—'

'Stop it, Charlie.'

'It's uncanny. They sound just like you. There's a man speaking on them, too—'

'I said *stop*.'

Charlie blinked, batting his lashes, his face a picture of innocence. 'It's a horrible feeling, isn't it? To know someone has violated your privacy like that. Manipulating it to make it look like you were breaking the law. You really should look at updating your security systems, Mummy. I mean, people could get the wrong idea if they didn't know better. Just think what the authorities would say. They might even think *you* had something to do with poor old Amber vanishing.' He paused. Licked his lips. 'It's a good job I tipped them off when I did. Otherwise you could have found yourself in real trouble.'

I stared at him. He was so pleased with himself, his eyes radiating malevolence. He was a monster. 'What did you do, Charlie?' I whispered.

'Why, I acted like a good citizen. I sent an anonymous message telling them to check out a school on the other side of the city. I mean, whoever hacked your phone was most likely hiding there.'

'An anonymous message?' I croaked.

'Well don't thank me too much. I probably saved you from being locked up. And I certainly saved Amber. Anyway, from the looks of it, they got the culprit in the end. I can see your phone's been safely tucked away in your room ever since. Right where it should be. Although, on the other hand, there have still been some very strange search requests popping up on your browser, so maybe your system is still vulnerable after all. Just this morning, there was a raft of strange searches on news sites for someone called Jason Freeman. Or is that Jazz Freeman? Most bizarre.'

I was shaking now. 'Charlie, I want you to promise that you're going to stop looking at my computer. Do you hear me?'

He only laughed, though. 'Oh, Mumsie. There's no need to be so melodramatic. I'm just keeping an eye out for you. Just to make sure you're safe. After all, you never know who's out there. Watching you.'

'Charlie…' I began, but his screen clicked to black before I could carry on.

He was gone.

In the months that have passed since then, I've not heard anything else from him. His school have been in touch a few times to request a meeting. Apparently, he's stopped attending classes altogether. I never got back to them. As far as I'm concerned, he can do what he wants. He's on his own now. We all are.

Though I've thought about it almost constantly, I've also resisted the urge to punch Jazz's name into my computer again. I have to accept I'll never find out what happened to him. Sometimes I think that's a good thing. In the absence of hard facts, I am able to make up a version where things go well for him. Where he is rewarded handsomely for cooperating with the authorities. Where they really do use his DNA to develop a vaccine. Where we are all saved. Or else, I picture him escaping from a high security detention unit in the dead of night. In this version of the story, against all reasonable probability, he rescues Amber, too. Perhaps they break back into the school together and somehow manage to tow his boat to the ocean. And then maybe, just maybe, they set sail and find the damn thing floats after all. They chart a course for the unknown. They are both finally free.

Of course, I don't really believe these stories. Still, as long as I don't find out the truth, there is always hope. Perhaps I should be thankful to Charlie for that. By taking away my privacy, he has injected a little uncertainty back into my life.

Besides, it's not like I don't still have secrets. Oh yes. I have things that can't be so easily stolen. Things that aren't on any hard drive or cloud. At least not yet. Things that are buried so deep down inside of me that even Charlie can't drag them out into the light.

A souvenir. Proof that I lived. If only for a little while.

But I won't be able to keep it a secret forever.

In the next few weeks or so it will be time for another visit from my friendly government gynaecologist. Then the game really will be up. I might be arrested and thrown into prison myself. Or sent to a government facility for observation alongside Amber. Who knows? Maybe in this story *I'll* be the hero. The one who saves the human race. Or at least, the one who dies trying.

Either way, there will be no hiding you any more.

Everyone will find out.

Charlie. Colin.

The police.

And then my own, private little world will be flattened for good. As comprehensively destroyed as the one outside.

And perhaps that's a good thing. After all, isn't that what I've wanted all along? A true levelling. A chance to start again, and maybe even get it right this time.

A blank page.

But it won't be blank for long. Even now, I can feel a new story stirring inside of me. Dividing and multiplying. Letter by letter. Word by word.

I don't know what it says yet.

But I'm praying it's something good.

Acknowledgements

Though this book is dedicated to my mother, I very much have both of my parents to thank. Without their unconditional love and support, neither I, nor this book, would exist.

Family and friends.

Kind strangers and discreet enemies.

Tom, Lauren, Lucy, Ditte and all at Legend Press.

My agent Laura Macdougall and all at United Agents.

Ed Homer for his awesome illustrations.

Jonathan Davidson and all at Writing West Midlands.

Everyone who still believes in the power of books.

My two beautiful boys, Elliot and Felix, both of whom are a little bit like Amber and nothing at all like Charlie.

Simone, for making anything possible.

A side note: I almost died writing this book. Like the punchline to some sinister cosmic joke, I was struck down with a mysterious skin infection that left me hallucinating in a hospital ward, unable to walk. I owe a huge debt of gratitude to the nurses and doctors who looked after me when I was at my lowest. The NHS is a glorious old lady, an incomparable national treasure that should be nurtured and protected at all costs.

One last thing: while writing *Skin*, I simultaneously wrote and recorded an album with my band, Absent Fathers. While it's not a soundtrack exactly, I've come to think of it as an accompaniment of sorts. If you'd like to hear it, search for Absent Fathers on Spotify, Apple Music or YouTube. The album is called 'Swimming Lessons'.

If you enjoyed what you read, don't keep it a secret.

Review the book online and tell anyone who will listen.

Thanks for your support spreading the word about Legend Press!

Follow us on Twitter
@legend_press

Follow us on Instagram
@legendpress